Beneath the Mistletoe

BENEATH THE MISTLETOE

WIP Authors

Mimi Barbour, Deborah A. Clifton, Genevieve McKay, Jo-Ann Carson, M.A. Reitsma, Wendy J. Merritt, Megan Riley , Sandra Hunter, Phyllis Chubb, Tracy L. Tinkler-Denouden
Canada

This is a work of fiction. Names, characters, places,
and incidents are either the product of the author's
imagination or are used fictitiously, and any
resemblance to actual persons living or dead,
business establishments, events, or locales,
is entirely coincidental.

Beneath the Mistletoe

by multiple authors of WIP

No part of this book may be used or reproduced
in any manner whatsoever without written permission
of the authors except in the case of brief quotations
embodied in critical articles or reviews.

Contact Information: mimibarbour66@gmail.com

Contents

Beneath the Mistletoe

A WIP Christmas Anthology

~*~*~*~

Compelling holiday entertainment!

This fabulous Canadian collection encompasses ten diverse stories and many genres, but they all have one thing in common. They are written for the holidays and Christmas is the theme.

You'll love turning the pages to read these imaginary tales for the winter season. So... enjoy the work created by these Canadian authors and lose yourself in a world of thrilling entertainment.

Please Keep Me by Mimi Barbour

Holiday Heartwarmers Series – Book #1
by
NYT & USAT Best-selling author, Mimi
Barbour
Copyright © 2016

~*~*~

Christmas is family time in Carlton
Grove…

In this beautiful holiday love story,
Belinda Page, a single mom of a very
intelligent four-year-old daughter, is at her
wits end trying to keep up with the baby

genius. When the child throws herself into a lake to rescue a puppy, Belinda is frantic. Turning to the man who saves both babies, she seeks his support – until she finds out he's one of those hated Carltons. After all, it was at their home where she'd gone to a party, been drugged, raped and left to deal with the consequences of that distressing evening she couldn't quite remember.

Dr. Reed Carlton, an introvert who feels uncomfortable around most people, can't believe his luck. He's finally found Lindy; a girl from his past, a fond memory that has haunted him for over four years. Except that once this Lindy learns who he is, she hates him. What was that all about? At least her daughter and the puppy were on his side. But would their affection be enough for Lindy to accept him into her family's life.

Praise

"As far as I know, I have read everything Mimi Barbour has published, and I bought most of them. I keep coming back because I love her sense of humor and style of writing and I always fall in love with her characters." ~ *Reviewed by A. Chambers*

"As a writer myself, I think that one of the true marks of an excellent author is solid, believable character development, and in my opinion, Mimi Barbour is the master of character development!" ~ *Reviewed by author Flo Barnett*

Dedication

I want to dedicate this first novella, **Please Keep Me,** to Debbie Turner, the wonderful lady who came up with the title and got the **Holiday Heartwarmers** Series started.

Have a wonderful Christmas Season, my friend. May you be blessed with family, friends and lots of fun.

XO

Mimi

Prologue

Dark and frightening, the night sounds of busy birds, buzzing insects and muted traffic from the faraway streets created a surrounding racket that disturbed the terrified puppies. Rustling of the tree branches added to the discord, as did the wind sweeping up dry leaves and forcing them against solid objects where they splattered and crumbled.

The overwhelming, surrounding scents were tantalizing and yet not familiar and therefore, not comforting. Only the smell from the teats and the warmth of their mother's body was yearned for and missed.

Inside the cardboard box, the one female puppy communicated with her two brothers; *he's gone!*

Scampering to the corner of their flimsy prison, she thought back to the fight that had ensued between the man and her mistress before she and her brothers had been thrown here.

"Amelia, you kept those mutts? Before I left last week, I told you to get rid of them."

"But, Jimmy, they were too little to be weaned from Bella. I was waiting until this weekend to try and sell them." Her mistress's lovely voice had sounded placating and miserable all at the same time.

"Who's going to buy these three? Their mom is a fat, ugly, overly-friendly lab with no guard skills; don't know why I let you talk me into keeping her. And that vicious Samoyed brute across the way, who's no doubt their father, is meaner than the devil who owns him."

"Jim, they're cute pups. I bet I can get a few dollars for them."

"Sure, and until then we have to listen to them kai-yiying all the time, clean up their messes and feed them. No more! I want them gone. It's bad enough we have to trip over that bag of bones without having to deal with her stupid offspring too. Never mind! Since you're as useless as a garden hose in a forest fire, I'll take care of this myself."

He yanked the three pups out from under the tummy of the keening dam where they'd burrowed in fear. Grabbing a nearby box, he hurled them inside. After a short drive in a car, he carried the carton for a few minutes and threw it down.

"Good riddance!" Those were the last words

the puppies heard from him. The fading sounds as the man crunched away were terrifying.

Whimpering at the memory, after multiple tries, the female puppy bounced until her front paws gained purchase on the box's edge. Straining her neck, she peered out.

The moon, riding high in the starlit sky, provided illumination for the snoopy pup. *I think it's a park*, she told the other two, whining, sharing her thoughts.

Chubbs, her roly-poly brother, subsided lazily in his corner, his furry body falling over and staying there. *What are we going to do?* Little beady black eyes watered as he howled pitifully.

Stop that caterwauling! It hurts my ears. His brother's normal cranky manner was evident in his insensitive attitude. *We'll sleep now, and in the morning, Sis can go and find us some help.*

Okay! That's a good idea, right, Sister? Chubbs yawned and curled up next to his brother. Both were asleep in seconds. Only their sister snoozed with one eye open, guarding their new dwelling.

In the morning, sounds of human voices woke the three. Again, the female bounced in the corner until she had her front paws clinging to the side of the carton. In the distance, she saw a lot of water. There were people running along its edge. To her left, there was a grassy field where humans were playing a game with a big brown ball.

Cranky wanted to see the world she was

describing. When he got close, she used his butt as a ladder and worked her way up and over his head, landing ungraciously in a heap on the grass outside of their container.

Go, Sis. Find us help! Chubbs and the Cranky pup whined together.

Chapter One

Reed Carlton couldn't believe that his three brothers had talked him into a game of touch football, and on Thanksgiving yet. A day he'd normally be working. Or at home recuperating from too many shifts at the hospital where, as the youngest and easiest-going of the staff, he worked as a surgeon.

Since they'd recently opened the new surgical wing at the local clinic, he'd been playing catch-up with all the cases that had been put on hold for months. It seemed that everyone over the age of fifty and within a hundred mile radius had been waiting for some form of surgery. There were so many hip and knee replacements scheduled, it was a wonder anyone could still move around.

Carlton Grove, Washington, the small town where he'd grown up had become quite a thriving metropolis in the last decade and their hospital had had no choice but to expand and include facilities that the population demanded.

"Reed, throw it here." Gathering his drifting thoughts, he looked over at his youngest brother and grinned. Harley was the most energetic and he normally managed to wear the rest of them out. Reed tossed the ball and watched as Harley, making a wily maneuver, snapped it from the air, dodged the three on the other team and headed for the goalpost. A line drawn in the dirt with a couple of branches planted at either end signified its importance.

In the next play, Reed received the ball and headed to the same goalpost, hoping to get in the clear so they could score again. This time, Harley, overly enthusiastic, heaved the ball way over Reed's head in the direction of the lake. Hurrying to retrieve the slippery object, Reed raced over the hill and his heart slammed into his throat at the scene playing out below him.

A furry white puppy ran to the top of the slope by the edge of the lake and had lost its footing. It slid and then rolled, ass over tea kettle, over the bank and into the water.

Meanwhile, a small child in jeans and a hoodie raced into the water with no hesitation, obviously intent on saving the puppy. As Reed watched, he could see they were both in trouble. One minute the little one was waist-high and reaching for the dog, and the next, he was in over his head struggling to find footing. And the pup, now in the kid's clutches, fought to free itself, which only made matters worse.

Oh-oh! Reed and everyone who had ever swum in that lake were aware that the shore was dangerously uneven. One minute you'd be safe walking on ground in low water, and the next step would take you down. Dead, rotting vegetation on the lake's bottom made it slimy and greasy in some places, dangerous in the extreme. Unable to balance, and with a wriggling puppy to contend with, the boy went under, taking the dog with him. Reed dropped the ball and ran faster than he ever had before.

Chapter Two

"Hollie?"

Belinda was furious at herself. One minute she'd played the polite stranger to tourists looking for the closest restaurant, and the next, was repaid by her naughty daughter taking off—God knew where.

The child was a terror, never listening to her, always thinking she could do as she pleased. A constant battle went on between the two. Only this morning, she'd been forced to bribe Hollie with a walk in the park if she'd go to her daycare after lunch and behave like the other children in her class.

Hollie had wrinkled her nose and looked disgusted. "The girls play with dolls and stuffed animals. And they giggle about everything. They're goofy, Mommy. And the boys fight over the same toys. Or whine. *Those* goofballs whine a lot."

"Hollie, baby, you're exaggerating. They're nice children. I spent my assigned afternoons helping out at the daycare, and I never saw a goofball in the crowd."

"*You* don't have to play with them. I don't want to. But whenever I try and go off on my own to read, Miss Dummy makes me stay with the others."

"*Hollie!*" Belinda hid her smile and remonstrated with her daughter over the mispronunciation of her teacher's name. "You know darn well her name is Miss Dumry. Please don't make that mistake in school or she'll send you home again."

"I know." Hollie lowered her face, but not before Belinda had seen her tears. "She doesn't like me. I guess it's 'cause I don't like her neither."

"Of course she likes you, sweetheart. She's just very busy. There're so many children that she hasn't any time to pay special attention to just one."

"No! It's 'cause she's always checking her phone for messages and texting her boyfriend."

"I'm sorry, baby. Mommy's working really hard to try and save enough money to get you into a better school, one you'll love." Belinda was careful to call it school rather than daycare, knowing that would appeal to her disruptive little genius a lot more.

With an advanced curriculum, Hollie'd behave better. A grin broke through Belinda's worries. She decided she was probably the only parent who had a four-and-a-half-year-old child suspended from the relaxed, public daycare system.

Thank goodness she'd managed to sweet-talk them into only making Hollie stay away for a week and not forever. They'd taken her daughter's disappearance on an unaccompanied walk in the empty grounds as a serious matter and used terms like 'uncontrollable' and 'single-minded'. This daycare had been the third placement Belinda had arranged for her high-strung little rebel and she'd begun to run out of options.

Hollie's problem was that she was just too intelligent. Bored easily, she found the other kids to be babyish and silly. Belinda felt heart-sick every time she thought of the private school she had in mind where the program included all kinds of activities that would appeal to her baby's cleverness. Stuff like painting with water colors rather than crayons, working in plaster making leaves and other realistic impressions, and not doodling with colored plasticine.

They taught them a lot more about the world around them and her baby would soak that all up and beg for more. Plus, the teachers were highly qualified and the class sizes realistic. Unfortunately, who had the kind of money to pay their ridiculous rates?

Lately, overwhelmed with the sole responsibility of Hollie's welfare, Belinda wondered if she'd done the right thing in choosing to keep her baby. Friends who'd strongly suggested an abortion were no longer people she hung around with. Her family, struggling to put her two older brothers through college, had no extra money to help. Instead, they'd advised her to go the adoption route.

She'd done neither. And now, she was pretty much on her own—same as always—and left to deal with the outcome of that choice.

"Hollie!" *Where was that child?*

A scream tore through her worry and Belinda stiffened with instant panic. The hairs on the back of her neck began doing that creepy thing they did when a person's instinct told them there was trouble. Her pulse tripled and distressing heart tremors quickly followed. Breathing normally became inefficient and she panted instead. *That was Hollie screaming.* Belinda, throat clogged with fear, began running. *Oh, Lord, what now?*

Chapter Three

Once Reed hit the water, he knew he had to get to the little guy. But since the puppy had wrenched away from the reaching arms, he figured the best way to gain control would be to grab the pup and take it along with him. Lunging for the animal, he hit a low spot and his feet lost purchase. One minute he was wading through the cold lake, and the next, he was in over his head.

Knowing it was too late to change his mind, he dove for the pup and grabbed its thrashing hind leg, and then turned for the boy. Except that the kid had somehow managed to snag his neck from the back and was choking him so hard that panic gripped Reed's senses.

Fighting to remain calm and not let go of the

distraught pup, he tried to flip the boy onto his front where he could better control his movements, except the boy was having none of it. And instead, sensing that Reed was trying to dislodge him, he squeezed even harder. In trouble, Reed went under again. He swallowed a mouthful of water and came up choking.

Knowing he only had seconds to take control, he let go of the pup and wrenched the little hands away from his neck. Once unlocked, he yarded the frenzied thrasher over his shoulder and hugged him close to his chest.

"Calm down, son. I have you. You're okay now. Stop fighting me."

Whether the kid heard him or not, Reed didn't know for sure. What he did know was that the boy had seen the pup on its own, and not understanding that animals could swim, he thrust away from Reed and threw himself toward the mutt yet again.

Bellowing so he'd be heard, Reed followed. "He's okay, boy. The dog can swim." Reed hauled the sopping wet little body back in his arms, only to have to physically subdue the child. "Listen to me." Reed shook the body to get his attention. "I'll get the puppy."

Finally having his feet on the ground where he could stand, he lifted the kid high over his shoulder. Then, to make sure there would be no further argument, he grabbed the bedraggled puppy, swimming for all he was worth in his free hand, and waded to shore where a group of people now waited.

Dripping with water and fury, Reed glared around him, hoping to see someone who would claim both daring little monsters.

The woman who ran forward, reaching for the mischief-maker, was reasonably rational, or so Reed thought until he saw the luminous terror glinting in her drenched brown eyes.

A feeling of déjà vu hit him like a sucker punch in the gut. *Lindy?* Before he could say a word, she'd wrenched the child out of his arms, lowered them both to a crouching position as if her knees didn't have the strength left to keep them upright and was kissing the tiny face nonstop, hugging the body and rocking them both from side to side.

Sobs broke from her, excruciating sounds of fear and self-reproach. "Baby, oh, Hollie. You scared Mommy so much. Never, ever wander away from me like that again."

"Mommy, I found a puppy. He's mine."

Reed, watching the two, felt a shifting in his heart region and unfamiliar soft emotions flooded.

Dazed and obviously half out of her mind, the woman he knew as Lindy agreed. "Yes, okay, honey. I love you, baby."

Since everyone's attention was on the re-joined family, the canine mischief-maker who'd started the whole spectacle shook herself hard to get rid of the water and fell over from the exertion. Then she wiggled her way to the woman's knees, scrambled between the clutching pair and jumped up to add her kisses too.

Both the woman and, as it turned out, little *girl*, opened their arms in welcome to include the canine into their circle of love. The pup craved the attention and squirmed so she could lather both their faces in a frenzy of adoration.

Just then, Reed's brother, Harley, approached. After making sure Reed hadn't suffered unduly, he commented, humoring everyone in the crowd, "It's just a mild case of puppy love, folks. Thanks to my brother, hero of the day, it looks like both babies are fine."

Chapter
Four

Reed's middle brother, Terry, had had the forethought to fetch blankets from the car and appeared, passing the dry wraps to Reed.

"Thanks, bro." Reed took the blankets and approached the small family. He dropped the smallest cover over Hollie and Lindy made sure it enfolded the tiny body. She'd calmed somewhat and instead of kissing her baby, she now had the child by the arms and was doing what all mothers did in dangerously stressful moments; she was mothering.

With her expression full of tempered wrath, she wrenched the child away from her and shook the thin shoulders to get the attention she needed. Her eyes drilled the little girl's and the words she used would not be misunderstood. "Baby, what have I told you over and over? You left me. You must never do that. I need you to stay beside me all the time."

Pitifully, the little head hung from drooping shoulders. "I'm sorry, Mommy. I didn't know I went so far away. I only wanted to play with my puppy. But then he fell into the water and he needed me to help him." Her chubby hand reached forward and gently patted the woman's face, while big earnest melting brown eyes stared out from under a mass of curls that spiralled like a ginger halo around her little pink-cheeked face.

Lindy visibly melted and her control broke. Reed figured that her love and the recent worry for her daughter must have taken the starch out of her backbone. As if she needed some support, Lindy glanced up and caught his stare. "Tell her what she did wrong. I don't know how to make her understand."

As all eyes turned in his direction, Reed felt the onus shifting to his shoulders. Not knowing what the hell Lindy expected from him, nonetheless, he crouched down and faced the stubborn child still gripping the listless pup hanging over her arm.

Small but fierce, the kid looked defiant. Her bottom lip protruded and her brown eyes revealed anger and resentment. Yet he saw the fear she hadn't the ability to hide and that made the damn nervous tick explode in his right cheek. A warning bell clanged in his head. *Be Careful!*

The pup snapped out of her daze and took his measure also. The two stared at him. It was like nothing he'd ever faced before. Uneasy, he smiled at them and both pair of eyes looked wary, yet waited trustingly.

A second emotional deluge caught him unexpectedly. A mind that in a flash could answer any medical question put to him had nothing in its banks to deal with this dilemma.

What the hell did this woman expect of him? Given that he was the Carlton brother who never had much to say, the situation left him panicking. In fact, his family had often joked that their reserved brother had chosen the best possible route as a surgeon because most of the time his patients would be unconscious.

Without meaning to, he reached out and wiped away some drops of water from the child's face. They had escaped from the damp spiralled curls that bounced around as if they had a life of their own. Her eyes measured him, watchful, but she didn't flinch.

He heard the pup's pleading whine. Slowly, kindly, so as not to startle the little girl, he took the uncomfortable creature from her hurting grip and gently lowered her to his own knee. His big hand almost enveloped the small body as he petted the wet quivering animal. "You mustn't squeeze so tight. It hurts her."

When the first sob broke, not a sound could be heard. "I didn't mean to. I love her." As if she couldn't handle any more of the stressful situation she'd found herself in, the kid threw herself at Reed, her arms strangling as she blubbered her sorrow against his neck. "Don't be mad at me. I didn't mean to be a bad girl. But I had to help my puppy."

From the second he felt her tiny body melt against his, Reed's arms reacted. He hugged her to him, whispering brokenly, "Shush, sweetie. We're not mad. But you have to promise your mom not to ever run away from her again. Okay?"

"Okay." A reedy voice answered, but the arms still clung and the face still burrowed, seeking his warmth.

"Promise?"

"Okay."

"Uh, huh. You have to say the words. Then you have to mean them." Suddenly, a thought interrupted. Separating them, he watched her wary expression, "Do you understand what a promise means?"

"Yes." She tried to look away but he didn't allow it.

"What does it mean?"

"It means I'm going to be in a lot of trouble if I say those words."

Chapter Five

A lot calmer after she'd seen Reed laugh, Hollie left his arms and was now working on Belinda. "The puppy's mine, Mommy, she loves me."

The creature began to whine pitifully. First she stared at Belinda and then Hollie, her little black eyes full as if tears were brimming.

"Look, she's begging. She's saying, please keep me."

As soon as Hollie had flung herself in those male arms, the pup, lowered to the ground to leave his hands free, had begun bouncing up and down, yipping her consolation. Now she was plastered against Hollie's side, gazing at her with pure worship.

Because of her daughter's pointing finger, automatically Belinda's glance fell on the now fluffed-out white canine, and damned if those black eyes and grinning snout weren't beseeching her just like Hollie had said.

"No, baby, you can't keep the puppy. She must already have an owner." Hoping someone in the crowd would step forward, she deflated when no one did.

Belinda couldn't believe the manipulation her little genius was working on her. And at a time like this when she was particularly vulnerable. Hollie had even added those magic words to include the puppy's make-believe appeals. *Please keep me! Really?* Weakness overcame her usual refusal. After all, she'd just watched her child survive a dangerous, near-death situation.

"She loves me, Mommy."

"No, Hollie. You know we can't look after her." Proud that she hadn't been swayed, Belinda recognized the hint of weakness in her tone and hoped her smart daughter hadn't caught it.

What made the situation worse was that this was a constant argument between them. Hollie had pleaded for a pet non-stop, and though Belinda would love to cave, she couldn't. So she always used the same argument. "*Not yet, honey. We can't look after a pet because we're never home. But one day, I promise.*"

Belinda forced her eyes away from the entreaty in Hollie's, and noticed that most of the bystanders had faded from the scene. Only Belinda, Hollie and her savior were left to hear the puppy's heartrending whine.

Suddenly, the furry body scooted over to Belinda to snuggle as close as possible. Now it was two against one. *Oh, God!*

Belinda's heart dropped. First she looked at Hollie, and then at the puppy. Two pairs of eyes begged the impossible. She couldn't bear taking on any more responsibility. Her hands covered her mouth, but not before a moan broke loose.

"Sorry, sunshine. The pup belongs to me." The commanding male voice saved her ass and an overwhelming urge to do the same as her daughter had done just minutes earlier took hold. If only she could throw herself into his arms, wrap hers around his neck and sob with relief.

Instead, she shot him a look of gratitude and for the first time since the incident happened, she paid attention to Hollie's good-looking rescuer.

Short dark hair damply clinging to his head only created more focus on the soft brown eyes of the handsome devil. She recognized regret in his expressive face and knew he had stepped in to save her over the puppy—that he wasn't the real owner. *How sweet was that?*

Endearingly, he didn't try and hide his disgust at his lack of control. His stance revealed his annoyance. But when he saw her searching, he grinned lopsidedly and shrugged.

It was the grin that struck a chord. Memories long buried fought to be more than a fleeting vision, but faded almost as quickly as they started. One thing was for certain, she'd never met the man before because he wasn't someone any woman would be likely to forget.

Chapter Six

What the hell are you doing? His soft-hearted rescue, a position he'd never experienced before, had appeared and spoken before passing the words through his brain. And now that organ was laughing hysterically at his blunder. *Too late, you idiot! You can't take the words back. Look at Lindy's relief.*

It was true. Overwhelmed with gratitude, the woman wore a huge smile. "I'm sorry, baby. The dog belongs to this gentleman. You must give her back. And then thank him for rescuing you."

Hollie looked at her mom and then at Reed. Her wobbling lip almost unmanned him, but he waited to see what she would do. Shoulders again drooping, blanket now laying on the ground at her feet, she bent over and kissed the furry head. Then her little hands pushed the uncooperative dog toward him. "She's too little to know she's yours. Don't be mad at her. I guess she likes me." Sniffing audibly, she finally picked the puppy up and handed her over.

Reed looked at Lindy, whose eyes were still begging for support. He'd felt low before in his life but never like his belly was scraping the gravel. Still, the relief shining from his former one-night-fling's eyes couldn't be ignored. He had to carry on with the lie.

He took the beast from the little hands and held her against his chest, getting his chin bathed by the rough tongue and puppy breathe. "She doesn't recognize me yet because I just got her very recently." *Yeah, like a few seconds ago!* "I'll have to train her to stay, ahhh... where I put her." Reed had no real intention of keeping the animal. As soon as he could escape from this awkward situation, he would find out if anyone knew where the pup came from. If not, he'd find a home for it. Someone among the staff at the hospital would take the little pain-in-the-ass off his hands.

"What's her name, sir?" Hollie couldn't seem to let go.

"I haven't named her yet." Without even pausing to consider the question, he asked, "What would you call her?"

"I'd call her Cloud."

No hesitation. Hollie answered and he had to ask. "Why Cloud?" The name surprised him. He'd expected Fluffy or Snowball, or something equally childish.

"Because she's white, soft and round like a cumulus cloud. I love clouds. Did you know there are a lot of different ones?"

Shocked stupid, Reed only nodded, his eyes flying to Lindy, who was trying not to let her pride be overcome by a smug grin. Intelligent beyond her years, the kid must be a handful.

Securing the blanket around her daughter yet again, Lindy picked her up and stood. She faced him as a stranger, a warm smile of appreciation lighting her beautiful face.

Reed, holding Cloud, got to his feet and waited, trying to decide if he should remind her of their last meeting almost five years earlier, the weekend of his May 12th birthday. He watched her expression, peered into her oblivious gaze and decided she had no idea who he was. Strangely, that hurt. Made him decide the hell with reminding her of a night he'd spent years remembering.

Lindy smiled. "Please, what's your name? I want to thank you, and it seems too informal to call you sir like Hollie."

"I'm Reed Carlton. I work as a surgeon at the new hospital here at the Grove."

Lindy's expression closed and her smile faded. "You're a Carlton?"

"Yes." He'd never had to apologize for his

antecedents before. But for the first time in his life, he felt compelled to say he was sorry. And if it would bring back the smiling girl from minutes earlier, he'd seriously consider changing his name to Wojciehowicz or Stubbs.

Stiff now, her previous warmth vanished, Lindy spoke in crisp tones, an order her daughter knew better than to ignore. "Hollie, thank Mr. Carlton for saving you today. He was very brave and we're both grateful." So saying, she forced her hand out to shake his. Pulling away as soon as his fingers closed around hers, she leaned her daughter closer and waited.

"Thank you, Mr. Reed. Me and Cloud are very happy you were there."

"Me too, sunshine. Be good and listen to your mom, okay?"

"Okay." Reaching with her small hand, he thought Hollie was aiming for the wriggling puppy. Not so. He felt her little fingers gently pat his cheek. "Be nice to Cloud. Maybe we can meet in the park, in the mornings on weekends and I can play with her."

His eyes flew to meet Lindy's. She shook her head, the movement quick and furtive, her eyes now empty of their previous warmth.

Huh? What just happened? "That's a deal, honey. I'll watch out for you."

Chapter Seven

Of all the men in a city of over seventy thousand and rising, Belinda couldn't believe that Reed Carlton would be the one to save her baby. After all, the Grove was big enough that she'd gambled on never having to deal with a member of the family she'd detested for almost five years.

Maybe it wasn't fair of her to blame the entire Carlton clan for what had happened to her. But since her disgrace had occurred in their ostentatious home, and she had no idea of the actual culprit, it was just easier to condemn the host. Who, of course must have been a Carlton, maybe even Reed himself. Truthfully, she didn't know because she couldn't remember. How could she when she'd been drugged and virtually raped?

Just the thought of what had happened to her that May weekend was enough to make the sandwich she'd gulped down earlier feel like it would be making a re-appearance.

Stop thinking about it! You have to live here, there's no other choice.

Carlton Grove was where her family was and though they weren't able to help her financially, they did allow her to bring their grandchild to stay overnight when she had late shifts at the pub where she bartended. Without that second income, she doubted she could manage to bank even a penny of the wages from her other job.

Rushing now, Belinda zipped around their tiny apartment chosen because it was close to the park. Quickly, she bathed Hollie and made them both ready for the day.

Later, after listening to the little one chatting continuously about Cloud and Mr. Reed, pretending to pay attention with the occasional nod and hum of agreement, Belinda stopped her old beater and dropped her little monster munchkin off at the day-care.

"Hollie, remember your promise? We agreed that if I took you to the park this morning and we played on the swings, you would be a good girl this afternoon. Since it's your first day back, you must find a way to get along with Miss Dummy and behave..."

Giggling, her hands over her mouth as if to stop

the laughter, Hollie scolded, "You mustn't call her that, Mommy. Remember? It's Miss *Dumry*."

Red-faced, trying to hide her own smile, Belinda glanced around to make sure she hadn't been overheard. "Sorry." She gently slapped her own mouth and said, "My bad! Miss Dum*ry* hopes to find more time to be with you, so be nice. Okay?"

"Mommy, if she'd put her phone... O-*kay*! I'll be good."

Belinda kissed her and watched as her little hellion ran off to join with a group of the others, mostly boys, and observed Hollie pushing her way in and then taking over the conversation. No doubt, by the end of the day, everyone would have heard about her morning's exploits.

This didn't bother Belinda near as much as what had happened earlier, while they were still at the apartment. She'd left Hollie in the bath so she could call her mother to make arrangements to drop her daughter off after supper. She had her regular housekeeping job for the afternoon, had time to make them supper and then do a late shift at the pub.

Returning to the washroom, she'd spied her daughter in the mirror. Hollie had been rocking, hugging herself and crying softly, tears streaming from her sad eyes. Piled in front of her sat a mountain of soft white bubbles closely resembling a cloud.

Chapter Eight

Reed stood holding the crying puppy, soothing her as she wriggled to get down. Finally, he lowered the fluffy animal to the ground and then had to run and scoop her up again as she took off, following the woman and child now some way ahead.

"Oh, no, you don't! They can't take you, Trouble. Hey, settle down." The pup had a mind of her own and was frantic to get to the little girl who kept glancing back and waving sadly.

Finally, Reed had to wrap Cloud inside his blanket and turn the other way before the puppy stopped fighting him and relaxed with a whine of dismay.

"Harley! Man, I'm glad you waited." Reed sloshed his way to where they'd parked, glad to see his brother leaning against the car, a cellphone held to his ear and a smile plastered over his face. As soon as he saw Reed, he shut down the conversation and stood. "Hey, bro, quite a morning you've had, super hero of little children and puppies."

"Zip it, dumbass! Here, take the mutt."

Harley stepped back and held his hands up in denial. "Nope. I don't want the headache, man. It's all yours. Sure is a cutie though."

"Just hold her so I can get these wet clothes off me. I have a set of sweats in the car."

Shaking his head vigorously, Harley laughed. "I ain't falling for that old trick. You've gotten away with it more times than I want to remember. That animal is all yours."

Pissed and showing it, Reed's voice deepened. "Did you by any chance see where it came from? Or notice anyone looking for her?"

Harley laughed out loud once more and shook his head, obviously enjoying his brother's predicament.

Sighing with disgust, Reed used the towel to make sure Cloud was dry, opened the rear door and shoved her carefully onto the seat. Then he closed it and went to the trunk. "Look, you're a cop, right? You're supposed to be so observant. Did you see anyone searching for a missing... ? Stop grinning like an idiot and shaking your head. It's beginning to make me want to hurt you. "

Harley cracked up. Not intimidated by his older brother's grouchy disposition, he finally straightened his face and solemnly answered. "I already told you. I didn't notice any unusual behaviour, but I can put an APB over the system to see if we can apprehend the nasty varmint who'd leave a teeny-weeny, adorable little puppy all alone in a park in the hope that some big-hearted, pea-brained shmuck would take pity on it."

"Jesus, man, with that smart mouth, I can't believe you passed the academy."

"And I can't believe you're a wealthy young surgeon who hangs out alone in a big old house, I might add, with a fenced-in yard, never goes anywhere and lives like a hermit. Guess it's your ugly face that's the problem. Must be why you never have any girlfriends."

"Yeah, right. At least I'm not a slut like you, always with a new chick on my arm, breaking their hearts every time you cut them off. Don't know how you sleep at night with all those rejected women calling you to reconsider."

Purposely, Reed used this example to get at the now straight-faced man glaring his way. One time Harley had left the speaker on his phone open and the whole family had overheard a female voice begging him to give her another chance. When he needed taking down a notch, they used this to tease the best-looker in the family of handsome boys.

Harley stiffened and straightened. His face lost its teasing look and his voice turned to steel. "That bitch did me wrong, not the other way around. And no one makes a fool of me and gets a second chance to do it again. And... in case you never figured it out, the females I spend my time with are all women who know the score. Until I meet 'the one', they're only pit stops on the course."

Knowing he'd overstepped the boundaries, Reed reached out and grabbed Harley's arm to shake it consolingly. "Sorry, man. That was shitty. I didn't mean it. Guess my temper's still working on high. I know you'll find your one and only. Hell, you've been talking about her as long as I can remember. But, I'm different. I'm a moody, introverted prick and I like my own space. Can't imagine any woman wanting to put up with the likes of me and wouldn't take the chance if I found one."

"Don't blame you. She'd obviously have mental issues to even consider taking you on." Harley, now visibly relaxed, patted his brother's hand before it disappeared. Reed didn't touch people often and when he did, it mattered. Being a smart man Harley apologized also. "I shouldn't have teased you, bro. Sometimes the devil gets into me and I can't resist. Look, I'll ask around and see if anyone knows anything about the pup. But my guess is that whoever dumped her here wanted her gone and couldn't be bothered to find it a home.

My advice is to either take her to Mom or to the pound. She's cute. She'll be adopted."

"Yeah, well, I can't do that. I kind of promised the kid that I'd meet her in the park sometimes and let her walk Cloud. I can't go back on my word."

"Cloud?"

Reed shook his head. "It's a long story."

"So what were you planning to do if you'd have sucked me in to adopting the mutt?"

Reed grinned. "I'd have played uncle and taken the nuisance on outings, just like I expect you to do now."

"Yeah, like that's going to happen."

Chapter Nine

Mindlessly cleaning the house of her oldest client, Belinda tried to come up with some plan where she could somehow keep the little puppy and make her adored baby's dream come true. The image of Hollie sobbing into her hands had broken her heart, as it would any loving mother who knew the one thing her child most wanted, she'd just refused to give to her.

Plus, it had been obvious to anyone with eyes and a heart that the two little ones had bonded from the beginning. Belinda had heard Cloud whining after they'd walked away, and she had seen Reed chasing the pup when she had tried to follow them.

But, no matter which way she jiggled her daily

routine, there was no time in her busy schedule for the care of an active puppy. Especially one that looked like she'd be growing into a fairly large dog.

After all, not only would she need to be housebroken and have a fenced-in yard, she'd have to be fed, walked, groomed and trained. And... those things didn't happen in a few spare minutes. As it was, Belinda gave every bit of her free time to her daughter and those precious hours never felt sufficient.

Most days, guilt had her questioning all her decisions. *Does this laundry, baking, vacuuming... really need to be done, or should I use the precious time to play with Hollie?*

Also, the expense of taking on a pet just didn't fit into her overextended budget either. Already she did without a lot of ordinary comforts in order to save her pennies.

Completely lost in concentration, she knocked over a vase which brought her back to the present. The oil she'd been waxing into the antique furniture gave off fumes of cleanliness and old times that usually cheered her. But today, no matter how gleaming the tables looked, her heart was heavy with uncertainties.

Falling snow caught her attention. She straightened and stared out of the bay window at the luxurious gardens surrounding the older home. Because of the weirdly mild autumn, huge baskets of fall mums were still vying for attention.

Now, all were slowly being buried under a white comforter.

"Belinda. You have sighed more than that old furnace does in the winter, and trust me, it's on its last legs and needs replacing. Can't you please tell me what's on your mind? If there's anything I can do to bring back your usual happy face, I'd like to help."

"So now you're telling me I sound like a crappy old furnace and look like a grinning computer icon. My day can't get much better." Laughing to take any sting from her words, Belinda went to her employer and, leaning over her wheelchair, she gave her a gentle hug.

Maeve Wakefield giggled, the sound brightening Belinda's spirit. "Put words in my mouth—go ahead—see if I care. But don't ever make light of how much I appreciate everything you do for me. It's because of you that I'm able to continue living here. Your help makes it possible."

"You pay me, Maeve." Belinda cut in softly.

"Not nearly enough. For one thing, I've never seen you just walk around here, you're usually moving at a sprinter's pace. And you know darn well I couldn't manage without you cleaning my house, doing my shopping and laundry, preparing a lot of my meals and even taking out the garbage. Those care-givers who come in and dress me and come back in the evening to put me to bed do help too. I appreciate you making those arrangements with them. You look after all those things, so do you see what I mean? It's only because of your constant attentiveness that I'm able to stay home."

"It's been my pleasure; you know it has, Maeve. I don't know what I'd do without you and this job."

"I just wish I could pay you more so you wouldn't have to take on the extra night work. Maybe I'm being silly hanging on to the old barn. I should probably sell and look for some place smaller?"

"Maeve, we're not getting into that nonsense again. I love helping you here at Cherrylane. If you moved away from your memories, you'd be sick at heart, and if you add that to the already weak valves you're living with, there's no telling what would happen."

The two laughed comfortably together and Belinda began sighing with relief for having gotten out of a tight spot. But... she should've known better. Previously having been a lawyer, and a damn good one, the seventy-eight-year-old hadn't forgotten the original thread that had started the conversation. "Sit down here and tell me what happened to give you such a pinched look and sad expression."

Taking a final glance at the shining room full of treasures, gilded mirrors and frightfully expensive keepsakes, then peeking at her watch and seeing she had a few minutes to spare, Belinda did just that.

"Hollie fell in love this morning." Telling a story to Maeve had to be done with drama. She wasn't the type who appreciated a boring tale.

"Aha! Well, I won't ask when the wedding is since I do believe Hollie graduating elementary and high-school is compulsory, but you can tell me about her new beau?"

Laughing, enjoying the discussion as much as she knew she would, Belinda played along. She smirked while answering, "The name is Cloud."

Maeve's eyes twinkled and her wrinkled hands folded together before she dropped them in her lap. "Very interesting! He's either a Native American, or quite possibly a Doberman pincher. Which is it?"

"Ha! You're so smart. And quite close. From the looks of his coloring, his beady little black eyes and grinning... ahhh...snout, I would say *she's* more likely to be a Samoyed puppy."

"How precious! I love that breed. They make wonderful family pets, especially the females. Can you bring Cloud to see me?"

Losing her grin, Belinda stared at her red, chapped hands. "We didn't keep her. She was wandering in the park this morning, slid down the embankment and went right into the lake. My impulsive and irrepressible Hollie happened to see this and went right in after her, thinking to save the pup. Instead, she lost her footing and took a header. I arrived in time to see a man rescuing them both. He ended up with Cloud."

"The dog was his?"

"Not really. I think she's a stray. Despite all the onlookers nearby who saw what happened, not one stepped forward to claim the animal. And Hollie was wearing me down with her begging. Then Mr. Carlton claimed her. I believe he lied to help me, though I begrudge having to accept this gesture. Quite possibly, if I'd known he was a Carlton I wouldn't have, but it's too late to back down now."

"I don't understand."

"Hollie made him agree to let her walk the puppy if we were able to meet in the park on weekend mornings." Belinda didn't hide her frustration fast enough. Wily Maeve had eyes like a hawk.

"And that's a problem, why?"

"Because I hate the Carltons—plain and simple. It's because of them that I had to change my life, give up my dreams of being a nurse and ended up as a single mom."

"My goodness, Lindy, what in the world did they do for you to feel such resentment?"

The nickname made Belinda hesitate. Maeve was the only person who called her that from time to time and, whenever she did, memories tried to break through which left Belinda feeling a strange yearning.

Shaking off her reaction, the overwhelming

urge to tell her story took hold. Seeing Maeve waiting, and trusting her more than anyone else she knew, she finally decided her painful experience needed to be shared.

Plunging in before she changed her mind, she began. "When I was young and foolish, visiting my folks for the May weekend from college, I'd gone along with a group of friends to a party at the Carlton home. Normally, I didn't hang around with this group; they were wilder and way more unconventional than I was. But one of the girls who I'd grown up with asked me to come with her. She'd invited me to go with her so many times that I felt bad for all the refusals.

When we arrived at this big house, there was a party in the wild stage; booze everywhere and couples were being far more than romantic—if you know what I mean. Not used to this kind of behaviour, I'd all but decided to leave when one of the cool girls I'd known in high school gave me a glass of beer and welcomed me so nicely that I decided I was being a prude. Then someone asked me to dance and, without a thought in the world, I left my drink on the table and didn't return to it for some time. When I did, I was so thirsty that I drank it and that's the last thing I remember. The next day, I felt achy and sore and had a hangover. Mainly, I was scared because I couldn't recall any events from the night before. My girlfriend told me I'd had a fabulous time, had flirted with all the guys and had even disappeared with someone. She thought it might have been one of the Carlton boys, but she wasn't sure."

"Oh, oh!"

"Yes! As you can imagine, I was very embarrassed. Then three months later, I was totally devastated."

"And Hollie was born Christmas Day."

" As you know she was premature."

"Goodness me, Lindy, I'm saddened by your story, but aren't you being rather harsh on this fellow who rescued Hollie today? After all, he could be her father."

Oh, my God...

Chapter Ten

Belinda held out the first weekend after the incident, refusing to go to the park. Instead, she took Hollie to her parents' home one afternoon for her mother's birthday party, and she arranged a movie the next day to take the pouting child's mind off where she yearned to be. But she just didn't have the stamina to withstand the barrage of 'please' that her determined little monster fired at her for the rest of the week. All she could do was pray that Reed Carlton didn't show up this morning.

Dressed warmly, Belinda followed her excited daughter along the walkways toward the lake and breathed a little easier when she didn't see any fluffy small white animals nearby.

Dancing along, excitement lighting her pink cheeks, Hollie wore a new red hat and matching sweater her mother had knitted for her to help pass the long lonely evenings watching romantic sitcoms on television.

All the snow was finally gone from the freak snowstorm they'd had the day after Hollie had fallen into the lake. The cold spell had given over again to warm weather, but the smells of winter close by made the day extra beautiful.

"Stop running to and fro, Hollie, you're making my neck sore trying to keep track of you. Let's give Mommy's tired legs a break, and sit here on the bench and I'll tell you a story."

Grudgingly, Hollie came and plopped down beside her mother and sulked. "Mr. Reed said he'd bring Cloud. He promised."

"No, baby, he didn't do any such thing. It was a casual 'maybe' and you know it."

"But he winked at me, Mommy, and that means a promise."

"Where in the world did you get such a goofy idea?"

Oh, no!

Bouncing with delight, Hollie took off at a mad dash to meet up with the yipping puppy who was in a panic to get to her. Their meeting in the grass brought tears to Belinda's eyes. Both canine and child were so delighted to be together again that the kisses and licks were all mixed together in a hugging frenzy of love.

Reed, holding an empty leash, approached and

stood near the bench. "May I?" He gestured at the seat.

Rather than sit near him, she stood instead. "I was just going to walk. I-I need the exercise." *Liar!*

"You weren't here last weekend. I came both days."

"Are you accusing me of being a bad mother?"

He swung to face her. "What? Why in the hell would you think that? I just wanted Hollie to know that I hadn't broken my promise."

"Oh, you two. It's enough for me to try and control that little devil, and now I have you siding..."

"Hold it, Lindy. I wasn't accusing you of anything, or trying to make you feel bad."

"What did you call me?" Furious beyond reason, she spat out words at the same time as she glared her anger.

He backed up a step. "Isn't your name Lindy?"

"My name is Belinda Page. No one calls me Lindy."

Awkwardly, Reed put his hands behind him. "I'm sorry. We met once a long time ago and you introduced yourself then as Lindy. I recognized you, but you didn't seem to remember me, so I never said anything."

Oh, my God! It's him! He must be Hollie's father.

A sickening feeling of dread overcame her and she was forced to sit down again on a different bench. Pain seared her temples, pressing relentlessly, pounding into her panic. Hugging herself to control vicious accusations from spewing, she bit her lip and hid her face.

"Lindy, here let me help you." He gently forced her head toward her knees and rubbed her back.

His touch soothed but she didn't want his hands on her. She couldn't look at him. *Oh, God!*

"Take deep breaths. That's good. Slowly."

She shied away from his hands. Her mind raced, thoughts fighting over each other to be heard, to make sense. Though she followed the instructions from the soft-spoken male voice, she tried to conceal her reactions to his touch. *I need to get away!*

"Mommy, what's wrong?" Both child and puppy had come running and were now fussing over Belinda. Hollie tried to hug her around her head and the pup whined pitifully. She heard the fear in her little girl's voice and that was enough to give her the strength she needed to snap out of her pity-party. Feeling the puppy's tongue on her cheek, giving her own brand of comfort, Belinda gave Cloud a cuddle and took the time to breathe deeply.

"I was a little dizzy, baby. But I'm fine now." She caressed Hollie's worry away from her face and held up the excited canine. "Cloud. You've grown." Gathering the quivering mutt close, she let the animal shower her with affection.

Hollie, obviously satisfied her mom was fine,

turned to the hovering man. "Mr. Reed. You came like you promised."

"Of course! I think Cloud knew she would see you here. She pulled me so fast to the lake area; I had a heck of a time keeping up. I was worried the little monster would drag me along behind her if I fell."

Seeing her laugh at the mind-picture of the little puppy pulling along the big man, Hollie's giggles had him chuckling also.

Belinda, fearful of the child racing off again with her furry friend, rose carefully, steadying herself by holding onto the back of the seat and made a suggestion. "Let's take Cloud for a little walk now, because it'll soon be lunchtime and we'll have to go home to eat."

Hollie's demeanor changed instantly. Stiff with resentment, she appealed, "We can go on a *long* walk. I'm not hungry."

Belinda watched Reed hide his smile and turn away.

"Yes, baby, but little puppies tire very easily. Their legs are short and not as strong as a big girl like you. We'll go around the park and that should be enough for one day." Though her voice started out in a gentle humorous tone, it had changed by the end of her sentence. It became firm and meant business, and Hollie knew not to argue.

Reed attached the leash to the puppy's collar and handed it over to outstretched chubby hands.

The two were off at a run.

"Hollie Page. You stay in my sight, you hear me?"

"Yes, ma'am." A grin and nod were shared, and then all her attention became focused on her furry companion.

Chapter Eleven

"Hollie's very good with the pup. And Cloud adores her." Reed knew he needed to fill in the silence. It was obvious that Lindy was still suffering from her earlier predicament. He just wished he knew what he'd said wrong.

Lindy's answer took time but she eventually replied, "It's all I've heard about for the last week: Mr. Reed this, and Cloud that. She was furious at me for not bringing her last weekend."

"Truthfully, I expected to see you. Even Cloud seemed disappointed when there was no sign of Hollie. She whined when I took her away and pulled so hard at the leash that I had to pick her up."

No way would Reed tell her how he'd dressed

in a new outfit, groomed the pup for an hour and had even bought a chocolate-covered candy apple as a special treat for Hollie. Disappointment had ridden him for days and was most likely felt by anyone who had the misfortune of working in his surgeries.

He'd told himself he wouldn't come today. He'd work. But when the time came he'd booked the morning off, and here he was trying to understand why the woman he'd been so attracted to seemed to hate the very sight of him.

Since she didn't answer, he added, "I wasn't accusing you. Please don't think that—"

"No, don't apologize. It's me. I'm behaving badly."

She faced him, her cheeks still pale. Melted chocolate, her brown eyes highlighted by curled dark eyelashes didn't quite hide her raging emotions. Pink lips quivering slightly, lush and full, drew his attention. She'd changed in the last few years, filled out—seemed more mature and even more beautiful. "I have to ask you something. Did we meet at a party at your house five years ago?"

Reed studied her pallor and quickly put his hands behind him, stuffed them in his back pockets, a habit he had for self-protection. He stared at his shoes and took a minute to decide his answer.

Unsurprisingly, his mind raced into the past

and he was reminded about an incident as a carefree young teen. When he'd impulsively reached out to a distressed girl, he'd gotten his face slapped and his heart broken. The girl he'd believed returned his affection hadn't had the finesse to deal with a boy's sensitive nature. Head over heels in love, he'd trusted that she'd cared about him in the same way. Not so. He'd learned a huge lesson that day: *don't ever open yourself to a female. More than likely, you'll live to regret it. Keep your walls up and stay behind them.*

She waited, staring, not moving. He sensed her anxiety and it made him ultra-nervous. *For pity's sake, just tell the truth.*

"Yes, we did. Look, I tried to find you again but you'd disappeared." Watching the varied emotions she couldn't hide, he stopped talking and waited. Didn't she remember the incredible night they'd spent together? She'd flirted with him, come on to him but with a naiveté and sweetness that had hooked him big time.

Not one to party, that night he'd been celebrating the end of his finals and had gone a bit crazy. When she'd shown up, acting the sexy siren, she'd just been too damn perfect to ignore.

And he hadn't regretted that decision. At first, when he'd realized she'd never been with a man, he'd tried to stop but she hadn't let him. He'd never been with a virgin before, but she'd been sweet and giving, leaving him with the feeling that he'd been special.

After they'd satisfied their hunger for each other, he'd gone to get them some wine and a platter of goodies. When he'd returned to his room, she'd disappeared. He'd searched frantically, asked everyone if they knew her but many had left and those still around had no idea who he was talking about. In the end, all he'd had from their encounter was the beautiful memory and her first name.

"What do you mean I disappeared? How did I do that?"

Feeling like he was walking through a live minefield, Reed hesitated. Then he decided to speak truthfully. "Lindy—it's what you asked me to call you—we hit it off that night. Both of us were infatuated—"

"Mommy, you were right! Cloud is tired. She's whining for me to carry her. I guess we better rest for a while."

Reed couldn't decide if he welcomed the interruption or not. Lindy's eyes were huge, watching his face closely. It appeared as if she wasn't breathing, so enthralled was she with his words.

The sigh she let escape ended in a tiny imperceptible cry that shot straight to the muscles in his throat and made swallowing impossible. He watched her struggle to shake off the spell, but not before he recognized the frustration she couldn't hide. With her hands gripping each other to still their trembling, she finally answered. "Yes, okay, sweetheart. Maybe it's time that Mr. Reed, I mean, Mr...."

"Please, just call me Reed."

She searched his eyes and then nodded. "...time for Reed to take Cloud home for her nap."

No! Clamouring in his head, the instinctive word made one thing very clear to him. He didn't want this meeting to end. "Look, we haven't had much time to be together. So, can I take you ladies for lunch? There's a restaurant just at the entrance to the park called Di's where the owner is crazy about Cloud and allows me to put her under the table while I eat. We can go there if you like?"

Watching the by-play between mother and daughter, he had no idea how she withstood her baby's arguments, enhanced by pleading eyes and trembling lips, for as long as she managed. He'd have been a goner after the first *I-promise-to-be-a-good-girl–forever* tearful plea.

Chapter Twelve

Sitting together in the booth at Di's, Belinda wasn't exactly sure how she got there. Certainly, Hollie had played a big part in making up her mind. Guilt had ridden her hard at how seldom she could afford to give her baby a meal in a restaurant. Plus, she knew how much it meant to the little girl to have more time with Cloud.

Once the waitress had fussed over the tired puppy and they'd settled her on the mat under the table, she'd taken their orders and left them to move on to the other customers. Hollie, sitting on the floor near Cloud, was happy in her own little world, and had left the two adults facing each other with just the well-washed table top between them.

Looking anywhere but at Reed, Belinda studied

the cozy place and saw an atmosphere and faded furnishings that hadn't been updated in decades. It reminded her of the diner she'd practically lived at with her high school friends. The good food smells that attacked the minute they'd walked in were making her mouth water and she realized just what a treat it was to be waited on and having her meal served to her.

"I'm glad you came." His words seemed to surprise him, make him uncomfortable, as if they escaped his mouth before gaining his permission.

Speaking low, she shared, "Hollie doesn't get to eat out very often. It's a wonderful treat, so thank you for inviting us." Belinda stopped talking before she made a fool of herself. As much as she yearned to go back to their earlier subject, fear and shyness stopped her questions.

"My pleasure. Really!" He put his long-fingered hands on the table and stared at them in a funny way before he looked at her, his eyes full of warmth. "After you left the park that day, it took some time to settle Cloud. She fretted terribly for hours. Strange as it may seem, I think those two bonded... ahh, I'm not making much sense but you had to be there to see the little monster grieve. Finally, that night, I had to bring her into bed with me and hold her close so I could get some sleep. And trust me, if anyone would have told me I'd be doing anything so asinine, I'd have laughed and told them to get real."

Belinda saw his cheeks redden before he bent over to check under the table. It was as if his confession had escaped without him meaning to say anything. Sensing his discomfort and not being a person who liked to see others in distress, she quickly cut in, "I think that was sweet of you. Many would have shut her in a bathroom or the garage."

He straightened. "Only one person has ever accused me of being sweet." Their eyes met, and there was an emotion in his that had her breath catching and her heart beating so fast she swore the pulsing in her chest must be visible.

As if the words were forced, she admitted her own situation. "It was the same with Hollie, only she carried on for days. I have a strict rule that she must sleep in her own bed, but that night I had to share it with her, to soothe her. She refused to understand why we couldn't keep *her* puppy."

"You could have. You knew it wasn't mine."

"No. That's just it; we don't live that kind of a lifestyle. I work two jobs, and as much as I would have loved to have Cloud, I have no time left over to raise another baby."

Lost in his searching gaze, warmth and gentleness making the green hues in his brown eyes darker and more intense, she didn't notice when his hand enfolded her fingers to stop their unconscious fidgeting. It was the brush of something against her leg that dropped her back to earth with a thud. *Hollie!*

"We need to talk." A frantic urgency had entered his low voice, and she felt pulled between mothering her child and losing herself in the chaotic emotional whirlpool he created with every glance.

Ignoring his insistence, she pulled her hands from under his and reached down to her child. "Sweetie, come with Mommy now. Our food will be here soon and you need to wash your hands before you eat."

He leaned back, watchful, waiting for a response to his plea. Before she could whisk the child away, he tried again. "Lindy? Answer me. When can we meet?"

"No. I mean, not yet."

"When?" His right eyebrow rose and steel entered his voice.

"I don't know. Excuse me. We'll be right back."

By the time she'd returned with the munchkin, the hamburgers had been delivered, along with Hollie's strawberry milkshake and a huge basket of flavourful fries.

Being considerate, Reed had fetched a higher chair for the little girl to sit in but when she spotted it, mutiny appeared and she crossed her arms, her mouth forming the stubborn pout that Belinda knew well.

Reed stepped forward. "Here we go, Sunshine. They have the special chairs for little girls to use.

Let me help you." He reached to lift her and Hollie backed away.

"Those chairs are for babies."

Looking nonplussed, Reed nodded first. Within seconds, he realized his mistake and his head changed direction. "Not really. They're not *just* for babies; the owners have them for anyone who wants to... ahh, sit up higher." Looking for help, he glanced her way. Belinda quickly shook her head and grinned. Let him suffer his own folly. She'd experienced her daughter's displeasure often enough, she had battle scars no one saw—didn't mean they didn't exist.

"I'm bigger when I sit on my knees. They're strong and it's healthy exercise. I do yoga with Mommy and it's one of our poses. Right, Mommy?"

Her hands outstretched, Belinda shrugged at Reed and watched him surrender gracefully.

"Okay, swift, you got me there. A yoga chick; heck you must be older than I thought."

Giggling proudly, Hollie answered. "I'm five on Christmas Day. I'm just kinda short."

Chapter Thirteen

Right after they'd eaten, before Reed could pin Lindy down to a date and time for their next meeting, she'd rushed Hollie along and vanished.

Driving back to the hospital for his afternoon appointments, he remembered the little girl's proud statement: *I'm five on Christmas Day.*

Suddenly that fact hit him like a rock on the side of his head. He swerved, his foot ramming the brakes hard. Stunned, his brain opened an inner calculator and he quickly added the months from the night in May when they'd been together. A quick sigh of relief followed.

Thank God! Hollie couldn't be his.

Why sadness washed over him, he didn't know, but a faint inner glow faded and his heartbeats slowed. The brainy, curly-haired angel with dimples and the attitude of a little warrior wasn't his. He swallowed the sigh and pulled into his reserved slot. Gripping the steering wheel with both hands, he lowered his forehead and for just a few minutes he let himself wallow in unexpected desolation—*she wasn't his.*

Upon reaching his office, he spied his receptionist talking with his next patient, one of his favorites.

"Ah! Here's Dr. Carlton now."

"Maeve, my dear, how are you today?"

"Could be better, Dr. Darling. Could be better." Maeve coughed and the harshness in her voice deepened. "Now if you'd stop being so damn finicky and write me a large prescription for some of those pain-relieving narcotics you're hoarding, I'd be perfect."

Smiling at their nonsense, he answered. "Sweetheart, if you'd quit trafficking the ones I give you, they'd last longer. How many times have I told you to stop sitting on that street corner and selling the product?"

Giggling at their silliness, Maeve clapped her hands. "Okay, you got me there. I'll be good." She coughed again, and he helped her sit upright.

Wheeling her chair into his office, Reed proceeded to take her blood pressure and then he checked the information on his computer screen. "How's your breathing, darling? Is it getting difficult? Are you wheezing? Any chest pains? Having trouble sleeping?"

"Not really. But I'm tired all the time. My housekeeper has taken on all the chores for me because I'm pretty useless. She wants to hire someone to come and sleep in the house with me at night so I'm not alone, and I admit that I've given it some thought. I guess it's the stranger in the house aspect I'm not comfortable with. During the day, she's organized caregiver visits and an alarm button, but those dark hours can be lonely."

'I'm glad she's looking into it. You should have someone with you all the time now."

"Now? Okay, spill the beans. How long do I have, Dr. Carlton? I know you couldn't operate..."

"You mean you refused to let me."

"Yes, well, I didn't want to be any more of an invalid than I already am. I just wanted to live these last few months in as normal a way as possible, stay in my house and enjoy the life I have left. You said yourself that my ticker is wonky."

"Darling Maeve, I never said your *ticker* was *wonky*." Reed grinned. "I would never use medical jargon with a patient who wouldn't understand such technical terms. I remember distinctly using layman's words when I explained that you suffered from mild congestive heart failure. A heart attack was just a possibility. One I felt you had to be aware of. There were other procedures we talked about, such as radiation or chemical therapy that I thought might stave off the end, but you refused them all."

"Yes. I know. I'm a stubborn old wretch who's made up her mind. Rather than take any chances, no matter how slim, I wanted my last months to be special. And it's been wonderful. I've put all my finances in order, so I'm ready to go out of the world like I came in, kicking my legs and screeching like a banshee."

Reed laughed, couldn't help himself. The spritely lady sitting in front of him was a jewel and he would miss her terribly. But from the results of her latest scans and blood tests, she would begin fading more quickly now.

"I'm going to have a technician deliver an oxygen ventilator to you which you must begin to use constantly. You'll find it helpful for sleeping especially."

"Will it stop this infernal cough?"

"Sure, it'll soothe you and help your breathing ability a lot. I'm also giving you a different prescription for antibiotics and one for relaxation. You must take them as directed. Maeve, it's time for you to have someone with you during the day as well as the night, a person to help you with the new equipment. Do you have anyone you can ask?"

Maeve shook her head. "As you know, I never had any children and my sister died a few years ago, unfortunately preceded by her only daughter. So, no, there're no relatives. But I could ask my housekeeper to move in with me, I suppose. She's a lovely girl and has a small child of her own. Since I've willed everything to her, she might choose to move into the house anyway."

"Good. Ask her. It'll make all the difference to you in these last few months having someone to be with you. Otherwise, we'll have no choice but to bring you into hospital."

"Aha! You just let the cat out of the bag. I only have a matter of months now. Yes, I can see by your long face that the end is close. I'm not at all unhappy, Dr. Darling." Maeve reached out and took his hand, smiling as his warm fingers wrapped around her thin claw-like ones and squeezed. "You've been good to me, my friend. Please know how much I've appreciated having someone listen rather than just give orders. Bless you, Doctor, and thank you."

Chapter Fourteen

"Maeve, tell me again why your doctor won't operate." It was a question Belinda had asked before, and each time Maeve had looked away and made little of her response, putting Belinda off with a nonchalant shrug and a silly excuse. Furious that the medical community could be so uncaring with her precious friend's life, Belinda had been tempted to interfere. If Maeve's faculties were questionable, she would have. As it was, her friend was sharper than most her age.

Maeve shrugged. "Oh, you know, they have so many patients. I'm just one of hundreds. Besides, I have no complaints about my treatment. In fact, Dr. Darling has been wonderful. But he's insistent that I have someone live with me now or it'll be the hospital for me and I would hate that. So I'm asking if you and Hollie can do it."

Belinda leaned over and gave her a gentle squeeze. A scent of roses wafted around her boss. Since the lotion had been one of Belinda's birthday presents to Maeve, the odor pleased her. "Of course we can move in here with you. Hollie will be ecstatic to be this close to special Auntie Maeve at Christmastime and she'll love having the yard to play in, especially if we're lucky enough to have snow this year. Plus, I'll feel a lot better being with you during the night, rather than constantly worrying when you're alone."

"It's settled then." Maeve slapped her knees and settled back in her chair. The white curls haloing her wrinkled face bounced with satisfaction.

"What about the evenings when I'm at work? There's a friend of Mom's, you've met her before, that lady called Freda who lives close by. She's babysat for me periodically when the family was away, and she's strapped for cash most months. She might like to earn a few extra dollars to come and stay with you and Hollie during those hours. Should I ask her? She wouldn't charge much so I can probably pay her from my tips."

"I'll pay her, you mean. After all, you'll be changing your life for me."

"We'll work it out." Belinda had noticed the ventilator resting on wheels over in the corner and decided to take the plunge. "So, Miss Maeve, suppose you tell me about that contraption over there and how it works."

"Oh, we'll let my doctor explain. He's promised to come over tomorrow afternoon so he could explain everything. I couldn't make any sense of what the delivery fellow said. Spanish accents and my ears just don't go together. Guess I'm too old."

Belinda smiled. "Your Dr. Darling does house calls?"

"For me he does."

"That's wonderful. I'll be here. I can't wait to meet him." She turned away, hiding the determination from Maeve to give the idiot a piece of her mind for not taking better care of her friend.

Too many patients... bah!

Chapter Fifteen

Belinda wiped the counter and settled back to washing glasses. It was quiet tonight in the bar area; most folks were in the dining room having a meal. Other than taking the occasional wine orders, she had the time to scan the room, see that the few regulars were settled and happily occupied with filled glasses. She let her mind wander.

Modern, yet warm and inviting, the wooden booths and tables scattered around the fair-sized room were tidied and waiting for the customers she knew would eventually appear. The greens, grays and blues used in decorating the walls and light fixtures presented the low-lit room with a convivial and inviting atmosphere.

Modern music played in the background, kept

low for her own enjoyment and it wouldn't be turned up to fight with the noise of people having a good time until later when no one cared.

Having left Maeve's house to pick up Hollie and deliver her to her parent's home, she'd explained that it would likely be the last time the little girl would be overnighting with her grandparents for a while. Smiling at the memory of Hollie's glee, she allowed the satisfaction to take hold.

"Auntie Maeve wants us to live with her? In her house? Even me?"

"Yes, for the third time, she wants both of us to live with her."

"I'll be a good girl, Mommy. I won't run around or yell very much. Maybe we could get Mr. Reed to bring Cloud over to see where we live and meet Auntie Maeve. She'd like that, wouldn't she? Then I could play with my puppy in the yard."

Belinda sighed over Hollie's noticeable use of the pronoun 'my'. "We'll see. I can't make any promises, munchkin. You do know that Auntie Maeve isn't well, I've explained this to you before, remember? She'll need a lot of sleep and then one day she won't wake up. Do you understand?"

The silence trembled. A sigh escaped the little girl, one of acceptance. "Yes, she told me she can't wait to go to sleep because soon she'll get to live with the angels. She's lucky. I wish I could see the angels."

Belinda smiled, swallowing the instant shot of dismay those words evoked. "One day you will, baby, but for now, you need to stay and look after Mommy."

Lost in her own world, reliving earlier moments, Belinda didn't see the man who approached the black granite counter and took a seat at the end of the bar until he lifted the menu.

Shock had her hesitating, but his welcoming grin started her feet moving forward. "Hi, Lindy."

"How did you know I worked here?"

"Hollie told me while you were in the ladies' room after lunch."

She tried to hide her smile and knew she'd failed when he returned it. Cheekily, she added, "How did you know I'd be here tonight?"

"I didn't." His playful wink had her raising an eyebrow and trying to suppress her pleasure. "I've checked in every night for a drink and figured I'd catch you sooner or later."

"You lucked out tonight. I'm only here for a short shift to cover for a friend. If you'd been a half an hour later, you'd have missed me."

His satisfaction was obvious. "Good. Then you'll be free for dinner."

"I wasn't angling for an invitation—"

"I know that. I never believed you were. But I want to get to know you and you don't really give a guy a chance to make that happen. You haven't returned my calls, and I know I used the right number because I heard your voice message."

Sheepishly, she looked down at her hands locked in a tight grip, one thumb peeling the nail polish off the other. "I didn't know there were messages. It's a new cell phone and the girl where I bought it set up the voice mail. I've forgotten her instructions on how to recover calls."

His face lit up and the smile he sent her way had her knees knocking. My goodness, the man had charisma. When he looked into her eyes, she felt herself drowning in twin sensations of lust and – could it be – hope?

A server called her name and broke into their moment. Quickly, she filled the order, moving briskly and efficiently. Then she called to Reed and got his preference for a beer and the brand. While filling the mug, she glanced quickly in the mirror and felt thankful she'd changed earlier into her favorite soft blue sweater and the slacks that showed off her long legs and flat tummy.

Because she was only twenty-seven and lived alone, she'd spent way too many lonely nights working out, stifling frustration by doing exercise and yoga.

Be glad, girl. It's paid off.

He'd picked up his beer and brought it closer to where she'd gone back to washing glasses. "Lindy, *will* you have supper with me tonight?" Mistaking her hesitation, he added. "We can stay here, if you prefer. Most nights I eat alone so you would be doing me a huge favor if you'd have a meal with me. We could share our stories and bring each other up to date. Besides, it'll stop me from being bored with my own company and passing out with my face in the spaghetti."

Laughing at that mind picture, she studied him and saw the exhaustion the poor man suffered. "It might be best if you ordered take-out and got an early night."

Chuckling, he shook his head. "Trust me, that's my customary pattern. Sharing a meal and conversation with a woman not connected to the hospital would be a treat beyond anything you could imagine."

"Then, since Hollie is at my parent's house tonight, I'd like that." With her heart beating to where she thought she could pass out, where it made breathing difficult, she hoped he hadn't taken her explanation about Hollie's whereabouts as being a hint she expected more than dinner. Feeling absurdly tongue-tied, her usual state around men, Belinda held her breath.

"Great!" Waving his phone and grabbing his beer, he grinned like a man feeling happy. "I'll let you work while I go and answer some e-mails in the booth over there, until you're ready."

While she worked, her mind travelled back in time. Understanding clearly that her theories about being drugged and raped didn't make sense with a man like Reed Carlton, Belinda knew she needed to rethink her story. What had happened to her on that May weekend when she'd conceived their precious daughter?

Chapter Sixteen

They'd decided to move into the dining room where it was less noisy and designed for couples to enjoy an intimate meal. Now waiting for their seafood choices, Reed tried small talk to help Belinda to relax. He'd never known a woman so nervous and yet alluring.

Her appeal today re-sparked his hunger for her body. This girl had lingered in his memory, an ideal for his other partners to surpass. And it hadn't happened. She'd come between him and romance too many times.

Remembering her beguiling smile, the one she'd given him as he'd entered her body, the sweet caresses on his face and chest while they'd been attached, moving together as one to reach their climax, came to him both in dreams and moments like this when he'd relax his guard.

Lindy had made him feel like a star that night and he'd never forgotten her magic. No other woman had ever given as much, loved as sweetly or lived in his head, as she had.

Since she'd been on edge from the moment they'd sat down in their booth, Reed decided to clear the air. Acting like a person with a secret, one that didn't make her happy, she'd looked everywhere but at him. Her flyaway auburn hair was being sifted and tugged at continuously and the trembling in her hands was obvious, no matter how much she moved them. He couldn't stand the building tension a moment longer. "You wanted to talk."

Her eyes flew to his, wide, distracted and filled with dismay. She started to rise. "I think this is a mistake."

Reacting quickly, he rose and blocked her way, his body touching hers. "Please don't. I have no idea what's wrong, but I'd like to try and work things out." She'd stopped and was listening. Aching to touch her, yet afraid of her reaction, he leaned slightly closer and whispered, "I lost you once and I don't know why. We were beautiful together and you left me, ran away. I can't lose you again." Electricity speared between them, he felt the air sizzle and knew she felt it also. Her breath caught and the fact that she leaned against him, letting him support the weight of her body, letting his hand creep around her waist to give her his gentleness, he just knew she'd once again connected to him with that strange vibe they seemed able to generate whenever they were together.

He leaned his face against her neck, his breath disturbing the wisps of hair and she trembled, a small moan escaping. Careful not to make her feel he was in any way overriding her wishes; he slowly guided her back to the booth and then slid in next to her.

Taking her hand, he placed a kiss on the palm, folded her fingers over it and said, "Lindy, I'm not a romantic man. I work too hard and I'm lousy with people unless I like them. But when I care for someone, it never goes away. That night long ago, you made me care about you. Why did you disappear after what we'd shared?"

Tears emerged, filling, overflowing, and she looked at him, casting her spell once again with those incredible eyes. The rest of the world receded leaving only the two of them lost in their discovery of passion. Hands gripping, needing the touch, the connection, they basked in their joy of finding the other.

He leaned toward her and she met him. They kissed; drawing sustenance, then pulled back and again searched each other's souls. Incredible thrills worked throughout him until his mind spun crazily.

Food, heavenly smells of garlic mixed with seafood being placed on the table in front of them, brought him back to earth with a thump. Unwanted separation irritated Reed, driving him insane. He waited impatiently while the waiter poured the wine and fussed with the meal. Biting his tongue to stop himself from telling the idiot to bugger off, he hid his frustration.

Finally they were alone once again. He looked at her and saw her paleness. Reaching for his wine, he lifted it and motioned for her to do likewise. "To our future."

She clinked her long-stemmed glass against his and looked into his eyes. "Yes, to the future."

They drank a sip and he spoke in a quiet intimate tone. "Lindy, let's enjoy our first meal together and leave the 'talk' for after. We've plenty of time and I'd love to know more about you and Hollie. Would that be okay?"

Chapter Seventeen

Belinda felt a gigantic weight lift off her shoulders when Reed requested they get on with their meal and leave their talk for later.

"I'd really like that, actually. I'm starving and these shrimp look fabulous. I know the customers rave over them, but it's the first time I've ever had the good fortune to eat here."

"What? You don't get to eat where you work?"

"Some of us do. But we still have to pay a discounted price and so I bring sandwiches from home."

"You must be on a tight budget." Reed's eyes had narrowed and his interest was sparked. He was a man listening and she felt relaxed enough to openly share.

"Well, that's not unusual for a single mom. My expenses often exceed my budget. You know how it is. Besides, Hollie hates the local play school where she goes and I'm saving to put her in a private school that caters to children who are more advanced."

Reed smiled. Teasingly he replied, "And which parent doesn't think their child is the next Einstein just because she can count to a hundred?"

"True, but Hollie can do it backwards from a thousand." Smirking at his astonishment, Belinda added, "She can name most types of clouds because she watched a show on T.V. She also knows the differences between the dinosaurs and what they eat. The stars and planets are another area she's partial to. Should I go on?"

"Okay, wow! I see what you mean. She's gifted all right."

"Yes, she is. I did fairly well in school but never scored higher than average. Neither did anyone else in my family. Therefore it's hard for us to deal with a mind like hers."

"My parents felt the same way about me. I was advanced for my age, not exactly like Hollie, but I got bored very quickly with regular classes and was thrilled when I reached the higher grades and was more challenged."

Swallowing her glee to finally have answers to questions she'd had to put aside, Belinda said, "Then you'd understand why I think it's so important to get her into this special school."

Reed nodded and asked a lot more questions until, with a shock, she realized they'd not only finished dinner but were at the coffee stage and the restaurant section was closing.

Reed picked up on her astonishment. "They want us to leave. We could go back into the bar, if you want? We never did have that talk and I think we need to as soon as possible, don't you?"

She made up her mind. "Yes, we should." She wasn't quite ready to tell him that Hollie was his child but she did want answers to other questions and after tonight, she didn't want to wait any longer. The noise level streaming out of the bar helped in her decision. "Maybe we can go to my place for coffee? The bar's kind of busy."

"Nothing I'd like better."

"For coffee."

He winked and agreed, "For coffee."

***

"I'm sorry the place is so small but it has everything we need." Seeing Reed move around her tiny apartment brought it home to Belinda just how little room she and Hollie really had. Moving into the kitchen, she waved him to a stool across the counter and began the preparations for their drinks.

"It's cozy and familiar. Looks like the place I lived in off campus while taking residency. Only my rooms were never this tidy."

"I bet. I have brothers and if you're anything like them, well, let's just say my mother would throw her hands up in disgust." She laughed, remembering how many times she'd tidied up after them so there'd be peace in the house.

"Yep. That was me."

Picking up the plate of homemade cookies along with her tea, Belinda carried it into the other room and placed it gingerly on the coffee table. She sat on the end of the couch, hoping Reed would choose the chair next to her. Instead he sat beside her, leaned back and took a sip from his cup. "Hmm... good. I'm a coffee freak so I know when it's bad."

"I'm a tea granny; otherwise I'm up half the night." Realizing their conversation was absurd, she slapped her tea down in front of her and clasped her hands. "I want to talk about the night we met."

"Sure."

"About what happened."

"You mean when we hooked up?"

"Yes. How did we get to be together?"

"Don't you remember?" Reed placed his mug on the table, his movements slow and precise. There was a note in his voice that caught her attention. Her news had made his features tighten and he looked incredulous. "You don't remember anything at all. How we met? And danced?"

Realizing this news had gotten to him, she

spoke softly, explaining. "No I don't. I was drugged."

"What?" He swung her way, anger filling the grooves in his face, replacing the smiling man who'd looked so comfortable just minutes before. "You were taking drugs?"

Shaking her head, she stammered. "No! No, they weren't m-mine. They were put in my drink. Look, when I got there, a girl I knew handed me a beer and being shy and out of place, I drank it. Next thing I remember is dancing wildly with a bunch of people and then nothing until I woke up in a bed alone, naked and terrified. I got dressed and left."

During her explanation, Reed awkwardly put his coffee onto the table. With his face turned to stone, only his eyes showed emotion and they were furious. "You were drugged at my house... in my home? Is that what you're telling me?"

Inching away from the angry man, Belinda nodded. "There's no other explanation." Staring him in the eye, she let him read the truth. "I've gone over it a million times. I always thought that the person who slept with me had to be the one who'd drugged me. And I could never forgive such behavior."

"I didn't drug you, Lindy. Believe me. I would never stoop so low to get a girl into my bed."

She reached out tentatively, touching his arm for only seconds before shooting her hand back into her lap. "I know that now; now that I've met you. I can't figure out why it was my drink someone messed with, unless it was meant for another girl. My memory's vague about that whole night. All I remember is how packed the rooms were and the loud music, so many kids all milling around, laughing, drinking, dancing—it was crazy."

"Yes, it was crazy. And you were beautiful, you know, wild and having so much fun. I couldn't take my eyes off you. We danced together, a lot. Then you came on to me and I couldn't keep my hands off you. You were hot for me too and I figured you knew the score, knew what you wanted. Lindy, if I'd known you weren't yourself, I'd never have touched you."

"You couldn't tell I was intoxicated?"

He closed his eyes for a minute and travelled back in time. But soon he shook his head, his voice sincere. "No. I was celebrating that night for having passed the finals. And you were so full of fun, carrying on a bit wildly, but I figured you were as hot for me as I was for you. God, I'm sorry but I was cooked myself. I hadn't had a good night's sleep for months and the booze hit me big time."

She concealed her face, embarrassed by his description. Then he started talking again and she listened to every word, her breath suspended.

"I did try and find you, Lindy. You fascinated me and I was obsessed. The memories still haunt me. You were a virgin and so beautiful. You wanted me and I couldn't say no. Now that I think about it, it must have been Ecstasy that you took"

"Please tell me I wasn't performing for everyone?"

"Nope, just for me."

"I can't imagine."

"You were beautiful."

"You already said that. I must have been acting like a slut."

His hand slashed the air and he pointed toward her. "Don't ever say that." Anger sliced through his words and made her stare in astonishment. "You were soft and loving, as if it really meant something to you being with me. There was no... sluttiness whatsoever. Shit, Lindy, I'm not good with pretty words, I get all twisted up when I have to think of the right things to say." He reached for her hands and cradled them in his. Then he placed his forehead against hers. "I promise. It was beautiful. We were... good together." He leaned back to stare into her eyes and she felt herself drawn into his magic. She couldn't look away when he moved closer. "Like this."

Chapter
Eighteen

His lips touched hers gently, questioning, getting permission, begging, and Belinda couldn't refuse his request, didn't want to. She'd kept her eyes open, as had he, and they looked at one another for as long as possible until passion ignited.

Lost in the excitement of the moment, she opened to him. Desire like none she had ever known sprang between them. Floating above her normal world of worry, she just let herself feel and– oh, God– it felt so right.

Her body reacted, craving what only he could provide. Panting, breath catching, passion took over and every logical reason she should stop this craziness from happening fled.

"Reed..."

"Lindy, I need…"

"Oh, God, yes…"

They began tearing at each other's clothes, ripping, pulling, working to get shed of anything that kept them apart.

Breathing harshly, kisses not nearly enough to slake their thirst, they stroked and caressed, writhing to get closer. Rubbing against each other, he caressed and squeezed her breasts until she cried out.

"Yes! That feels wonderful. Yes!"

"You're so beautiful, Lindy. I could never forget you, ever. You're like a drug in my blood, keeping me from caring about any other woman. It's always been you."

"I need you, Reed, need this. My God, it's been forever. Hurry!"

Totally naked now, Reed laid her back and covered her body with his, entering the wet haven waiting, throbbing, craving for his specialness. "Oh, God, sweetheart! I've missed you."

She lovingly caressed his face, kissing him everywhere, clinging, giving, loving. A climax began to build, slowly at first, and then, with every kiss and caress, every thrust he made, it doubled in strength. She panted each moan until she couldn't wait another second. "Reed!"

"I'm here. It's good, baby. I'm here." He moved faster, lifting her higher and then he gave one last heave and she exploded—flashing, igniting, bursting, sensations rioting, her body pulsating, clenching. Writhing in joy, she clung.

Inside her, wrapped around her, he buried himself deeply, arched and shuddered.

Together, they both reached heaven.

***

Satiated, they relaxed. He waited for her to speak. Having no words, other than his favorite which pounded in his brain: *beautiful!* Together, they were beautiful.

Is she crying? He'd moved away from her so he could gather her close to cuddle and stroke. Glancing down, he saw that her eyes were closed and her lips trembling. He couldn't stand it if she regretted what to him had been so bea... perfect. Leaning over, he kissed her lips to stop the wobbling and then he kissed her closed eyes to coax them to open.

It paid off. She looked at him, so open in her honesty, so bewildered in her behavior.

"See, I told you. We're beautiful together." He hadn't known what words he'd say until they came out of his mouth and made her eyes fill up. Her smile brought instant relief.

"I see what you mean. We're a little like tinder and sparks."

He grinned. "Okay, I might be tinder, dry and thirsty. But, baby, you're all sparks. You incited me just like you did the first time. Now do you understand?"

Staring into his eyes, she playfully blinked her long lashes. "Do you think I could do it again?" Her smile invited.

"Oh, baby, you already have." He leaned in for a kiss, his rekindled tinder nudging her stomach.

She giggled for a few seconds and then stopped....

Chapter Nineteen

The next day, Belinda decided to pack some of her belongings to start the move over to Maeve's house. Hollie, her little chatterbox, hadn't stopped talking from the minute her grandfather had dropped her off.

"It's my day to go with you to Auntie Maeve's, isn't it, Mommy?"

"Yes, munchkin. While I'm working, you can visit her a little and then you can help me unpack. Hurry, because we need to get there a bit earlier than usual."

"Why?"

"Why? Because Maeve's doctor will be there to pass on some instructions for her care." *And I'm going to give the idiot a piece of my mind. How can a doctor, sworn to save lives, be so incompetent?*

Finally to get some peace, some alone time so she could revisit the night before, Belinda set Hollie to packing her own belongings. Giving her a box and instructions, which she knew would never be followed, she left her daughter busy and happy.

Soon she started gathering her own belongings and stopped when she reached for the pillow on the sofa. Lifting it to her face, she smelled Reed's cologne, closed her eyes and returned to the wonders of the night and the man who attracted her more than anyone else she'd ever met.

Making love with him had been beyond satisfying an urge, more like feeding a craving. As if her body had remembered his, they'd been good together, perfect... in his words... beautiful.

Eventually, they'd ended up in her bed until early in the morning, when he'd reluctantly left to go back to his own house for a shower and to get ready for the hospital and morning surgery.

Before he'd left, he'd forced a promise that they'd be together again soon. Unaware of why she'd agreed, he'd left in a bubble of happy anticipation, whereas she only dreaded their next date. Knowing how important it was that she tell him the truth, she groaned and again buried her face in the pillow. No doubt, as soon as she told him he was Hollie's daddy, the man would back off and it would be him not answering *her* messages.

She stopped dead. The pillow fell from her

hand. Thinking of daddies reminded her they hadn't used any protection last night. *Oh, no! Not again!* Her knees gave out completely and she sank to the floor.

She couldn't be that unlucky, could she? Her brain kicked in and a thought popped up. They had a test now that would reveal the truth within twenty-four hours.

Okay, a stop at the local drugstore had to be made before she could go on to Maeve's. Premonitions swamped her mind, memories of another time when her prayers *hadn't* been answered. A sick feeling began attacking her stomach until she was forced to take deep breaths so she wouldn't lose her lunch. *Give me a break this time. Please...!*

Chapter Twenty

"Maeve, has Dr. Darling been here already?" Belinda arrived expecting to see a strange car in the driveway. "I wanted to have a word with him."

"He called to say he'd be a little late due to an emergency. He knew I wouldn't mind. He's a very busy man, works far too hard and has saved a lot of lives since he came home to practice here in Carlton Grove. He's the best of the Carl... Oh, there's the bell now, Lindy. Would you mind letting him in while I say hello to my favorite playmate?" Maeve patted her knee and beckoned to the child to climb aboard. "Come sit with me, Hollie."

Having been tutored by her mother to take care, Hollie gingerly lifted herself onto Maeve's knee and cuddled close. "Hi, Auntie Maeve. Mommy says we're going to live with you from now on."

"Would you like that? It's going to be Christmas soon. We can find a nice big tree for the living room and decorate it together."

"And I'll be spending the night with you, right?"

"That's right."

Clapping her hands, giddy and excited, Hollie hugged the older woman, careful not to squeeze too tightly. "I'm so glad. Maybe we can go shopping and you can help me buy Mommy's Christmas present."

"Of course I will. We'll have such fun."

***

First, Belinda stopped at the hallway mirror, ran her hands through her hair and checked that her lipstick was still noticeable. She wanted to look presentable to the jerk who she had full intentions of berating.

She opened the door and the handsome man who looked up from his phone seemed just as shocked as she felt.

"Reed!"

"Lindy. Why you must be the person who takes such good care of Maeve. The one she brags about all the time. She calls you her sweet housekeeper." He smiled, delighted with his conclusions. "I fully get it now."

"She told me her doctor's name was Dr. Darling." Belinda's feet seemed glued to the floor and she held onto the door, not opening it far enough to allow him entry.

He chuckled. "That spritely gal does have a way with nicknames, doesn't she? That's an old joke. You see I've always called her darling when I tried to talk her into certain... ahh, procedures. Her usual retort is... don't you darling me, and now she calls me Dr. Darling in retaliation."

He stepped forward, expecting her to let him in but she couldn't move. For too long she'd held a grudge against the idiot who she'd decided hadn't given proper care to Maeve. Now to find out that the idiot was none other than the man she'd slept with last night was more than she could handle.

Weak-kneed, tears close, she tried to make some sense of the confusion drumming in her head. "I don't understand." She turned away and moved quickly to sit down. "Maeve's doctor is an old fool. It can't be you." Tongue loosened by shock, she blabbered the thoughts that had free range in her head. "I was going to give him – you — a good talking to. For not operating. For giving up on her. Lung cancer can be managed with surgery. Yet you aren't doing any. She's dying and you aren't trying to save her."

"Darling—"

"Don't you darling me either! I'm not an old woman who you can manipulate. I want answers."

Reed stiffened. "I can't talk about my patient with you, Lindy. You know I can't."

"But I can." Maeve wheeled into the room and stopped next to Reed. She slid her hand into his and clung. "Hollie is fetching me some water so we don't have a lot of time."

"I'm sorry, Maeve." Belinda didn't know what else to say. She'd been caught messing in the other woman's affairs, but she just couldn't stand by and see such an injustice.

"Lindy, Dr. Carlton, who has always been a darling and patient man, tried continuously to talk me into surgery. He thought I had a good chance of surviving for longer but he couldn't guarantee what level of functionality I'd be left with. You see, I'm also in the beginning stages of congestive heart failure which means that any operation is doubly dangerous. So it was my decision to enjoy the months I had left, be able to live them as normally as possible, and let the cancer eventually take me when my time came."

Belinda stifled a cry but not before it was heard by the others. Reed hurried to her side and sat next to her as if shielding her from the pain of Maeve's words.

Maeve wheeled closer and reached out her hand to her. "Please don't cry. I've had a wonderful life, especially since you and Hollie came into it four years ago. You've been like a daughter to me and Hollie is as sweet a grandchild any old woman could have. With you moving in to help me, it will make it possible for me to spend the last of my days in my own home, and I can't tell you how happy that makes me."

Hollie sped around the corner, carefully holding a tall glass only half filled with water. "Here's your water, Auntie.... Reed!" Hollie quickly passed over the glass and then ran, leaping into Reed's open arms. She hugged him, exuberance spilling out—happiness lighting her pretty features.

"Hi, sunshine. So you're the little angel that Maeve keeps talking about. Now I see the resemblance."

Hollie laughed. "I don't look like Auntie Maeve."

"No. I was talking about the pretty angel I saw in a book recently. All you need are the wings."

Giggling, Hollie gave him another hug. That's when she noticed her mother's face and saw the tears. "Mommy? Are you alright?" She wiggled away from Reed and ran to Belinda. "Mommy?" Fear rang in her voice and was just the strengthening agent Belinda needed.

"Yes, munchkin. I'm just happy that Reed is Maeve's doctor and he'll be helping us look after her." Belinda patted Hollie's arms and ruffled her hair.

"Can he help us get a Christmas tree too?"

Chapter Twenty-one

It took some time for Belinda to wrap her head around the fact that Reed was Maeve's doctor. For so long, she'd held a grudge against the unknown physician that it took a lot of head-straightening to let go of her resentment.

Understanding that Maeve would not be having surgery hit her hard, took away her last hope. At most, her friend would live a few more months and Belinda would be left alone to parent Hollie. Never again could she bring those silly worries or proud accomplishments to Maeve. The ones most parents shared. The older woman's simple logic had soothed her many times when she couldn't see things clearly herself.

Working away like a zombie, cleaning out the

upstairs bedrooms Maeve had designated for her and Hollie, Belinda's mind teemed with everything that needed to get done.

She'd settled Maeve for her nap and had left Hollie happily working away in her new Christmas coloring book they'd picked up at the drugstore this morning....

Drugstore! How the heck could I forget?

Her hand dove into a pocket and found the three packages of different brands of pregnancy sticks she'd wasted money on. But she had to know. Would last night's uncontrollable desires kick her in the ass again this time? Would she have to pay for the rest of her life for a night of enjoyment? It had been spectacular, mind-blowing, but...

She dropped the dust cloth and sped into the bathroom. Sitting on the edge of the bathtub, she stared into the mirror across the room. Slowly she approached and looked into her eyes.

What will you do if it shows positive? What – will – you – do?

She closed her eyes and thought back to the first moments she had found out about Hollie. How terrified she'd been, alone, and questioning everything she believed in. She remembered the litany. *This was her baby. Hers! No father in the picture. She was alone.*

Could she do it?

Would she do it?

A little baby...

The answer had come over her like a rush of knowing. She wasn't a child herself this time—and she had skills. Life promised challenges but then hadn't she always thrived on them?

Shaking herself away from the past, she lifted the first stick and unwrapped it. By golly, if she had another hardship to face, there'd be no negativity. Emotions flooded inside, love and gladness. If she was pregnant— right from the beginning—this baby would only know how much it was wanted.

Chapter
Twenty-two

Reed woke up on Christmas morning, ruffled Cloud's silvery softness and let the daydreams roll before starting the day.

The last few weeks had been hectic as hell and the night before weariness had caught up and slammed into him like a knockout punch from Mohammed Ali. Tuckered, he'd hit the sack and felt a lot better for the full eight hours he'd gotten.

Thinking back over the last couple of weeks, astonished at the amount they'd accomplished, satisfaction flooded in when he thought about how settled Lindy and Hollie now were with Maeve. They'd worked hard to set up Christmas for the old lady and her little sidekick, and last night, before he'd kissed Lindy good-night at the door, he'd taken one last look around and felt great.

The tree they'd bought from a farm on the outskirts of town sat in the corner beautifully decorated and glowed with Maeve's old-fashioned twinkle-lights and the many ornaments she'd squirrelled away over her years of being a Christmas freak.

More twinkle lights had been intertwined with the garlands that were plastered in the main room and hallway, making a surprising display that had turned out rather classy and not the overkill he'd expected.

Hollie, vibrating with happiness, had made the work fun. He'd never wanted to please anyone as much as he'd found himself wanting to please the little dynamo. Free with her hugs, he'd cherished every moment her arms had wrapped around his neck and she'd squeezed him with affection.

Even Maeve had dug her way further into his heart and the hours they'd spent together gave him a huge amount of satisfaction. Remembering made him smile. The Sunday before, when they'd all worked together to get the outside of Maeve's house looking as fancy as the inside, had been a blast. Snow falling added the perfect touch and Hollie had glowed. Hitting him in the face with a snowball, her crowning achievement, the munchkin's giggles had infected them all.

"Why, you little monster, who taught you to throw snowballs like that?" He'd picked her up and heaved her over his shoulder, pretending to smack her well-padded bottom.

"My mommy. She can hit anything so you'd better duck." Before he could, another snowball had smacked him in the back of his head. As soon as he'd released her, Hollie had ended up rolling in the snow, laughter convulsing her little body and Cloud hysterically licking her face which only added to her merriment.

He'd turned to face the attacker. "Why, you monster's mommy, it's more than past time to teach you a lesson." He'd chased Lindy, thrown her over his shoulder and play-smacked her bottom as well. And she'd giggled in the same way as Hollie had.

Thinking back, Reed realized that those special moments were what he'd been missing from his whole, boring, predictable life.

He pictured Lindy, the girl, who'd burrowed her way inside him years earlier. Now, Lindy the woman had become as necessary to him as the food he ate or the air he breathed. Glowing, the center and essence for everyone around her, she lured him back day after day. He couldn't stay away from her magic.

Smiling, happily knowing that he'd wormed his way into their circle, he decided the first step had come when he'd made her accept help for their move from him and his two brothers.

It turned out to be a wonderful day and it had

solved one mystery they'd all pondered over. Harley, his younger brother, had shared some great news. He'd recently met the woman who owned Cloud's mother. Long story short, the lady's crazy brother had taken a dislike to the puppies. Against her wishes, he'd thrown them in a cardboard box and abandoned them in the park.

At first, Belinda had worried that she might demand the return of Cloud but Harley calmed her fears.

"Amelia's fine about Reed adopting the little monster mutt. I told her how he spoils Cloud, buys her the best puppy chow from the vets and even lets her sleep with him, the big softie." He'd grinned at Reed's discomfiture, looking happy that he'd put the spotlight on his older brother.

"She won't insist that Reed return Cloud?" Reed heard the worry Lindy couldn't hide.

"Nope. Don't you worry; she's just glad that the puppy has found a good home."

When she'd leaned over and loudly whispered to Harley, he'd found himself grinning like a besotted fool. "The man dotes on her, you know. Even bought her a pink rhinestone collar and had her name etched on the fancy dangling bone. You'd think he'd bought it for Hollie, she was that pleased."

Watching his girl charm his favorite brother, having them bond to gang up on him, had made the day better.

His plan of bombarding her with his presence; wiggling his way into her life, seemed to be working. She began including him with everything they planned.

A movie night, a dinner date, even evenings spent watching television, they'd done it all, but he hadn't talked his way back into her bed. No matter how hard he tried to beguile her, work his charm, she'd held him off—gently but firmly.

His disgruntled sigh woke the puppy, who yawned and wriggled then came searching for her morning rub. While satisfying Cloud's needs, Reed thought of his own. Something stood in their way, stopped his and Lindy's romance from moving forward. A few times he'd sensed she had a secret to share, but the time had never seemed right the moment had always been lost.

Thank God, each night she'd come to the door with him and say good-bye. Their only intimacy was when she'd see him out. Those brief moments were his favorite time of the day. She'd let him hold her in his arms, but her kisses were chaste and not in any way an invitation to take more than she offered. Every time he'd tried to open a conversation about the situation, she shut him down, gently but firmly.

He didn't know how much longer he could stand it. Every time she sat near him, his heartbeats revved up and his hands itched to touch. Memories of their encounter rode him, making him remember. Being a man in love...

He shot up in bed unexpectedly and the unprepared puppy, now scrambling on the floor, whined and shook off the shock.

In love?

Chapter
Twenty-three

Belinda moved over to the window side of the bed and turned in the direction where she could see the dark being gradually invaded by the soft glow of the morning sun. She stretched and then snuggled under the warmth; better take these quiet minutes to snooze. Soon Hollie would wake up and then Christmas would officially begin.

Over the last few days, she'd made up her mind: this was the day she had to let Reed go free. Pain radiated, driving her into a fetal position. Just the thought of losing him slashed a wound through her heart she didn't think would ever be repaired. But she couldn't keep him. It wasn't fair to tie a man down with responsibilities he hadn't asked for nor wanted.

It would have been better to end it earlier but she couldn't break Hollie's heart before Christmas. Both her baby and Maeve had built up such a hullabaloo for the holiday that she couldn't darken the mood, not for them, and especially not for her.

Therefore, the moments she spent with Reed were bittersweet and to be stored for the future. Through his actions, the special smiles, the soft touches, him trying to get her alone, she sensed he wanted more but instead, she kept him at arm's length. How could she lead him on when she knew their time was limited?

The squeaking door warned her someone was pushing it open slowly. Whispering, Hollie called out, "It's Christmas, Mommy. Can I come in?"

"Of course. Merry Christmas, baby. Come and snuggle under the covers with me. It's a bit too early to wake Maeve, and we promised Reed we'd wait until he arrives before we open our gifts."

Hollie leapt into the bed and wriggled her cold little body into Belinda's waiting arms, her icy feet landing on Belinda's legs. "Hollie Page, where are your slippers?" Belinda reached down to scoop Hollie's feet into her warm hands for a rub.

"I forgot. Mommy, I peeked downstairs to see if Santa had come, and he did. Oh, Mommy, there're scads of presents everywhere."

"Baby, I asked you to wait. Did you go all the way into the room?"

"No. Just to the doorway and then I came to get

you. You know Santa ate his cookies and the milk glass was empty. I told you we had to leave him a lot. He gets hungry carrying so many parcels."

Belinda swooped in for a hug. "I guess you were right, sweetie. I bet he enjoyed them." She ruffled Hollie's snarled curls and started to finger-comb them into some semblance of order.

Thinking back to the night before, after Maeve and Hollie had both gone to bed, Reed had helped her assemble Hollie's new purple bicycle. Afterward, he'd scoffed down the majority of the shortbread, commenting how much he liked the red sprinkles and green icing.

Seeing as how Hollie had been the decorator, which he couldn't help but notice from the uneven mess, she'd grinned and whipped away two for herself. She remembered how he leaned in to lick the crumbs from her mouth and they'd ended up kissing hungrily, before she'd firmly pushed him away.

Hollie patted her face to get her attention. "Mommy? Do you think Reed will like my present?" The question had been asked and answered at least a dozen times.

The little artist had diligently painted him a special picture and had spent quite some time choosing the perfect frame. She'd drawn the whole family, including Maeve in her wheelchair, herself being held up in the arms of a really tall, dark-haired man who wore the largest smile, and of course Cloud, who sat proudly in front of Belinda.

Answering yet again, Belinda kissed her cheek. "He'll love it, munchkin. I wish I had one too. It's so beautiful." Belinda meant that sincerely. It was a five-year-old's rendition of love and a happy family, a treasure to keep forever.

Together with Hollie, Belinda had shopped for Maeve, Reed and her parents by going to a studio to have her and Hollie's portrait professionally taken. Since Maeve had offered her frames from the stack of old ones she had stored away, one expense had covered all her gifts.

Hollie twisted in her arms, grinning at her mom. "Santa *might* bring you a surprise too you know? But only if you've been a good girl."

"Cheeky monster. You know mommies are always good girls." Belinda tickled her before lifting her high, crawling from the bed and heading for the bathroom. "Let's get washed, brush our teeth and see if Maeve is ready to get up in case Reed comes early."

Chapter
Twenty-four

Belinda had never experienced such a lovely Christmas Day. Not only did they have a blast unwrapping their presents together, Hollie, excited about her new bike, had thanked her mother with so many hugs and kisses that she'd made Belinda glad she'd dipped into their savings and spent the money.

Once the child found the big, beautifully wrapped box from Reed, her eyes had grown huge with childish delight. While he placed it in front of her, she'd clapped her hands and danced on the spot.

"Since you made me such a wonderful present, I hope you like the one I found for you."

"For me?"

"Yes, it's all yours, Sunshine."

"Can I unwrap it?"

"Of course."

"Mommy?"

"Go ahead, Munchkin."

Saving the elaborate bow first, Hollie tore off the pink, shiny tinsel paper and suddenly plopped her butt on the floor. Her hands cradled her cheeks while tears gathered and the wails began.

"It's a dollhouse. Reed bought me a dollhouse."

Belinda bit her lip, terrified that her daughter would hate this symbol of what little girls were supposed to like.

Throwing herself into his arms, Hollie hugged him hard. "You bought me a dollhouse... *to build.*"

Reed had looked beseechingly to her for help, but Belinda didn't know what had gotten a hold of Hollie so she couldn't save him this time.

"I hoped we could build it together, little Darlin'. Would you like that?"

Planting kisses all over his cheeks, Hollie resolved their worry instantly. "I love this. I love you, Reed." More kisses. "Can we start now?"

"No Sunshine, it'll have to wait for another day. Let's let your mommy unwrap her gift now, okay?" He handed Hollie a small box and motioned for her to pass it to Belinda.

Not sure what to expect, Belinda found her hands shaking when she unwrapped the exquisitely decorated jewellers box. Nesting inside on white velvet sat a delicate silver bracelet; one heart dangled with one word etched into it... *beautiful*.

Hardly able to breathe, Belinda shyly thanked him with words but her eyes let him know that she'd gotten the message and was touched.

***

While Maeve had a nap in the afternoon, Reed invited her and Hollie to Carlton House where they would meet his relatives and his cousin's children.

"But, Reed, we can't just show up. Goodness, your parents aren't expecting us. It'll be too much of an inconvenience."

"More like a shock," he said, laughter lighting up his features. "They'll be over the moon to finally meet you. I guess the word got out that I was seeing someone and they've been hinting for days about how nice it would be to spend some time together on Christmas Day. I believe my mother even bought Hollie a small gift for a just-in-case. She phoned me this morning to add more pressure."

His spontaneous hug, plus Hollie's enthusiastic pleading finally won her over. "Just for a short visit. We still have to get home to prepare our turkey dinner. Auntie Maeve will be expecting us."

Reed wrapped an arm around both girls to lead them to the closet for coats and boots. "I already told her I was kidnapping you both for a few hours and she was delighted. Now hurry up, or I might have to get my revenge on you two sassy snowballers since there's more snow coming down now."

Sure enough, the snow had increased to where it was hard to see the streets. Soft, thick flakes dropped non-stop and were an invitation to play, make a snowman, maybe snow angels. Belinda saw the glee on her child's face and lifted her away from temptation. Watching Cloud drill her nose through the snowbanks and then roll her furry mass in the white softness had all three of them laughing. Reed grabbed the frenzied pup and put her on the back seat of the car while Belinda coaxed the frown off Hollie's face. "Tomorrow, munchkin, we'll play then."

On the way to his parent's house, Belinda, sitting in the front of the car with Reed, caught him smiling at her. When she smiled back, he reached for her hand. Impossible to ignore or refuse his gesture, they locked fingers. His were warm and cradled hers gently.

Emotions passed between them, travelling through the link where their bodies touched, making normal breathing difficult. The effect the man had on her startled her silly.

Thoughts of what she'd planned for later froze the joy and replaced it with so much sadness that tears formed. Pulling away, she pretended to search for a tissue to wipe her sniffles, only secretly, she used it to dab at her eyes too.

When they arrived, he went around the car, opened her door and reached in for her. Affection lit his brown eyes to melted chocolate. Her knees weakened, making her stumble and he swept her close, hugging her to his body while he whispered in her ear, "You look so beautiful."

Stunned silent, she let him help Hollie from her car seat, pick up the happy puppy and escort them all to the front door of the house that she'd always thought looked like a mansion.

Unnaturally shy, sitting on her mom's lap while Cloud nestled in hers, it only took a lovely book about a lost little puppy from Reed's mother and a few invitations from the other kids before they swept Hollie and Cloud into their circle. Meanwhile, the adults treated Belinda with a kindness she never expected and it worked to put her at ease.

Soon she found herself in the kitchen with his petite, stylish mom, helping her to restock dessert trays. "You know, you're the first female Reed has brought to the house since a teenage fling broke up with him. It devastated him, changed him from being a happy, daredevil teen to a more studious, serious person. Don't get me wrong, he's always made us proud, working like a dog to get through medical school. But I have to tell you, I've missed his teasing, his stupid jokes and him laughing just because."

Belinda found herself hungry to learn more.

"Some guys are very sensitive during those years. I remember my brother had a similar experience, only he ended up winning the girl back and they're married today."

"I'm glad that didn't happen for Reed. I doubt he'd be a doctor now and the last time I saw her, she had four kids and big hips to show for them."

Laughing together, Belinda felt her heart melt when his mother, Stacy, had wrapped her arms around her and given her a squeeze. "I like you, Lindy. You and Hollie are welcome in my home anytime."

Following the lady into the family room, a heaping tray loaded with goodies, Belinda's stomach felt like a pile of smoldering cinders were stored there, waiting to combust. Panic cracked her calm and she began to tremble from pure wretchedness. Today she had to give all this up. Let Reed go.

How the hell was she going to survive?

Chapter
Twenty-five

Soon, dinner was over, the dishes done and both a very tired Hollie and an equally exhausted Maeve were in bed. The time had come—zero hour. Belinda couldn't put it off any longer.

Returning to the family room where Reed lounged, cuddling a sleepy puppy, she dithered. Glasses of wine poured and ready for them to enjoy told her he expected time alone with her. He'd turned on the showy electric fireplace, had tidied the room and, other than the Christmas lights twinkling everywhere, the dim shadows lent a romantic element she wished she could shut off but didn't have the heart to. Left with no more excuses, she approached and sat down where he patted the couch next to him.

If only she could use her pounding headache as a legitimate reason to put this torture off for another day. But by delaying the inevitable, the stress would most likely have her in a psych ward. This situation needed to get taken care of – now.

"I thought you'd never quit fussing and join me. You need to relax, baby. You're wound up tighter than what's good for you." He slid the sleepy pup on the other side of him and reached toward her. "Here, let me rub your shoulders—"

"No!" Belinda slid further away from his hands. "Don't touch me. If you do, I'll make a fool out of myself and you'll never be able to walk away without having me clinging and begging."

Her words made him smile; the honesty she didn't even think to hide must have gotten to him. "What's wrong, baby? Whatever you have to tell me we'll deal with. Then we can move on."

"That's just it. There's no 'we'. No 'we're moving on'. There's only you walking out. And me making do."

"Never going to happen. You know I'm crazy about you. And Hollie."

"Good, because she's your child too, so there." A deep breath stopped her from passing out and sliding to the shaggy rug at his feet.

"I know. Isn't it wonderful? I love—"

"You know? *You know?* Why didn't I know you knew? How could you keep it from me? Why didn't you tell me—"

"Wait – shouldn't that be my line?"

She glared her mommy signal that he better not mess around, and he answered quickly.

"At first, I thought it couldn't be. You know, because of her birthday being on Christmas. Then earlier today, when I wondered where her other birthday presents were, she told me she'd been born a really tiny baby in an *incubatery*, her word, and that you couldn't bring her home until Valentine's Day. So you celebrated her birthday then. In her little old-lady, Maeve-like way, she thought it *marvelous* because she could have separate special days. I thought it was marvelous too. Both her birthday being special and her being mine—ours."

Chapter
Twenty-six

Reed's hands cupped her face so he could look into her concealed tawny eyes. When she refused him access, his heartbeats accelerated and he felt bile rising, making his stomach clench, tight, hard—sickeningly.

Earlier, when he'd learned her secret about Hollie, he'd felt a deluge of relief. So this was what had been making her act strange the last few weeks. Why she'd held him at a distance. Understanding had swept over him and he'd breathed easy for the first time since he'd met her. Once she understood just how delighted he was, there'd be no more obstacles to their becoming a couple.

He slid his hands under her gorgeous silky, auburn mass and caressed her scalp, wanting to help her relax. Even without a doctor's degree, he'd have known she had a headache. Periodically, for the last few hours, he'd watched her kneading her temple. Massaging gently, he tried to coax away her pain.

He might not be a born lover, had little experience in the ways of females, but even he accepted that there was still something eating away at her. All day, watching her chew her lip and fidget with her hands, it had taken a lot out of him not to drag her in a corner and tell her he knew about Hollie, put her out of her misery. Explain how incredibly happy he'd been realizing the little angel he loved was his own flesh and blood.

Now he had to accept that she'd held something else back. What if this mystery turned out to be the clincher? The one he'd need to walk away from. Did he really want to know?

"Lindy, don't tell me anything that makes you feel so scared. Nothing matters. I don't care what you've done; it won't change the way I feel."

"It's not what I've done."

"Then for sure it doesn't matter."

"It's what *you've* done."

God no! Memories of another conversation intruded and panic, like a spear in his chest, drove deep. As a teen, he hadn't understood the jealousy in a young girl's character. The degree of intolerance, or for that matter, the degree of mean-spiritedness either. Being a friendly sort of a chap hadn't gone over well with his girlfriend and him smiling at other girls wasn't to be tolerated.

Never again had he let someone have that much control—until now. Why would he let another get close enough to hurt him, to devastate him? His self-protective nature tried to get him to stand, leave, walk away from the pain. Only this time, he couldn't. She was the mother of his child. He loved them both—so much.

"Whatever it is that I've done, I'm sorry."

"You don't understand. You need to know. I have to...." She covered her face, tears seeping through her fingers. "Please don't be angry."

"For God's sake, tell me. Let me make it better. I'll apologise, promise to never do it again, whatever it was that I did.... Are you giggling?"

"I am. I think I'm hysterical. But what you said about never doing it again was completely the wrong thing for you to say."

Flabbergasted, he held out his hands, palms up and smiled just a little. "Belinda Page. If you don't put me out of my misery right now, I'll be forced to kiss you until you do. I mean it."

Smiling, her tear-drenched face lifted and she leaned forward until her forehead met his. "You've gone and done it again."

"I have?"

"Oh, yes, you did it really good this time."

"I did? Can you just give me a little hint of what it was that I'm supposed to have done?"

"It'll be twins this time."

"Twins!" The shock took some time to catch up with his brain, but when it hit, he didn't miss a beat. "Two more like our Hollie?"

She'd stiffened, seemingly afraid to see his face, watch the blow—be disappointed at his reaction. He sensed her waiting, not breathing...

"Oh, baby, how can one man get so damned lucky?"

Afterword

Thank you so much for reading *Please Keep Me* – Book #1 of the Holiday Heartwarmers Series.

I loved writing this story and I hope you enjoyed reading it. If so, I would ask you for a favor. Wherever you purchased this book, please take a few minutes and leave an honest review. Authors enjoy hearing that readers like their stories, and hopefully, others will read your words and choose to buy them because of your sentiments.

My website at **http://mimibarbour.com** now has all my books listed with links to the various publishers to make it easy for you to return to where you bought the book and to find my other work.

While you're there, I'd really appreciate it if you would sign up for my newsletter so I can keep in touch.

http://bit.ly/mimibarbournewsletter

I only send out newsletters approximately once a month and you have my word that your address will never be shared.

Hugs, Mimi

Snow Pup
by Mimi
Barbour

Holiday Heartwarmers Series – Book #2
NYT & USAT best-selling author, Mimi
Barbour
~*~*~

In this delightful Christmas love story, Deputy
Shawna Mallory finds Billy McCrae – a runaway
boy sleeping in a mound of snow with an anxious
puppy guarding him. He's a sad child surviving a
terrible existence until she puts a stop to it and
becomes his foster parent. She's drawn to the
snarky kid and just wants his life to be happier, his
and the stray mutt who won't leave his side. Not

that the boy cares about the dog... or her. Then she meets his father, the one who abandoned the boy when he was five.

John Reid McCrae wants only one thing in his life to make it worth living. Years ago he'd lost his son to a bitter wife and now his goal is to get Billy back. He'll do whatever it takes, no matter who gets hurt. Until he meets the town's stunning deputy. Can he put his needs ahead of her happiness?

~*~*~*~

Prologue Book #2:

When Sis didn't return, it was hunger that eventually drove Chubbs from the box. Irritation had made him leave his cranky brother who'd nipped him in the flank and then ignored him when he'd wanted to play. But once ouside, it was curiosity that led him to the mound of snow that covered a body. Once he'd dug a little nest, there was warmth and the irrational need to stay close, to protect, to wait until someone came and then sound the alarm for help.

~*~*~*~

Chapter One:

So far, Deputy Shawna Mallory had searched everywhere kids tended to hang out in town and without any luck. The runaway, twelve-year-old Billy McCrae was nowhere to be found. Frustrated, she stopped driving and pulled the car into the lot closest to the park where the town's families spent a good deal of their spare time.

The tennis courts were closed due to the unusual snowfall. Normally they were full and had been until last night when the previous good weather had taken a turn for the worse. The soccer and football fields were empty too and even the lake looked deserted, whereas on normal days, there were always people running, walking, kayaking... Heck, you name it; the people of Carlton Grove did it.

Deciding to stretch her legs, Shawna circled the far side of the lake, keeping her eyes open in case she lucked out and saw Billy McCrae wandering around. She'd been looking for the youngster since early morning when his foster mother had called in that he'd gone missing.

Whipping out her cellphone, she let the precinct know where she was and about her plans to explore the park just in case the boy had hidden there. She'd already been to see his teacher, only to find out that the kid hadn't shown up yesterday either and had a tendency to use the school as a place to sleep rather than learn. After questioning the rest of the kids, she'd found that he had no friends and that unfortunate situation was solely his decision. He pushed everyone away who tried to get close.

Striding, long legs eating up the yards, she kept moving, her eyes searching, listening. Circling around some bushes, a yapping puppy obviously in a snit about something ran towards her. It was the cutest thing she'd ever seen. Fluffy silvery-white fur puffed out, which made its little black eyes and snout seem oddly abnormal against the white furry background. The mutt tried hard to converse, get her attention, rotating, then running over to a snow pile and back again. She chuckled at his antics.

"Hey, cutie? You look like a snowball yourself. Are you lost? Come and see Shawna." She held out her hand, knelt down and coaxed. "Come, Snow Pup. Come here."

Frantic, the dog ignored her hand and plowed into her knees, jumping to her face, nudging her and then running back to the snow mound that suddenly looked suspicious. Not waiting for her to explore, the pup began digging at the pile and suddenly a plaid blanket came into view.

Holy Moly, there was a body under there.

Also author of...

Many of Mimi's books can be found FREE on Kindle Unlimited!!

~*~*~*~

The Vicarage Bench Series
— Spirit Travel at its Best! —
She's Me (Book 1)
He's Her (Book 2)
We're One (Book 3)
Vicarage Bench Anthology (Book 4 – Books 1-3)
Together Again (Book 5)
Together for Christmas (Book 6)
Together Always (Book 7)

***

Angels with Attitude Series

— Angels Playing Cupid! —
The Angels with Attitudes Anthology (Books 1-3)
My Cheeky Angel (Book 1)
His Devious Angel (Book 2)
Loveable Christmas Angel (Book 3)
***

Elvis Series
— Make an Elvis Song a Book! —
She's Not You (Book 1)
Love Me Tender (Book 2)
***

Vegas Series
— Action–Packed Thrillers! —
Vegas Series – Complete Boxed Set
Partners (Book 1)
Roll the Dice (Book 2)
Vegas Shuffle (Book 3)
High Stakes Gamble (Book 4)
Spin the Wheel (Book 5)
Let it Ride (Book 6)
***

Undercover FBI Series
— Popular & Compelling! —
Special Agent Francesca (Book 1)
Special Agent Finnegan (Book 2)
Special Agent Maximilian (Book 3)
Special Agent Kandice (Book 4)
Special Agent Booker (Book 5)
Special Agent Charli (Book 6 – to be released

Fall 2017)

***

Holiday Heartwarmers Trilogy
— Truly a Christmas favorite! —
Holiday Heartwarmers Series
Please Keep Me (Book 1)
Snow Pup (Book 2)
Find Me a Home (Book 3)
Frosty the Snowman (Book 4)
Love of my Life (Book 5)

***

Mob Tracker Series
— She's unstoppable! —
Sweet Retaliation (Book #1)
Sweet Justice (Book #2)
Sweet Resolution (Book #3
Sweet Endings – (Book #4)

***

Other Titles
I'm No Angel
Hotshot Cowboy
Big Girls Don't Cry
Christmas Runaway
The Surrogate's Secret
Mimi's Mix (Box Set)
'Tis the Season (Box Set)
Hearts, Flowers & Romance (Box Set)
Red Hot Divas (Box Set)
A Touch of Passion (Multi-author Box Set)
Love, Christmas (Multi-author Box Set)

Unforgettable Romances (Multi-author Box Set)
Kiss Me, Thrill Me (Multi-author Box Set)
Mystic Lovers (Multi-author Box Set)
Wedding Pets & Kisses (Multi-author Box Set)
Hotshot Heartbreakers (Multi-author Box Set)
Sweet and Sassy (Multi-author Box Set)
Mystic Passion (Multi-author Box Set)
Unforgettable Heroes (Multi-author Box Set)
Sweet Heat (Multi-author Box Set)
Hotshot Charmers (Multi-author Box Set)
Unforgettable Christmas (Multi-author Box Set)
A Christmas She'll Remember (Multi-author Box Set)
Sweet and Sassy Christmas (Multi-author Box Set)
Beneath the Mistletoe (Multi-author Box Set)
Snowflakes & Christmas Kisses (Multi-author Box Set)

***

All Mimi's books can be found on her Amazon Author Page:
http://bit.ly/MimiBarbourAmazon
OR
Website: http://mimibarbour.com

A note from the author, Mimi Barbour

MIMI BARBOUR: New York Times & USA Today Best-selling romance author has written 5 series and over 30 books. She lives on the beautiful East coast of Vancouver Island and writes her books with tongue-in-cheek and a mad glint in her eye. The fans all agree that it's the fascinating characters she creates which makes her writing so entertaining and brings them back for more of her magic.

"The favorite part of my job is meeting the

characters from each new book. Designing them the way I want and having them act however I think they should. It's thrilling, especially when most of my make-believe folks are so very interesting. They're fun and surprising, and in most cases, people I would love to interact with in reality."

Write to me! I truly love hearing from my readers!

My website: http://www.mimibarbour.com/

Angels to the Rescue by Deborah A. Clifton

~*~*~

The world faces destruction again, but the angels come to the rescue.

The third world war has decimated the planet, and left communities lost, and living in the "dark ages" once more. Few pray to their deity. That was bad enough, but when the birth of His Son was forgotten, God wanted to start over again. He asked the archangels to come up with ideas before he sent an asteroid in the direction of Earth.

One man had not forgotten the true meaning of Christmas. The archangel, Michael, pointed to him as an example of a good person who could be one of God's prophets.

Michael and Ariel were sent to give the message on Christmas eve

Dedication

I dedicate this story to my children, who are my
human angels.
They have been my anchor in tough times, and
my best friends in good times.

Angels to the Rescue - a short story

World War III

By the year 2100, the planet was so over-populated that it could not contain the multitudes. 12 Million souls inhabited the Earth. People started migrating to the Moon, Mars, and the moons of Saturn and Jupiter. Even genesis ships with cryogenically frozen humans traveled to planets in other galaxies that seemed viable for life.

The people of Earth were spreading throughout the cosmos.

Climate change had changed the terrain of Earth. Many island nations sunk under the oceans. The coastlines changed dramatically. Land was lost. Technology was invented to build floating cities on the oceans. This was their solution.

Then cities in the air became possible. At first it was a marvel of engineering. The wealthy loved living among the clouds, but ultimately, they became floating slums.

From one of these slums rose a man.

***

A secret military force attacked from the sky on Christmas Eve 2200. It was as if the entire world exploded, instantaneously. No-one knew why or who was at the head of the invading force.

At least, not yet.

People were out and about shopping, not suspecting they were on the eve of the last war, World War III. It seemed the world erupted with every pent-up hate, every hidden resentment against those on the land. It was unexpected, after a hundred years of peace.

The governments of the world needed to get their communities into uniforms, trained, and fighting this new foe.

It was different from the usual wars or terrorist attacks. It wasn't even a civil war in the way civil wars were fought. These soldiers were trained, and knew what they were doing. When captured, they had poison pills, and committed suicide. Not one of them could be interrogated.

The war raged on for more than fifty years. Then it ground to a halt. Each side had barely anyone left to fight. There were not enough men to bury the dead. Large pits were dug, and the corpses were thrown in, and markers put on their graves.

Here lies the dead of the 110th Infantry. It was Ol' man Smith's unit, and he helped bury them.

Not many survived.

Who brought about this carnage? It was a man called Landon M., an occupant of the slums in the sky. He had a golden tongue, and a steel heart. He escaped the war when all the sky cities were blown up, and dropped into the ocean. No-one knew where he was, and eventually they stopped looking.

In the meantime, mega-cities were decimated, emptied, unliveable. They caved in on themselves like earthquakes had played shuffle board with the buildings. The smaller cities barely survived. Eventually, they too were abandoned. The people could not maintain them. So, they drifted into small hamlets and towns, where they grew their own crops, or mined metals and minerals for trade.

After the war, Ol' man Smith went into the woods for a long time.

Alone.

None of his family had survived the war. His wife was gone, his children had disappeared. His parents were enslaved, and died a gruesome death in a camp.

He felt bereft. He couldn't feel anything, not love, not hate, not revenge against those who had wronged him.

Pointless, because they were all dead.

Ol' man Smith couldn't remember how long he wandered the forest. He clambered over mountains, and survived off the land. He eventually discovered a cavern, and stayed. He remained alone with his thoughts, and memories. Until people drifted through. Many with wounds from the war, external and internal. They were broken, but in the forests and mountains, they found peace. Some stayed, then built houses under the mountain, in front of the cave. It became a community. Then children were born.

Ol' man Smith was amused when people called the hamlet, Smithsville. He was the oldest citizen, and it was a way to honor him. The town wouldn't have existed if not for Ol' man Smith.

He built a little hut in the woods amongst the trees, for those who wanted to pray or meditate. Ol' man Smith called it a prayer-hut. He would meditate for long lengths of time. He wanted his family back, but he knew it wasn't possible. So, he prayed they were in a better place, where there was no pain.

He had his old bible. He wasn't religious, but spiritual. Ol' man Smith thought religion had caused a lot of the disaster that happened on Earth. Some tried to start religions in the town, but he never attended their churches. When people saw his example, they followed it, and the religions died.

He told the children, "be your own religion. Do good, and it will come back to you many times over."

Decisions in Heaven

Uriel, one of the archangels, flew to the high plains where the Holy One, and His Son resided. He was the smallest of the archangels, and his little wings fluttered like a hummingbird. Uriel easily transcended the heights he needed to go.

He arrived, and landed with a soft sigh. He walked down a wide, white hall. It was open to the sky. This was his favourite place to be, other than in the presence of his Creator.

Finally, Uriel entered a large garden. It had a large imposing tree in the center of it. So large that you couldn't see the ends of the branches, or how high it was. The trunk was big and sturdy with roots showing here and there. It had no likeness on Earth.

God sat under it in a meditative pose, while Jesus paced. This was the first time Uriel saw Jesus looking worried. Since the angel had been created millions of years ago, he had seen Jesus only look happy, and serene. Of course, there was that time on the cross, but that was a microcosm in time.

Uriel bowed his head, "it seems there is no consensus yet, my Lords. Many would prefer to be done with the place, and start anew."

"No," Jesus said. The sharpness of His tone was unexpected. He stopped in front of Uriel. "There must be a way."

"It is not up to me, Lord."

God opened his eyes. "Son, there might not be a way. Even I cannot see a single future for my creation. I gave them free will. There are so many variables, which is why I decided to see if the angels could come up with some ideas."

"I know, Father."

"Go back, Uriel, and keep listening, and reporting. I do not want a repeat of the situation where a third of my angels, and an archangel rebelled. And, I really don't want to destroy my creation because of it."

"Yes, my Lord." Uriel bowed.

As he fluttered down to the angelic realm, Uriel mused about the difficult situation. He took God's Word seriously. He was created for it. *God also has free will*, he thought, *and He could destroy or create anything He pleases. He loved humanity for thousands of years. But prayers are feeble and rare these days. What's a God to do?* Uriel shook his head. He couldn't say.

The angels were meeting in Heaven in the angelic quarters, to discuss the events unfolding on Earth. Six archangels, Michael, Raphael, Gabriel, Jophiel, Ariel, and Azrael broke up to form workshops. Yes, earthly creativeness, and innovation originated in the spiritual world, and the idea of a workshop was one of them. Some people had easier access to that world than others, and it was called, genius. Many used it for good, but some aspired to power, and used their high intelligence for evil, with the help of Satan, their fallen brother.

While Uriel was gone, some progress had been made. Michael had convinced the angels in his charge that humans should be given a chance. Despite their wars, and unruly ways, many showed creativity, honor, love and worship for the One God. It was easy to convince his angels. They had all experienced the better side of humanity. The touch of a mother's hand against the cheek of her baby, the artist's inspiration, the hope and courage carried through the ages.

Being God's general, it was easy for Michael to understand war. He didn't like it, but there was a certain glory to it when fighting on the right side. But, the latest war was not like that. It was a carnage for sake of it, with those defending themselves unable to understand the reason for the war.

Ariel the protector of animals and nature, was not so inclined to be kind. She helped her measure of humans. Mostly comforting them as an animal. Her favourite was to appear as a lost black cat. She would purr, and allow herself to be stroked. It seemed to help lift the spirit of those in anguish. Now, she wondered how much she had helped them destroy their own environment.

"Behold the Earth. It is polluted. Many dear animals have gone extinct choking on the filth of the humans. Why should we let them continue this way?" It was a good argument.

Gabriel interjected, "Michael has a point. Not every human is bad. Can we not save some?"

"That's what happened last time. We saved Noah, and his family, and nothing really changed," Azrael said. "Eventually, the balance is altered to more bad than good." She and her angels were the ones who collected the souls of the dead. "It would give us a break." Azrael was wont to be sarcastic.

She was the so-called angel of death, but Azrael and the angels she led, were sweet looking. Their light shone in such a way, that the spirit of the dying person was happy to follow them. *Unless, the fallen angels took them.* She shivered at the thought.

"This is serious," Raphael said.

"I am serious," Azrael said. "We have seen the way men die in battle. They don't start the wars. Evil men do. If good men can be controlled by bad, then why should we continue to sustain their overall survival."

"I have witnessed the greatest artists creating music and paintings to honor God. But, in the last few hundred years, things have gone from bad to worse. The evil one has found his way into all parts of the world," Jophiel said. "This latest war has deadened the creative spirit of the humans, and they are battle weary. Perhaps we should wait another hundred years or so, until they are able to think and pray clearly. After all, they managed peace for a hundred years before."

"I agree, give them a time of reprieve. This war was more catastrophic than any I attended. My angels were overworked, and I saw many souls lost to the dark world," Azrael said.

"Yes, let us heal the world before destroying it?" Raphael said, sadly. "I have performed many miraculous healings in the name of Our Father. People have come to love the Word through those miracles. Millions in the heavens can attest to that, and are grieving the possible loss of their descendants."

They broke up to consider the words of Raphael. He was the wisest among them, so it seemed a good idea to listen to him.

***

Time went by, and Uriel once again flew up to the abode of God. He delivered a message.

"The angels have come to a consensus, Lords," Uriel said. "They follow Raphael's advice to give humanity one hundred years reprieve. In the meantime, bring up a prophet to spread the Word."

God's voice boomed across heaven, and even into hell.

"Let it be so. Humanity has one century then, We will see the choices they make." All heard it with their ears, and in their mind.

"Thank you, Father," Jesus said. "I know of someone. A humble man who has kept up the stories of the bible. The Holy Ghost is with him now receiving his prayers, and whispering in the way it does, in that small still voice."

"I am glad, My Son."

God went back to His tree, covering Himself with a sheath that appeared as if from the air. The tree formed a comfortable branch to seat its loving Master. And, God went back to meditating on the universe that He had created.

Christmas Eve

The children picked their way through the forest. It was a difficult path, and the cold nipped at their noses and brought a misty breath. They played with their mouth-mist, oohing and ahing to see if they could make shapes like ol' man Smith with his pipe. He blew rings forever, it seemed to the children. They giggled at the results.

They made a game out of who could get the most fir tree branches their mother requested. Of course, Xandra won. She was the oldest. Their dog, Mix, was disinterested in their game. He sniffed at the ground, and followed an intriguing scent.

"Come on, Mix," Xandra called. The dog left the trail of delicious scent reluctantly, and ran after the children, barking excitedly.

Xandra and Shawn were excited about the coming mid-winter celebration, when the days lengthened, and spring not far away. They ate honey balls, and decorated the doors of the huts with fir branches, and bits of colored glass. The main celebration took place in a large cavern. It echoed, and sounds reached far into the back of the cave. It was a good place for singing, and story telling.

Ol' man Smith was the best storyteller. He leaned on his walking stick, and his deep voice reached to the back of the cave, while he puffed on a pipe of herbs. He remembered the Last War, and told many tales from it. Some, of course, were far fetched and unbelievable, even to the children. They still enjoyed them. As for Ol' man Smith, he found it difficult to explain the war to those who never experienced one. So, he tended toward making them up as he went along. He got a kick out of it, when he saw the children's faces, eyes wide, silent. They hung on every word.

Ol' man Smith was telling them another story after their evening meal.

"It was loud, louder than you can ever imagine," he said. The words echoed through the cave. "My ears rang from the loudness."

One boy, always that one boy, interrupted, "louder than thunder?"

"Yes, even louder than thunder," Ol' man Smith said. "Not only from bombs, but guns. Oh, the big guns' sound was awesome. They could shoot way out into space. It looked beautiful, like fireworks, but deadly."

The same boy asked, "what's fireworks?"

"What? I suppose we don't have those anymore. Pity." Ol' man Smith's smoke puffed up into a curl. He never described the wonder of fireworks. How could he when it was part of the raging war? "Yes," he said. He frowned as he remembered the carnage of war. He still had nightmares, still dreamed of friends, and family who were lost.

The children thought he was asleep in his old chair. One of them poked Ol' man Smith, and he let out a roar, and they jumped with fright. He loved to tease them.

Ol' man Smith continued his story.

"There were many battles on the land, sea, and in the air. Even out in space. There was a colony on the moon. It was bombarded for no reason. Just because they existed. It was ravaged, blown apart, the surface forever changed. The smaller moon influenced the climate on the surface on the planet." He paused to take a puff. "Sometimes, we didn't know who the enemy was." He shuffled in his chair. "Isn't that weird ... to not know your enemy?" He changed his mournful ton, like a person shedding a heavy, gray coat.

He smiled.

"Did you know the mid-winter celebration used to be called Christmas?"

"Yes," all the children shouted out. The story was not new to them. Every year he told them the same story.

"Oh well, I'm sure you don't want me to tell you again."

"We do," the children shouted.

"I like the story 'bout the angels," the youngest boy said shyly. His eyes were big, and blue, and he illuminated innocence. Ol' man Smith's heart melted. He loved the young ones who knew nothing of war and strife. They gave him hope.

"Okay then, I'll tell you the story about a king who lived a long, long, long time ago. He was like no other king." He stopped. "Can anyone tell me what a king is?"

A hand went up, but someone was quicker than the boy. A girl said, "it's a person who's the boss of everyone." The children laughed. They were thinking of the same thing. There was a game, called whose-the-boss, popular among the older children. It involved climbing up a certain hill. The one who reached the top first, shouted out, "I'm the boss, so what are you?" And the children shouted back, "we're the ones who'll be the boss next time."

"That's about right," Ol' man Smith said. He knew the game. In fact, he invented it to demonstrate democracy. He continued. "This was no ordinary king, no boss of the hill. Angels and wise men attended his birth, even though it was in a barn. Shepherds sleeping in the field, minding their own business, were woken up by a chorus of angels singing about the new born king." He held up a picture of the baby Jesus, depicted in his well-worn bible. He was surrounded by angels, in the arms of his mother. "This is the king on his birthday which was celebrated on what was called Christmas day, our mid-winter celebration."

The younger children ooh-ed. "The angels are so pretty," Shawn said. "What happened to him?"

"It's a long story, and I'll fill you in on it another day." Ol' man Smith said. "But," he said mysteriously, as he looked at each child, "the world would never be the same from that day on." He looked out dreamily at the stars framed by the entrance to the cave. "Perhaps it was a good thing, perhaps not," he whispered.

Without warning, a bright light appeared in the space where Ol' man Smith was gazing. It had a purplish-blue hue to it.

The children screamed. Ol' man Smith gasped. He wasn't sure what the light was. He knew it was not an aircraft, or a meteorite. He'd seen many of those.

A UFO?

Mix crawled toward the vision. He made a small sound no-one ever heard the dog make before. *A whine of delight?* Xandra called to him, but he ignored her.

"Don't be frightened," a voice said out of the

brilliant light. "I am Michael, a messenger from God Almighty." Almost a whisper. In the light, one could make out arms spread apart, pale, almost translucent. As the light receded, large white wings appeared, each feather more perfect than a dove's. Michael was shadowed by the glory shining from behind. The little children ran to the figure.

"Angel," they called out. They seemed to know instinctively who he was.

The angel knelt and joyfully scooped them up in his arms. His face appeared as the radiant light faded, and it was one of kindness, and love. He looked at the older children and Ol' man Smith, as if to say, *you too*. And, they ran to him. Ol' man Smith was the last one to get to the angel's arms. The angel stood, and hugged the man.

Ol' man Smith cried. Tears streamed down his face. He was thinking of his lost family. Michael looked at him, as if peering into his soul. A thought appeared in Ol' man Smith's head. *They're all safe now.*

Michael turned away. "I bring news from the Most High," the angel said. He was talking to everyone in listening distance.

Ol' man Smith choked back his tears. "What news do you bring?"

"You, Craig Smith, have been chosen to go out and spread the Word of God to all the world. To tell your stories."

Like all the prophets of old, he was uncertain.

"But, I'm an old man, only fit to live out my life in this village telling stories to children. How can I travel the world again?"

"All is well, you are young again. Throw away your crutch and walk. See your arms and hands and legs have changed. You will live a long life, telling your stories of the Lord."

Ol' man Smith saw it was true. The children clapped. He looked different. He was his young self. Shawn pinched his leg to see if he was real.

"Ouch," Ol' man Smith said. "Obviously, I'm not exempt from pain.

Michael took a small bottle from his robe. It contained consecrated oil, blessed by Jesus himself. He took Ol' man Smith's right hand in his, and they knelt. After what felt like eternity, the angel lifted the bottle over Ol' man Smith's head, while he closed his eyes. Michael poured the contents slowly onto Ol' man Smith's crown.

"I anoint you, Craig Smith, a prophet of God. May you always be faithful, and honorable." Smith felt a power enter him. And, for the first time ever, he knew the wonder of God. Tears ran down his cheeks, and he shook. Michael let go of his hand, and Smith stopped shaking. He was afraid to open his eyes. When he did, everything looked different, even the angel. He could see his aura, and what an awesome aura it was. Violet, and azure interchanged with pure white, and golden light. The black cat was an angel too. It was surrounded by emerald, and gold.

Smith was distracted by a small voice.

"We can't call you Ol' man Smith anymore," Xandra said. "From now on you will be known as Smith the Prophet."

Some of the children's parents saw the light, and the angel within. Some even saw the black cat with the bright green eyes. They ran to the cave's entrance, fearing their children were in danger. Xandra and Shawn's father, Sam, got there first.

"What's happening?" Sam asked. The angel turned to face him, smiled, and disappeared. "What, who," he blustered, not knowing what to say.

"A miracle happened today, dad. Michael, the archangel appeared to us, and made Ol' man Smith young again. He is Smith the Prophet now."

The new prophet plopped himself into his usual chair, shocked at the events that had just taken place. The black cat jumped onto his lap, and curled into a ball, purring. The prophet stroked its fur, and realized how soft it was. Somehow, each stroke of his hand brought more confidence, and a knowledge of what he had to do.

Smith the Prophet stood up. He placed the cat on his old chair, where it started to groom itself.

"I have to go soon," Smith said. "I will spend Christmas here, and leave the next day." He walked out of the cave, and went to the prayer hut. The cat followed him, flicking its tail.

Everyone in the cave were speechless, and they all started to speak at once after Smith left.

"What just happened?" Sam asked again. He didn't expect an answer, but he needed to voice the question.

Christmas that year was the best the children ever had. Smith the Prophet told his stories, then he left them with a message.

"We all must love each other, and look to our hearts to seek the answers to what must come after. Do not waste your energy on building expensive churches. Pray in your homes. Search for the light within. Embody the true Christmas, being humble, grateful, and peaceful."

The End

A note from the author, Deborah A. Clifton

Thanks for reading my little story, Angels to the Rescue. I hope you liked it. It is in my genre, sci-fi/fantasy/paranormal/post-apocalyptic (I enjoy mixing it up), so I enjoyed writing it. I do love angels, and stories about them

May the angels be with you.

Debbie

Contact:

If you'd like to contact me, my email is writerdebbie1@gmail.comand mention this story.

Please follow me on my Facebook:
https://www.facebook.com/imvubuland
And,   my   website:
www.deborahaclifton.weebly.com

The Horses
of Winter by
Genevieve
McKay

~*~*~

Sarah Lawson has given up making Christmas wishes for herself. When her parents died in an accident she had to push all her dreams of a family and horses aside. Her only goal this holiday season is to find a permanent place for her baby sister Amy. Their latest foster home has everything Sarah could hope for; a farm in the country, a nice foster-mom, and the kind of stability that creative, scatter-brained Amy needs. The only problem; it's temporary.

When imaginative Amy finds a lost horse, she's convinced is a unicorn, Sarah is dragged on an adventure she'll never forget.

This could be the Christmas that changes everything. But is Sarah ready to take a leap of faith?

A short story
- The Horses
of Winter

The Horses of Winter
The horses of winter are at my cabin door
Gaunt-ribbed, tangle-maned
They paw the frozen forest floor.
-Elliot Lawson

"Sarah, there's a unicorn in Cecily's greenhouse!"

Amy stood panting in the doorway, the wild December wind tearing at her new scarf and winter coat. Her hat was gone and blonde curls whipped around her face in a tangled halo.

"Shut the door," I said automatically, dropping

my gaze back to the poem I'd been working on. I edged closer toward the stone hearth and the crackling fire. "You'll let the heat out."

The ever-present wind nipped at my cheeks and I nudged the thick, scratchy blanket tighter around my shoulders. The big farmhouse was always drafty and today the only warm spot seemed to be practically inside the dancing flames themselves.

"But, Sarah..." Amy's voice pitched sharply upward, "it's a real live unicorn."

"Do you want Cecily to kick us out before Christmas?" I said without looking up. "Then shut the door."

Amy heaved a big sigh and I heard her turn to wrestle the door closed with a reluctant thud. She was silent for approximately three seconds before she began bouncing up and down on the welcome mat again, working herself up.

"Sarah," she begged, "could you puh-lease come and see the unicorn? I promise you it's not pretend."

"Okay, fine," I said, slamming my book shut. Amy was clearly not going to give this up and let me work in peace. My homework wasn't going well anyway. I was supposed to pull a poem apart and write an analysis for my creative writing class. It should have been easy but, on a whim, I'd picked one of Dad's old poems, The Horses of Winter, and it wasn't giving up its secrets easily.

I stood to stretch my cramped muscles, then carefully folded the blanket into a precise square and set it neatly at one end of the sagging couch. "I'll come outside with you for just a few minutes, but then we have to help get dinner ready. Okay?"

Amy danced up and down and flung open the front door again so hard that it hit the wall with a bang, making the window pane rattle. "Come on!" she cried, plunging into the knee-high snow, not even caring that she would be a soaking wet mess when it melted.

Her boots had dropped chunks of dirty snow inside the door. I used my bare fingers to toss them outside and then prodded the watery trail left on the wood floor with my sock, wondering if I should go get a dish towel or something to dry it with. We hadn't lived here long enough to learn the rules, and while our foster mom, Cecily, seemed nice, she was also a little strange. And she hadn't wanted to take us in a month before Christmas; not at all. It was more important than ever that we, or at least Amy, stay on our best behaviour.

I'll leave it until we get back, I decided, carefully slipping on my new blue coat and matching gloves and scarf. *We'll just make more of a mess when we come back in.*

The coat was warm and puffy, wrapping me instantly in a protective cocoon. I felt a mixture of guilt and delight every single time I put the thing on. Outdoor wear wasn't cheap, especially when it was brand new and not from the thrift store. We'd always lived closer to the ocean so we'd hardly needed winter clothes before, but Cecily's farmhouse sat right up against the mountains where cold air loaded with snow swooped down from the peak to poke constantly at us with sharp fingers. That whole first week had been almost unbearable; we'd stayed holed up in the house with our teeth chattering and finally, Cecily had taken us shopping.

"Amy, you forgot your gloves," I called into the swirling snow, catching sight of her mitts balled up in a corner by the front door. There was no answer.

I pocketed the gloves, pulled on my boots, and followed my sister's tiny boot tracks through the rapidly falling snow. The prints didn't go in a straight line. Every few feet they'd leap off to the side of the path or disappear altogether. Here, a tiny snowman abandoned without a head; there, a flock of snow angels side by side in the snow. Amy was a sparrow flitting from one idea to the next.

I carefully pushed open the greenhouse door and peeked inside. "Amy?"

It was warmer inside and I shrugged back my hood so I could get a better look around.

The greenhouse looked like a cross between a barn and a big tent. The ceiling wasn't solid; it was covered in plastic, too thick to see out of, but thin enough to let the faint winter light stream in. The center was full of long, wooden tables piled with empty pots and dried up, spilled soil. Cecily had told us she started her young plants here in early spring; they were kept safe until they were strong enough to go outside. Her eyes had lit up when she'd described it, all green and fragrant and full of young, living things. It made me wish that I could be around long enough to see it in action. At least Amy had a chance of seeing it.

When I'm older, I reminded myself, *I'll have a small house just big enough for me and Amy and I'll have a garden of my own that nobody can take away.*

"Amy?" I called again, my new boots crunching across some dried up, discarded stalks that had been knocked to the floor. A few broken pots lay scattered beside them as if this end of the table had been swept clean, tumbling half its contents. There was a strong smell in the air, too; familiar and not entirely unpleasant, but I couldn't place it. "Where are you?"

"Over here," came my sister's despondent voice. "He's gone."

I glanced nervously back at the closed door, feeling like a criminal even though Cecily had told us we were free to explore the property as much as we liked. That didn't necessarily mean we could break into her greenhouse and go poking around, though. People were funny sometimes and there were invisible rules that could be broken without you even noticing. All it would take was one wrong move, one line crossed, and you could be sent away again.

"Amy?" I called, making my voice sound like Mom's used to when she was serious. "Tell me where you are."

"Over here."

I peered around the last table to see my little sister hunched down against the wall, knees pulled tight up against her chest.

"For heavens' sake," I said, kneeling beside her. "What's the matter?"

I didn't really need her to tell me, though; this was pure Amy all over. She'd get excited over an idea or story she'd dreamed up in her imagination, and then there'd be tears when she came crashing down to earth again.

"No unicorn, huh?" I said kindly.

"He's gone," she sniffled, "but he really was here. I wasn't making it up this time. I promise. Please don't get me in trouble."

"You're not in trouble," I said firmly, smoothing a tangle of hair behind her ear. Our last foster parents hadn't liked Amy at all and had punished her for pretty much everything she did. Who grounds an eight-year-old child for making up imaginary stories? I'd watched her spirit wilt day by day until I'd decided it was time to go. It had taken me months to convince Dee to get us out of there, but I'd done it.

"I believe you," I said, even though I didn't, and it was worth it to see her tear-stained face light up into a trembling smile. "Come on, let's get warmed up and have dinner ready for Cecily. She's in the studio and you know what that means."

Cecily was the most interesting foster parent we'd had so far. She didn't go out to work; in the summer, she grew organic vegetables for the farmer's market, and in the winter, she made the most beautiful pottery I'd ever seen. She made normal stuff like plates and mugs in all sorts of colours, but she also did these strange, abstract sculptures that she sold through a local gallery. She must have been pretty famous because she was always getting calls from people wanting to buy stuff from her.

Cecily was nice enough when she was around, but often she'd stay holed up in her studio for hours at a time and when she came out she'd have this far-off dazed expression on her face as if she were thinking about something else entirely. She hadn't even wanted to open the door when Dee had shown up with us out of the blue; she'd long forgotten that she'd signed up to be a foster parent at all.

"I'm sorry, I'm too busy," she'd called, peering at us through the window. "This is not a good time. Try again in Spring."

It had taken everything Dee had to persuade Cecily to take us in, but there was nowhere else for us to go and in the end, she'd let us stay.

"There are his hoof prints," Amy said, pointing

at some deer tracks that led past the greenhouse to the woods. "I wonder why he went away. He said he wanted to meet you."

"Oh, he talked to you, did he?" I laughed, nudging her shoulder. "And why would he want to meet me?"

I glanced down and froze, leaning forward so I could see the tracks better. There were dozens of deer living in the woods behind the empty barn. They tip-toed out early each morning, thin and nervous, long ears swiveling to catch any sign of danger, pawing holes in the thick snow on the barren hay fields to get at the grass beneath. I'd seen their tracks crisscrossing the entire property in their search for food, but these tracks were different. They were bigger and instead of pointy, cloven hooves they were oval shaped, the middle part printed with a heart-shaped "V."

"Hey, Amy, look at that. I think those are horse prints."

"Unicorn," she corrected. "He was a white unicorn and he said his name was Sam."

"That's a pretty plain name for a unicorn." I raised an eyebrow at her. "Shouldn't he be named Moonbeam Sprinkle Pants or something?"

"Sarah," Amy groaned. "You're being crazy."

"That's right, you're having conversations with unicorns named Sam but I'm the crazy one," I said, winking at her so she knew I wasn't serious. Sometimes she took things way too literally.

"Can we follow the tracks?" she said. "Puuhleeease?"

"Yeah." I glanced back at the house. "For a bit, anyway. We have a few minutes to spare. Here, put your mitts on."

She stood still long enough for me to work the mittens down over each of her cold, wet hands, and then she spun away, racing across the snow in a lurching gait, following the horse prints up the little hill we'd sledded down yesterday. We hadn't had a real sled of course but we'd done it anyway, sitting on slippery black garbage bags that rocketed us down the hill at top speed; better than any fancy store-bought toboggan.

"I'm cantering!" she yelled back over her shoulder. "Like a unicorn."

"Okay," I called out, "good job."

"Now I'm galloping!" she squealed, pushing herself harder until she inevitably tripped and face-planted halfway up the bank.

I held my breath, waiting for the tears, but she was in a good mood and she merely started rolling backward; a snow-suit wrapped log propelling down the hill until she lay panting at my feet, eyes closed and cheeks pink with cold.

"You okay?" I prodded her with my foot.

"No," she whispered, her head drooping to the side. She stuck her tongue out for full effect. "I'm dead and you'll have to bury me."

She was pretending, caught up in some inner

play, but this time it was too close to reality and I felt a shiver of fear run down my spine.

"Come on." I turned my back on her abruptly and headed off toward the woods. "You want to find your unicorn, don't you?"

"Sam," she corrected, springing to her feet and trotting beside me. "He told me he had a longer name but it was too hard for me to say so he said to call him Sam."

"Makes sense," I said, scanning the snow. "Look, he branched off this way."

We walked silently through the deepening snow, our breath coming in laboured puffs that grew worse the higher we climbed.

We must be halfway through Cecily's property by now. I knew she had sixty acres of land; there were the house and an old barn used for storage, the greenhouse, and Cecily's studio. The rest was part pasture that she loaned out to a local farmer to hay, part woods and the garden, but there was no fence and it was impossible to know when her land stopped and the neighbours began.

"Oh, no!" Amy sucked in her breath. "Blood."

The snow in front of us had been trampled in a huge circle, hoof prints marking the ground, but there were other flattened spaces where the animal had fallen hard. Splashes of blood were churned into the snow.

"Don't panic," I said sharply, shooting her a look. The last thing I needed was for her to lose her marbles way out here. There was no way I wanted to carry her all that way back kicking and screaming. I crept forward, holding my breath until I stood in the center of the crime scene. *So why did he stop here?* I kicked into the snow. My foot met something hard and I plunged my arm deep into a drift, clearing a space until I uncovered the culprit. A rusty bale of barbed wire, the end snaking out under the snow.

"Ah-ha," I said, carefully holding up the coil of wire to show Amy. It had sharp knots woven in it every few inches that snagged at my gloves, leaving small pinprick marks. The animal must have walked into it and gotten caught somehow.

"We have to help him." Amy stood stiffly, arms held out to the side and her breath coming in the rapid gasps that meant she was close to a panic attack.

"Right, but we have to stay calm. We know he got away, so that's one good thing, and we know he can walk, so that's a second good thing. Let's follow his tracks a little further and if we don't find him then we'll run home and get Cecily. She can call the police or someone to come help him, okay?"

Amy still looked like she would start wailing, but I turned my back on her again and marched away. "Hurry," I said. "Sam needs us."

That did it. She plowed after me and didn't say another word. We moved as fast as we could through the snow, half-running, following his tracks like hound dogs chasing prey. The blood wasn't so bad now, but it hadn't stopped, either. How long could he keep this up?

Just as I was ready to give up, there he was in front of us. He stood with his head hung low, sides heaving, speckled grey coat splashed with red. He looked like a painting; red and grey contrasting perfectly in an awful sort of way. Despite his condition, he was magnificent. He reminded me of the poem I'd been working on, The Horses of Winter, about these wild spirit horses who used to come and ferry dying people away against their will. It wasn't my favourite poem of Dad's; it was kind of depressing and I didn't like that he'd made the horses seem evil, but I could still hear his voice as he recited it, eyes lit up with the drama of it all. It was one of my favourite memories of him.

"Sam!" Amy cried. I came to my senses and grabbed her jacket just as she sprang forward. The horse flung his head up and stumbled a few paces away, his eyes rimmed with white.

"Don't," I said sternly, "you'll scare him."

Her lower lip trembled, but she nodded. "Sorry. I want to help him."

"We'll go up together, but very slowly so we don't startle him. He must be terrified."

"Yeah," she breathed. "It's okay, Sam, we're here to help. Good boy."

He lifted his head and flicked his ears in our

direction. He had a leather halter on his head that had come half-loose and ridden up over one ear so it lay partly obscuring his eye.

"Poor guy," I crooned, adding my voice to Amy's as we edged toward him, "poor horse, you just stand there and let us help you."

"Don't call him a horse," Amy whispered, "he's a unicorn."

"Uh huh." Up close he was huge, much bigger than any horse I'd even ridden, and built like a tank. I gingerly reached out to touch him with my gloved hand. He shuddered, but didn't move; he was done running. I stroked his neck softly, wincing as I looked at the red smeared on his beautiful, white coat.

Most of the damage was to his near front leg and chest; a hole gaped in the flesh of his upper leg, drenching his whole front end in a blanket of red. The other wounds looked pretty minor, but he'd have to be cleaned up before we could know for sure. He needed to get back home so we could call a vet.

"We'll have to wrap his leg," I said, thinking quickly. "We can't have it bleeding all the way home."

"We can use my scarf," Amy said, sounding surprisingly calm. She moved to unravel it from her neck, but I laid a hand on her shoulder to stop her. "No, let's use mine, just in case Cecily is mad that we got our new stuff all bloody. It's better if she's angry at me than you."

Amy frowned but didn't argue. She watched as I gave the unresisting horse another pat and then wrapped the scarf around his leg as best as I could. I tried to be gentle, but it needed to be a bit tight to stay in place and he tossed his head when I made the last wrap.

"Sorry, boy." I reached up carefully and slid his halter strap back over his ear. There was a brass plate attached to the halter and I leaned down, squinting in the slanting light to read it. "Silmarillion", I said, sounding the letters out. "Oh, that's the name of a novel. What a funny name for a horse."

"Yeah, he says it's easier to call him Sam," Amy laughed, "that's what everyone at his horse-home calls him."

"Horse-home, hey?" I said, gently pulling on the animal's halter until he took a hesitant step toward home. "So now he's not a unicorn?"

"Sure he is, but he says that only special people like me can see his horn. Most people think he's a horse. He says you can see it, too."

"Is that so?" I glanced at his forehead instinctively and then shook my head, laughing at myself. *You almost believed her for a second.* I inched the horse another few steps forward. He followed willingly but, even so, our progress was painfully slow. He could only move at a snail's pace and every few steps I had to adjust the slipping bandage.

The temperature dropped and now our breath came out in white plumes like frosted feathers. It took forever before we reached the spot where Sam had run into the barbed wire. My heart sank. We'd been out here so long and had made such little progress. We were never going to make it home.

"Amy," I said, looking anxiously at the fading light. "It's getting dark and I don't think we're going to make it to Cecily's before it does." I paused and looked down at her uncertainly. "See that tree way up there standing all by itself? We passed it just as we came up the big hill. Do you remember, we looked back and saw the farm?"

"Yes." She stared at me suspiciously, crossing her arms over her chest.

"Amy, you've got to be brave. Run to that tree and as soon as you're sure you can see the farm, I want you to run for home as fast as you can, okay? You need to get Cecily to call the vet and set up a dry place for Sam in the barn. He's going to need to get warm quickly or he'll get sick."

"But I want to stay with you and Sam," she said, her voice rising sharply like a knife, "he's my unicorn. I found him first."

"Amy," I said as calmly as I could. "This is not about you or me, this is about helping Sam. Do you understand? He could get really sick, maybe even die if we don't get him help quick. He's depending on you."

"On me?" she said uncertainly, looking up into my face to see if I was teasing her. Her mouth pulled down into a solemn line. Even though she was eight, most of the time she acted like an impulsive five-year-old. But sometimes her eyes seemed ancient, like she was someone's great grandmother reincarnated into a little girl. The look she gave me was spooky.

"Amy, he needs you. Stop at the top of the hill and wave to me if you're positive you can see the farmhouse lights for sure. Head straight toward them; if you run as fast as you can you'll be there in no time. Please, Amy."

She squished her face up, thinking hard and then she spun around without another word, flying across the snow at top speed. It seemed to take her forever to reach the tree; it must have been further than it looked. She appeared so small standing there all alone that I almost called her back, but the next moment she'd turned and waved both hands at me in the air, jumping up and down. She yelled something, but I was too far away to hear. She turned and leapt off the hill and we were alone.

I let out the breath I'd been holding and urged the big horse forward. "Come on, Sam," I whispered, "look how close to home we are. You don't have to make it much further."

It felt like hours for us to inch toward the tree but finally, we made it, and I allowed the horse to stop and take a break. Far below I could make out the lights of the farm, but from this height, they looked impossibly small. The sun had sunk long ago and the stars had come out, sprinkling the sky over our heads in a vast canopy of dancing lights.

I tugged on Sam's halter. He took another few faltering steps and then his legs folded and sank to the ground in the deep snow, groaning as he fell in slow motion.

"No!" I cried. "Get up, Sam, you have to keep moving."

It hurts, I'm so tired.

I froze, uncertain of where the words had come from. Had I gone crazy out here alone? Was it the hypothermia kicking in and I was seconds away from freezing to death?

The horse grunted and dropped his nose so it rested in the snow, his breath coming out in raspy gasps. His eyes flickered shut and he heaved a sigh. *I'll just rest.*

"No, Sam!" I wasn't about to let either of us die out here. I tugged on his halter hard and slapped him on the neck sharply to let him know I meant business. "I know it hurts, but you're so close. Get up now, just try, buddy. You're almost there."

With a moan and a mighty heave, he pushed himself upright, legs flailing until he gained purchase and stood trembling, blood soaked scarf-bandage half-hanging off his leg.

I re-wrapped it with aching, frozen fingers and

then stroked his neck, my hand leaving another dark trail down his white coat.

"Come on," I sighed, and this time he followed, lurching after me without stopping.

My feet were so numb that I'd long since stopped feeling any cold or pain. Somewhere dimly I thought that maybe that was a bad sign. I stumbled, steadying myself automatically against the horse's broad shoulder.

You're cold.

"I think we're beyond cold," I said, choking back a sob; hearing voices was not a good sign. "Don't think about it, just keep moving."

You are Sarah.

"That's right," I said out loud, giving in to my hallucination. There was nobody around to hear me anyway.

You're Sarah and you will ride me. We will jump big jumps.

"You're hardly in any state to jump anything," I muttered, tugging on his halter when he hesitated.

You are my person, Sarah; I have been waiting for you.

"Perfect, Sam, that's just perfect. Too bad we're about to die out here. And, even if we live, I don't have a home or any money for a horse. I can't even ride."

This is not your home?

"Sorry," I sighed, "it's not. Not really." I stopped, feeling a lump work its way up my throat.

This was the thing I hadn't told Amy. I'd overheard Cecily talking to Dee on the phone, telling her how well we were fitting in here. And then she'd dropped the bomb.

"I really only can take on one of them long-term though, Dee," she'd said. "I'm getting older and I just don't have the energy for two, no matter how nice they are."

"I have to make sure she takes, Amy," I told Sam, "this is her chance to have a real childhood. I don't want her being moved around again."

What about you?

I was quiet for a long time. "This is my last year in foster care," I said softly, my teeth now chattering so hard I could barely get out the words. "After that, I'm on my own. Amy is the only thing that matters. If I'm not living with her then I can't protect her, so I have to find a good place, a permanent place, for her soon. Dee says I should be able to get custody of her in a few years if I have a good job and a place for us to live. She could be safe here at least until then."

Sam, or the voice in my head pretending to be Sam, was silent and I scanned the dark trail up ahead, looking for landmarks. We'd come down the hill into the woods, but now we were too low to see the farm. I thought I was going in the right direction, but what if I was wrong? I could be leading us in circles. I pressed my lips together to hold back a sob; we just had to keep going, that's all. We walked and walked until I could hardly put one foot in front of the other.

"Sarah!" Cecily's anxious voice cut across the snow, but it sounded so far away and I was too exhausted to respond in anything more than a whisper. She called again and this time her voice was further off as if she were moving in the opposite direction.

"She's going away, Sam," I mumbled, resting my head against his neck just for a moment. I was so, so tired.

Sam stumbled to a stop, lifted his head and let out a bellowing neigh that shook his entire body.

I was so startled that I fell to the ground, clinging to his good leg with both hands so I wouldn't disappear completely in the deep snow.

"There they are," a man's voice now, getting closer as Sam's bellow still echoed my ears. Lights moved toward us and as I looked up, I saw that Sam was glowing as if there were light coming from inside him. A flash of silver over his head made me shut my eyes quickly.

"You're all right, Sarah," Hands gripped my shoulders and arms, drawing me upward. I stumbled again and someone strong scooped me up easily into their arms like I was as small as Amy.

"Take care of Sam," I whispered.

"As if we'd forget that big idiot. We've been looking for him all day."

"He's not an idiot," I protested.

"Easy does it, I was only joking."

The world spun and there was only the sound of boots crunching on snow and the stars circling slowly overhead.

"Here now, you're at the house. Your sister has been worried sick."

Warmth flooded over me, flowing from the open front door. He set me down on the couch by the fire and only then did I realize how truly cold I was. Every part of me shook so hard my teeth rattled in my head.

"We need some help here, Ellen," the man called and for the first time I looked at his face. He was middle-aged with the brown, weathered look of someone who spent all their time in the sun. His bright blue eyes were kind and edged by laugh lines.

"Oh, the poor thing." A woman appeared in the doorway to the kitchen. Her light brown hair was pulled back in a messy braid. "Did you find Sam?"

"He's out there and I think he'll be fine. The vet's on his way. He has a nasty gash on his leg. Seth put him in Cecily's barn."

"We should get him home, Arthur. He can't stay here overnight."

"Well, let's not fuss. You see to Sarah here, she's the one who rescued him, and I'll go check on that knucklehead."

He held up a hand when I shot him a glare.

"Don't get mad at me. I've raised that boy since he was a colt. There isn't a more annoying, accident-prone horse alive. He's escaped his stall and paddock more times than I can count and has needed sutures for some injury or another every year since the time he was born. But, he's family and we love him."

He grinned down at me, not looking away until I conceded a half-smile.

"You get warm and dry and then come on down and see him."

He turned and disappeared out the door, leaving me with Ellen.

"Okay," she said with an anxious look at his departing back, clearly wanting to be in the barn more than stuck babysitting me. "Socks and boots off first. I'll put some tea on."

As soon as she was gone, I slid off the couch and edged toward the fire, my hands shaking as I tried to pry off my sodden boots. My fingers wouldn't work right, they couldn't grip anything and by the time I had the first boot half-off, I whimpered with pain and frustration.

"Oh my goodness," Ellen appeared at my side and took both my hands in hers, peering worriedly into my face. "You're like ice. Here, get this stuff off quickly."

She pulled my boots off and ignored my protests as she peeled off my sodden socks and tossed them in a heap followed by my new jacket that was most likely ruined. I looked over at it longingly, holding back tears. It had been the one nice thing I'd owned in so long. "There's no time to be modest when you're freezing. Here's a blanket to wrap around you. Take everything else off as best you can. I'll run to get you some pajamas."

How does she know where to go? She disappeared upstairs. I shimmied out of my shirt and sopping yoga pants and wrapping the blanket tight around my shoulders. I really hoped nobody would pick that moment to come barging in.

Ellen was back with a pair of fluffy pajamas that weren't mine and an enormous pair of fluffy socks that looked brand new.

"I think those are Cecily's," I said, my teeth still chattering.

"They were the warmest things I could find," Ellen said in her no-nonsense voice, "put them on. She won't care."

She was probably right, but I still didn't like using Cecily's stuff. She might be okay with it now but later, when she had a chance to think about it, she might think of me as that poor, orphan girl who'd stolen her clothes. I didn't want her to associate Amy with anything negative.

"Put them on," Ellen repeated, heading back to the kitchen, "unless you want to sit around naked all night."

She had a point. Wrapping the blanket tighter around me I shimmied into the thick pajamas and pulled the socks on over my aching feet. To my surprise, everything fit perfectly, like a fuzzy second skin that wrapped me in life-giving warmth. I sat still with my eyes closed, luxuriating in the feeling of my body slowly thawing. The painful throbbing in my feet and hands at least meant that I was alive.

"Careful, it's hot." Ellen appeared beside me with a tray that held a tea pot and a chipped pottery mug, plus a plate of store-bought cookies.

My hands were shaking too badly to handle the cup Ellen set in front of me on the stone hearth, but I held my fingertips gently next to it for extra warmth.

"If you're okay then I'm going to check on Sam," Ellen said, already bundling into her coat and a huge wool hat. "I just need to see that he's all right; he's had us worried sick. Your sister's upstairs in bed. She was so exhausted when she got home that she couldn't stop crying and Cecily just put her to bed before going out to look for you."

I nodded and tried not to jump as the door slammed shut behind her. She must have been in a hurry to get away all this time.

"Sarah?" Amy stood uncertainly at the bottom of the stairs, her face puffy with tears. Someone had dressed her in her pajamas, too, and she had a pair of fluffy, white rabbit slippers on her feet that I'd never seen before. "You're alive? I thought you were dead."

"Of course, not silly," I said, "come sit with me by the fire."

She took a step forward and then stopped. "But what if you're dead, and this is just my imagination and you're not really here at all? What if you left me and went to live with mom and dad?"

My heart gave a little flip-flop of love for her, my tiny sister, who'd I'd been in charge of since she was only three years old. She was the thing I loved most in the whole entire universe. I would do anything to protect her.

"Well, if I were dead I probably wouldn't eat this entire plate of cookies by myself without even sharing any. Too bad because they're your favourite, too."

She didn't come closer; instead, she stood on tip-toe so she could get a better look at the plate. "The ones with the red jelly stuff in the middle," she said, her eyes lighting up. "And the sugar."

"Yep." I slowly picked up a cookie and took a huge bite. "It's a shame you don't want any."

"Okay, fine, I guess you're alive." She was at my side, crouching down beside me. "But don't ever go away again. I was scared."

"I didn't go away, silly, I was safe with Sam. Everything's fine." I pulled the plate closer and she grabbed a cookie with each hand, looking up at me sideways to see if I'd tell her off for being greedy.

"There's eight on the plate, so you can eat four," I said, pretending to be stern. "I'll be watching you to make sure you don't cheat."

She giggled under her breath and snuggled against me, her body a warm and familiar weight.

We must have fallen asleep that way because the next thing Cecily was there, shaking us gently awake and shepherding us to bed.

"Sam?" I asked groggily.

"He's fine. He'll be spending a few days in the old barn until he's well enough to move. The vet said he needs stall rest. Arthur and Ellen dropped off feed and bedding for him. He's snug as a bug out there."

She reached out unexpectedly and gave me a quick hug. "You did a brave thing, Sarah. That horse might have died without your help."

"It was no big deal." I yawned, steering Amy up the stairs to her room. She dropped into her bed like a log and was instantly asleep again; if she was ever really awake. I glanced around her room with approval, noting how well her few belongings fit in here. Years ago, I'd saved up for a cheap pink bedspread and flouncy pink curtains that we could take with us wherever we went. That way, every place we moved felt a little bit like home for Amy. Her small collection of plastic unicorns looked perfect on the dresser, too.

I stumbled down the hall and fell into my own bed, thinking of how nice it was that Sam was out in the barn and that I'd get to see him again in the morning. It had felt good having a friend to share my troubles with, even if that friend was a horse.

"Good night, Sam," I whispered into the darkness.

Good night, Sarah, we will jump the big jumps.

I laughed into my pillow. If I'd had known hypothermia would make me hear talking horses then I would have tried it a long time ago.

* * *

The next day, I woke up before the sun had fully made it up over the horizon. I carefully folded up the pajamas that Ellen had made me wear, vowing that someday I would have a pair as nice as that of my own, and pulled on a hoody and a well-worn pair of jeans. I kept the socks on, though. I wasn't quite ready to give those up.

I slipped past Amy's bedroom door, not ready for her company just yet, and tip-toed down the stairs to the front door. My jacket had been hung up and, to my surprise, it was clean and dry. I was sure it had been ruined last night.

My boots were still sopping wet, but there was a pair of Cecily's old gum boots by the front door and, even though they came up to my knees, they fit me reasonably well with my fluffy socks.

I quietly let myself outside and plowed through the drifts to the barn. It had snowed again last night, erasing all footprints and leaving only an untouched blanket of white. I loved the way that everything seemed so hushed after a snowfall, as if the world were holding its breath. Snow had always seemed magical to me; when I was little I believed all snowy woods held a hidden door to Narnia if I could only search hard enough. Even though I was too old for fairy tales now, the hint of magic still remained.

The morning light would have been perfect for taking pictures if I'd had a camera; shape and shadow blending so everything blurred together like one of those impressionist paintings Dad liked so much. He'd been a big fan of an artist named Seurat, who painted using all these tiny multi-coloured dots placed close together. When you stood back it looked like an everyday scene, like a picnic or a river, but when you got up close you realized that every inch of that painting was practically exploding with life and colour.

I shrugged off my thoughts and hurried the rest of the way to the barn, easing open the door and peering expectantly inside.

Crunch, crunch, crunch. Sam looked up eagerly from eating hay and gave a low nicker of recognition.

"Good morning," I called out to him, "you're okay!"

He bobbed his nose up and down then turned to press the back of his head against the wall, rubbing his ears as best he could against the rough, wooden boards.

"What are you doing, silly? Are you itchy?"

He bobbed his nose again and I approached slowly, reaching out to scratch the spot at the top of his neck just behind his ears. His eyes closed instantly and he tilted his head toward me, practically doubling in half to get me to reach the right spot.

"You are such a goof. You're obviously feeling better. Hey, stop that!"

I had to grab hold of the stall to keep from falling over as he pushed roughly against me, a horsey way of telling me not to stop the scratching.

"Don't be bossy, or you get nothing," I said, in the same voice I used on Amy all the time, the same voice my mom had used on me when I was pushy.

He seemed to understand; he stood up tall and opened his eyes wide, blinking a little as if to assure me of his innocence.

"Ha, I don't believe you," I said, peeking into his stall to check his bandages. I pulled my head back with a yelp and then carefully leaned over the stall again to where a boy around my age sat cross-legged on the floor at Sam's feet. He had on a winter jacket and toque, but his lower half was clad in a thick sleeping bag. He had a thermos of coffee in one hand.

"Sorry," he said, blinking up at me sleepily. "I must have dozed off for a minute. I've been up with the big guy all night."

"You slept here by yourself?" I said

incredulously, "in a freezing barn, at night, all alone?"

"Yeah, it's not a haunted mansion or anything. It was pretty peaceful, actually. No brothers and sisters bothering me, lots of coffee, good company. I'm Seth, by the way."

He stood swiftly, the sleeping bag dropping away to reveal a pair of ratty jeans like mine. He held out his hand for me to shake.

After an awkward hesitation, I slipped my hand into his and then pulled away quickly as if his skin had burned me. "I'm Sarah," I said, gulping. Making friends had never come easily and even something as simple as a handshake made me nervous.

"I know, you're the one who saved this idiot's life."

"No, not really," I said, feeling a slow burn rise up my cheeks. "Anyone would have done the same thing."

"Maybe." Seth shrugged. "But it still means a lot to me, to my family, I mean, that someone cared enough to look out for him. He could have died out there. The vet said he could have easily frozen to death or lost too much blood."

"He's a really nice horse," I said, changing the subject quickly. "Is he fun to ride?"

"He can be, if you keep his mind occupied. Once he gets bored then look out. He'll find a way to make your ride more entertaining for himself."

Sam looked up from his hay, sending the boy, Seth, another wide-eyed look of innocence.

"Yes, I know, we're talking about you, you big jerk."

I frowned and stepped back. "Don't call him names, I think he's wonderful. You're lucky to have a horse at all."

The boy looked at me in surprise and then broke into a grin. "Oh, he's part of the family and that's how we all talk to each other. He was actually an orphan you know; his mom died a few days after birth and we had to bottle feed him. The vet warned us that sometimes bottle-fed colts go funny in the head, but Sam never did. Well, not really; he's a bit strange sometimes."

"He's an orphan?" I said carefully, looking sideways at Seth to see if he were having a game with me. But his face was dead serious.

"Yep, we turned him out with the mares and foals once he was big enough, but he still prefers to be with humans first. I guess he sort of imprinted on us."

"That's neat," I said, then cleared my throat. "Do you think he missed his mom, though?"

Seth shrugged. "I doubt it. He was pretty young and we gave him everything he needed."

I turned to find Sam watching me intently, a wad of hay hanging out the corner of his mouth as if he'd stopped to focus on me mid-chew. His ears were pricked and he made a low, nickering sound under his breath.

A hard lump formed in my chest and, without thinking, I moved back to him and leaned over the stall door, wrapping my fingers in his mane and pressing my face into his warm neck. "I bet you did miss her, didn't you?" I whispered. I half-expected to hear him answer like I'd imagined last night, but he just nudged me with his nose.

"Wow, he really likes you." Seth's feet rustled in the straw and I drew back, watching as he checked Sam's bandage and gave the horse a pat on the rump. "I'd better put his blanket back on; he doesn't like wearing it but he needs to stay warm. Do you ride?"

"No," I said. Seth stared at me expectantly so I added, "Well, I rode a long time ago, but I had to stop because...because of things."

"What sort of riding did you do?"

"Nothing fancy, I did a bit of everything." *You rode pretty much every day for five years,* I reminded myself. I frowned, fighting to keep a hundred memories of life at the barn from flooding in. There was no point in focusing on the past. The only thing that mattered right now was the future. And it would take everything I had to afford to feed me and Amy; horses were definitely out of the question. "I've got to go. It was nice to meet you."

"Sure, maybe we could—" but I turned and fled before he could finish, back to the safety of the house.

Everyone was still asleep when I got back, but I knew Cecily and my sister would be up at any minute. I pulled some ingredients from the fridge and slowly mixed up a pancake batter: Amy's favourite breakfast. I set it aside to rest so it would cook up nice and fluffy and put on a pot of coffee to brew, putting in three scoops to make it strong just like Cecily liked. There were only two weeks before Christmas and everything had to go as smoothly and perfectly as possible until then. Cecily had to agree to keep Amy until I was old enough to take her to live with me.

As soon as I heard the floorboards creak upstairs I dropped butter in the pan and waited until it was just hot enough before I dropped the first spoonful of batter onto the sputtering surface. I made sure to sprinkle a few extra drops beside the full-sized pancakes. Amy loved when I made her these extra miniature cakes; she said they tasted better than the big ones for some reason.

"Oh, that smells heavenly," Cecily said, coming down the stairs still dressed in her tattered robe and faded slippers. I thought guiltily back to the new pajamas I'd stolen from her last night. She clearly needed them more than I did.

She stumbled over to the coffee maker and filled her special mug all the way to the top, not bothering to add cream or sugar. I winced as I watched her take her first, satisfied sip before she sat down heavily at the table, unfolding her sketch pad in front of her. I didn't know how she drank it like that; I needed about half a cup of milk and tons of sugar to get even the weakest coffee down.

"Thanks for lending me the pajamas," I said nervously. "I'll make sure I wash them before giving them back."

"What? Oh, no, you keep them. They were for you anyway, for Christmas."

"Really?" I said in disbelief. "Are you sure?"

"Hmm?" She looked up briefly from her drawing and smiled at me in a distracted way. "Of course, let me know if you need anything else; you're my guest."

I turned back to the stove so I wouldn't disturb her. *Guest means temporary*, I thought, my stomach clenching nervously.

The smell of pancakes filled the room and I heard Amy's feet hit the floor and come thundering down the hallway. I shook my worry off and deftly flipped Cecily's breakfast onto a plate, adding some apple pieces I'd sliced up and dusted with cinnamon. I set her plate down and put the maple syrup beside it, stepping back expectantly.

"Thanks so much, Sarah," she said, barely glancing at her plate as she stabbed her first bite of pancake with her fork. "I just can't see my way around this sculpture for some reason. I'm about ready to give up on it."

She winced as Amy came galloping down the stairs singing some high-pitched little kid song at the top of her lungs.

"Breakfast, Amy," I said, moving quickly to intercept her. "I made the tiny pancakes you like and there's juice there on the table for you. Sit quietly for a few minutes, okay?"

"Okay," she dropped her voice to an audible whisper, "was I too loud again?"

"No," I glanced over my shoulder to where Cecily was buried in her drawing, "but she's concentrating. Let's just sit down and eat our food, and then we'll go outside and see Sam."

"Sam!" she squealed loudly. Her face lit up, remembering that there was a horse in the barn. She spun around, knocking against the table and joggling everything on it.

"Damn it." Cecily used the edge of her housecoat to mop up the coffee that had splashed onto her page and sighed loudly. "Thanks for breakfast, Sarah. I think I'll take it out to the studio with me and see if I can make any headway on this project. You girls yell if you need me."

My shoulders sagged as she left the room and Amy looked up anxiously into my face. "I messed up, didn't I?" She slid into her chair, staring miserably at the pancakes on her plate. "Cecily won't want to keep us."

"Don't be silly," I said. "Who would be crazy enough not to want to keep a great kid like you?"

"Lots of people," she said glumly.

"Come on, eat up. We can't see Sam until we

finish all this food. I'll race you."

"Oh, right, Sam." She grinned up at me, her face unclouding so fast it was startling, and began stuffing food into her mouth as fast as she could.

* * *

The barn was empty except for Sam when we got there, but there were a couple sets of tire tracks in the snow so it looked like a few people had come and gone while we were inside. Sam looked up briefly from his hay, nickered low under his breath, and then dove back down.

"Sam says hello," Amy said helpfully, running halfway up the aisle and then stopping dead.

There was a cellophane-wrapped basket on the floor in front of Sam's stall. It was tied with a ribbon and there was a small card attached.

"Is it a present for us? What does it say?" Amy asked, clapping her hands together in excitement.

I unfolded the card carefully and read it out loud. *Dear Sarah and Amy, thank you so much for your help saving Sam. You two are real heroes. Please enjoy the basket. We'll be by this week to thank you in person.*

Yours in gratitude, Ellen, Arthur, and whole Plekowski family.

"Open it, open it!" Amy danced up and down impatiently while I set the basket down on one of the hay bales and picked at the ribbon wound tightly around the top. It finally came apart and we leaned forward to peer inside.

"Ooh, cookies," Amy squealed, "and hot chocolate. Oh, and books." Her voice fell at that last one and I shot her a look of concern. Our last foster parents had really gotten after her about her dyslexia and she'd started avoiding any sort of books, even the little-kid picture books she'd used to like, ever since.

"Amy, they're horse books and look, here's one with a unicorn on the cover, you're bound to like that one."

"Reading's too hard and I'm too slow," she said, picking up a box of gourmet chocolates. "I'll just eat these, you can have the books."

"But you'll love reading once you really, really find a book you like. It's like having all these doors to other worlds right at your fingertips. How about we read them together? We can take turns reading out loud to each other."

"You can read to me and I can eat the cookies?" she said hopefully, blinking innocently up at me like Sam had done earlier.

"Sure, it's a start," I said, reaching over to ruffle her hair. We filled our pockets with cookies and went to see Sam. Seth's parents had left a box of brushes by the stall door and I poked through it, wondering if I remembered how to use everything properly.

"Hey, big guy," I said, opening his stall door so Amy and I could slip inside, "you're feeling okay?"

He lifted his head and moved over to see us, nosing our pockets as if he could smell the cookies inside.

"I don't think you're allowed to have chocolate, are you? We'll bring you some carrots next time we come down."

I carefully pulled off his blanket and checked to make sure his bandage looked okay and then handed Amy a small round curry comb.

"See, it's like a massage brush. You go in circles to loosen the dirt and dead hair and to warm up his muscles. Just don't do his belly or this sensitive part here on his flank."

Amy used both hands to hold the soft, rubber curry and carefully moved it in circles over his coat.

I worked on the other side, and Sam munched away happily at his breakfast while we brushed him until his coat shone. Then I showed Amy how to carefully brush out his tail piece by piece so she didn't break any of the long strands.

When we finally headed back to the house we were both covered with dirt and hair and were very, very happy.

* * *

I left Amy downstairs playing with her art supplies while I ran to have a shower and get changed. When I came back down, my hair still wrapped in a towel, she and Cecily were talking quietly at the table. I stopped on the stairs, holding my breath so I could listen better.

"See, this drawing is me and Sarah saving Sam. Here's all the blood in the snow and here's you waiting back at the house for us and you're crying because you're worried about us."

"That's really good, Amy. I like your style. You girls definitely had quite the adventure, hey? You'll have lots to tell your friends at school when you get back."

"Oh, I don't have any friends," Amy said casually. "The other kids don't like me."

Cecily was silent for too long and I pinched the bridge of my nose hard in frustration. The last thing I needed was for her to think of Amy as a problem child who didn't have any friends. I wanted Cecily to think Amy was perfect.

"Why don't they like you?" she asked finally, sounding perplexed.

Amy shrugged. "Some kids think I'm weird, I guess because I'm different."

"Different how?"

"I don't know. At my last school, this boy threw a rock at me because I was talking to the squirrels at recess. It hit me right in the head and there was a big bruise. He got in trouble from the principal and the squirrels said they were going to drop nuts on his head whenever they saw him. Isn't that funny?"

There was a long silence while Cecily processed this new, probably alarming, information.

Amy looked up to see me standing there on the stairs and my face must have looked funny because her eyes opened wide in alarm. "Sarah, are you sick?"

"No," I said quickly, smiling at her, even though I felt like throwing up. I moved down the rest of the stairs and stopped behind her chair. "Of course not. You should draw a picture of what Sam's going to do next once he's all better."

"Okay," Amy said uncertainly, glancing quickly at Cecily who still stared blankly at the drawing as if her thoughts were far away.

"A horse," Cecily said, breaking out of her trance, "a horse lost in the snow; that might just work. I'll be in my studio if there's an emergency; otherwise, no interruptions, please. I might have a brilliant idea."

She turned and rushed out the door, not even bothering to put on her coat.

"Is she mad at us?" Amy whispered, not looking up.

"No, of course not, she's just busy right now. So that means we have to be extra good and helpful, and not get in her way. The more we fit in here, the longer we might be able to stay."

"Just till after Christmas, though, right, and then we have to go?"

Shoot, I thought, *how did she overhear that?*

"Maybe," I said, struggling to sound confident.

"I haven't decided yet. Maybe we'll stay here, or maybe we'll find somewhere better. But you don't need to worry about anything like that, Amy. Worrying is my job, not yours. The only thing you need to think about is what you want in your stocking from Santa."

"Not socks," Amy said quickly, making me laugh. Last year we'd had our stockings filled with socks, underwear, and school supplies from the dollar store. I hadn't minded; it really was stuff we needed, but Amy had been heartbroken thinking that Santa was mad at her. I'd been so angry that this year Dee had allowed me to substitute my meager clothing allowance for a gift card at a local toy store. She was even going to pick us up and drive us into town to go shopping. Other kids complained about their social workers, but Dee had been there helping me as best she could since our parent's accident had left us alone and penniless. I always knew she was on our side.

While Amy coloured, I tidied up the kitchen and living room, and then went upstairs to make our beds and make sure our rooms were clean. Amy's looked like a whirlwind had passed through, her covers balled at the end of her bed in a heap, colouring books, a few broken crayons, and her three plastic unicorns dumped in the middle of the floor mid-play. She could never seem to remember to pick up after herself no matter how much I reminded her. I wondered if all kids were this difficult to train.

The day passed quickly and it was nearly dark by the time the knock came on the door.

"There they are," Ellen said, pushing through the door before I could get there to open it. "There are our little heroines. Come on girls, get your coats and bundle up warmly. We're going on an adventure."

"Yay!" Amy said, leaping up, but I clamped my hand down on her shoulder before she got too excited.

"Sorry, I'll have to run it by Cecily before we go anywhere with someone we don't know."

Ellen stilled, her eyes opened wide and then she broke into another smile. "I called her already and she said she was on a roll and not to disturb her again; I'm guessing she had a breakthrough in that project that's been bothering her? I told her to keep going and that I'd take you girls out to dinner and give you a tour of the stables."

"Please, Sarah?" Amy bounced up and down beside me. "Please, can we go?"

"Sure," I said, deciding that it was very unlikely that Ellen was out to kidnap us and bury our bodies in the woods somewhere. "Do we need to get dressed in better clothes for dinner?"

"No, jeans and boots are perfect. We're pretty casual in this family. Hurry, though, I have a car load of hungry kids out there and we can't keep them waiting."

I wrote a quick note to Cecily explaining where we'd gone and then followed an increasingly hyper Amy out the door.

A huge, dark, SUV sat running in the driveway and I had a sudden urge to turn around and go back inside to my peaceful reading spot by the fire. It was too late to turn back now, though; Amy was already climbing in.

"Kids, this is Amy and Sarah, you be on your best behaviour while they're our guests."

A sea of faces stared at us curiously and I felt my own face redden under their scrutiny. I looked for Seth and blushed even deeper when I found him watching me from the front seat with a grin on his face.

"So, no farting or dirty jokes, you mean?" A boy around twelve said, giving Amy a wink. She stared at him with wide eyes and then giggled.

"No putting spiders in their food?" A younger boy said helpfully.

"Yes, that's a perfect example of what not to do," their mother said, "hop in, girls. Ignore these hooligans, they're all right once you get to know them."

"What do you mean, *all right?*" The twelve-year-old demanded. "We're spectacular children, fantastic examples of a modern-day breeding program."

"Oh, right," his mom said, rolling her eyes, "that's what I meant."

We settled into our seats and the door slid shut, locking us inside with no escape.

"I'm AJ," the boy said, holding out his hand formally for us both to shake, "and even though Seth is the oldest here tonight, I'm really the one in charge. If you have any trouble with this lot then you come tell me."

There was a rumble of laughter that he pretended to glare at. "The thing to know about us is that we're all extraordinary. That's Seth in the front seat, he's going to the Olympics, Katie's away at Space camp in Florida, she'll be an astronaut soon, I'm a wizard of finance who's going to keep this family from bankruptcy, Julie's off volunteering with old people tonight; she's studying to be a Saint, these three are triplets if you can believe it and that's extraordinary enough, and that's Rosco."

"But how am I 'trordinary?" said the littlest dark-haired boy, strapped in his car seat.

"Yet to be determined," AJ said, grinning at his brother.

"You mean, you're all from the same parents?" Amy opened her eyes wide, staring at the three identical looking kids in the very back seat. They all had the same curly red hair and freckles and I had no idea whether they were boys or girls. She'd been used to living in families that were a mixture of foster kids and real kids so I could see her point. "But, how many are there?"

"Um," AJ looked up at the roof of the car as if he were thinking hard and counted on his fingers, "let's see, seven...no, eight, counting myself there are definitely eight. And, if our parents have their way they probably have more coming."

"Stop teasing them, AJ," Ellen said, smiling at us in the rear-view mirror. "We have absolutely decided to stop at eight. We really reached perfection when we had Rosco so no need to keep trying."

I listened wordlessly to the friendly banter around me and felt a pang of longing for the family I'd missed out on. Would mom and dad have had more kids if they'd lived longer? Would we have been a big, happy family always laughing and joking and teasing each other? Amy could have flourished in a family like this where her wild creativity would have been considered extraordinary rather than shameful.

Dinner was at a noisy Italian family restaurant where this loud pack of children fit right in. My mouth watered at the delicious smells coming from the kitchen, and when my lasagna and garlic bread made it to the table it was worth the wait.

"Ooh, Sarah, this is so good," Amy said around a mouthful of spaghetti. "You should learn to make this. When Cecily forgets to make dinner next time, we won't go hungry."

There was a moment of silence and Ellen looked up from her dinner with a frown. "Are you girls getting enough to eat over at the farm? Cecily is a good soul and a great artist, but she's not the most practical person in the world."

"Yes," I said quickly. "It's perfect there. Everything's fine."

Ellen stared at me a fraction too long before returning to her food and a lump of fear lodged in my belly. What if these people stuck their noses in and decided that Cecily wasn't fit to be a foster parent? All my plans would be ruined.

I ate the rest of my food automatically, but I couldn't shake the worry that had taken hold of me. I caught Seth giving me a few questioning glances. Each time he did, I made sure to smile and look like I was having a good time.

After dinner, we all piled into the SUV and drove back toward home. But instead of going to the farm we turned into a paved driveway marked on both sides by low stone pillars. It couldn't be more than few miles from Cecily's place. I guessed that the backs of the properties might even be able to touch if they were angled just right.

"Wow!" Amy said, "look at all the lights!"

I turned to look where she pointed and saw a big stone house decked out with more Christmas lights than I'd ever seen in one place. There was a lit-up sleigh parked out front towed by eight life-sized reindeer and a big inflatable snowman that lazily waved one arm back and forth in greeting. It looked like a scene out of a magazine.

"Yeah, we sort of go a little crazy around Christmas," Ellen said with a laugh. "It's the one time of year we actually clean the house, decorate, and invite people over. Wait until you see the barn."

We didn't have long to wait, the barn loomed up out of the darkness, standing almost as big as the house but more tastefully decorated. A single strand of golden bulbs traced the roof line and only a solitary glowing reindeer stood out front. The big double doors stood open and light streamed out across the snowy laneway.

"Go on, girls," Ellen said. "I have to get these young ones to bed. AJ and Seth will show you your surprise."

"For us?" I said suspiciously. "What sort of surprise?"

"A nice one, silly," Seth said, appearing beside me. "The only kind of surprises we do around here. Don't worry."

I followed him reluctantly inside, keeping a close eye on Amy, who trotted along after AJ, gazing up at him as if he were her new hero. At least he didn't seem to mind her non-stop chatter.

"Oh, this is really beautiful," I said, stepping into the spacious barn. It would have been beautiful even without the decorations. One wide, concrete, aisle ran down the middle of the barn and there were wooden horse stalls on either side of it. Glossy, well-bred horses of all shapes and colours poked their noses out and nickered at us curiously, clearly expecting treats.

Someone had hung green garland laced with red bows above the horses' heads and fake candy canes decorated all the stall doors. It looked like a fairy tale stable.

"Come on," Seth said, tugging on my hand, "your surprise is in the arena."

I pulled my hand away quickly, embarrassed by the sudden contact and then felt myself blushing, even more, when I did.

AJ laughed, and I hurried past the curious horses, completely mortified. I stopped when I found myself in a big indoor arena. The lights cast a golden glow over everything, but my eyes were drawn to a man I recognized as Arthur who was holding a large brown horse and a small white pony by their bridles.

"Ooh," Amy squealed, "a pony! Can I pet him?"

"Sure you can, kiddo, he's a she, actually. This is Powderpuff, she's very friendly."

Without hesitating, Amy ran up and wrapped her arms tightly around the pony's neck probably cutting off its oxygen supply completely.

"Don't worry," Seth said. "Powderpuff taught most of us to ride. She has the patience of a saint. Come meet Lexington. You'll love him."

I followed him hesitantly, glancing over at Amy to make sure she was safe and not being too annoying.

"He's my old Event horse. He's mostly retired, but we pull him out for trail rides and for guests to use. We even hoisted Grandpa up on him this summer. He's bombproof."

I reached out and gently ran my hand down the horse's dark neck. His thick fur was like velvet and he bobbed his nose up and down in greeting, looking at me with kind, wise eyes.

"Here," Seth said, passing me a helmet. "I'll help you get on him if you like."

"Oh no, it's okay," I said, trying to push the helmet back into his hands. "We don't need to ride. Thanks, though."

I looked over just in time to see Arthur lift a now-helmeted Amy up onto the tiny pony's back. My sister had a grin on her face that spread from ear to ear and her eyes were sparkling with happiness. I hadn't seen her look like that in, well, in forever.

"Come on, Sarah," Amy squealed, "get on your horse. I'll race you around the ring!"

"Oh no," I muttered to Seth, "you've created a monster."

He laughed good-naturedly and led Lexington over to the mounting block. "Most kids want to gallop and jump right away. It's in their nature."

"I guess so. I mostly liked just spending time with the horses."

"It's about half and half for me," he admitted,

holding Lexington's reins while I carefully put my foot in the stirrup and eased aboard the horse's back. "I love the adrenaline that comes with going fast and jumping high. Nothing beats it. But I also like figuring out how horses tick; unlocking their weird behaviours like a puzzle and turning difficult horses into good ones. And I like taking care of them, too. I like it all, I guess."

I smiled down at him and nodded, really noticing him for the first time. He was a pretty nice guy and his large, dark hazel eyes were an added bonus. Too bad I wouldn't be sticking around long enough to get to know him. Maybe one day I could make enough money so that Amy could come up here for lessons.

"You remember how to hold the reins?"

"I think so, it's been a while."

I gathered the reins slowly, appreciating that Seth wasn't the sort of person to hover and give you instructions non-stop. He watched me carefully but didn't interfere when I gently brushed my calves against Lexington's sides and allowed the big gelding to move forward.

This is kind of nice, I thought, *I never imagined I'd sit on a horse again.* The steady rocking motion brought back all kinds of memories I'd locked away. The barn had been my whole life; when I was old enough to go by myself, I'd bike down in the mornings to ride and help with chores and not come home until late afternoon. Sometimes I'd be so late that my parents would have to come find me. They'd pretend to be mad but they never really were.

"Sarah, are you okay?"

I looked through blurry eyes to find Seth staring at me anxiously. "Of course I am," I sniffed, wiping my tears away quickly. "There's just dust in my eye. I'm fine."

I was about to swing down and go wait in the barn for Amy to finish when Arthur led her up beside me on a bored-looking Powderpuff.

"Sarah, this is so much fun!" Amy squealed. "Is this what you did when you were a kid?"

"Yep," I said, "it was a long time ago."

"Did you go fast and jump? Did you go to horse shows?"

"All that," I said, "and rode on trails bareback and swam our horses in the lake."

"Wow, you were so lucky."

"Yep, I sure was," I said, now wanting nothing more than to get back to the farm so I could cry in peace. Coming here and being around horses was a mistake. I didn't need to be reminded of everything I'd lost. I had to focus on what mattered now, and that was Amy's happiness.

Well, she certainly is happy now, I thought, looking at her beaming face, *I shouldn't ruin her fun by getting all emotional. She might not have the chance to ride again until she's older.*

We walked around the ring together, Amy

chattering non-stop and dropping her reins every few steps so she could lean forward and bury her face in Powderpuff's mane.

Arthur kept a tight hand on the pony's bridle, but Seth had retreated to the edge of the ring when he saw I was somewhat able to steer the elderly Lexington in straight lines without doing any damage and left me to my own devices.

"Good boy, Lexington," I whispered, reaching down and tentatively patting the horse on the shoulder. It wasn't his fault it was painful for me to be here, that every minute spent riding was like another dagger in my already bruised heart.

"Should we try some trotting?" Arthur asked, grinning at Amy.

"Trot and gallop!" she squealed, bouncing up and down on that poor pony's back and kicking it softly in the sides.

Arthur laid a firm hand on her knee and shook his head. "Amy, you have to be kind and respectful to your pony at all times. Powderpuff looks like a toy, but she's a living creature who doesn't like to be kicked. You'll have to learn to ask her politely."

"Okay," Amy said, sobering instantly. She shot a worried glance at me but I looked away. It was a lesson she needed to learn; one most kids needed to learn once they started riding. Horses were not machines; they were thinking, breathing animals who felt pain and sadness and discomfort just like we did.

Arthur showed her again how to hold the reins properly and then how to sit lightly with long legs that draped over the pony's fat sides. Once she was centered, he pulled Powderpuff into a brisk jog while Amy bounced and laughed along beside him, grabbing the pony's mane to keep her balance.

I couldn't help but laugh and I looked over and smiled at Seth. He and his wonderful family had made Amy so happy; she would never forget this Christmas. Ever.

"All right, your turn." Seth pushed off from the wall and sauntering toward me. "Trot him on the rail for a bit and see how he feels."

"Oh, it's okay," I said, even though part of me wanted to give it a shot. "I'm fine watching Amy."

"It's only fair if you get to have fun, too, you know. Come on, one trot won't hurt you. Try it once and see if you remember how."

"Fine, just once around the ring, though."

I didn't really remember what to do, but I nudged the ever-obedient Lexington to the rail and then gently squeezed my legs together. After a long hesitation where I'm sure he tried to figure out what on earth I wanted, he broke into a shuffling trot that left me bouncing on his back just like Amy had. Automatically, I rose up and down in a slow posting trot, mostly to relieve the discomfort of his jarring gait. And as soon as I found the rhythm it became easy and my face broke out into an involuntary smile. "Good boy,

Lexington," I told him as he marched around the ring; now that I had the hang of this, I didn't want it to end.

"Do you remember how to ask for a canter?" Seth called.

I didn't, not really, but my body must have because I shifted my outside leg back and squeezed gently with both legs, and was instantly rewarded with a slow-moving rocking-horse canter.

"Sarah, you're galloping!" Amy squealed, but I was too busy concentrating to respond.

Lexington went around on auto-pilot and it was only once my legs started feeling like jelly that I reluctantly pulled him back to a walk.

"That was so much fun," I said breathlessly, patting Lexington on the neck in gratitude. "Thank you so much for letting me ride him."

"You're welcome," Seth said as he dragged a small pole to the edge of the arena then went back for a second one. "You're actually doing us a favour. Lexington doesn't get nearly enough exercise. He loves to get out and be part of things. Have you caught your breath yet?"

"Yeah, I'm good."

"Okay, trot him around the outside again, but this time steer him over the poles."

"No way," I said, "you're not seriously asking me to jump."

"Of course not, I'm just asking you to trot over these teeny tiny ground rails, it helps him lift his knees and stretch."

"All right," I said, sensing a lie, but I didn't want to stop, either. Who knew if I'd ever have the chance to sit on another horse again.

"That's it, just find a nice steady rhythm and then trot down the long side."

I followed his instructions, and even though it was a ground pole and not a jump, I automatically folded my upper body forward, just a bit, in anticipation. Lexington's ear flicked back in question and he broke into a gentle canter, jumping each pole with about two feet to spare. Amazingly enough, I stuck with him and let out a whoop when he cantered away from the second pole.

"Perfect, just keep cantering and bring him around again."

I wasn't going argue with that. I let Lexington keep in his rocking horse canter and we popped over the non-jumps again, leaving me breathless with happiness. Even though I hadn't ridden in so long, this felt like I was home, like I belonged in the saddle.

Could I get a job working in a stable when I'm older? I brought Lexington gently down to a walk. The possibility blossomed slowly in my mind. Maybe I didn't have to just flip burgers or some other minimum wage job that made me miserable. Maybe I could actually do something I liked.

"You're hired," Seth laughed as if he'd read my

thoughts.

Excitement flashed through me until I looked over and saw that he was only teasing. Heat prickled my cheeks and I leaned forward to pet Lexington's neck to hide my embarrassment.

"Thank you, big guy," I whispered, pulling my feet from the stirrups and swinging down from the saddle. I managed to land without falling over, but my legs were shaking. I hadn't used those muscles in a long time and I knew I would ache like crazy the next day. Still, it had been completely worth it.

* * *

Ellen showed up to drive us home while we were still brushing the horses.

"You should have seen Sarah," Amy told her excitedly, "she jumped the big jumps just like Sam said she would."

Ellen's eyebrows crinkled in confusion. "Sam, you mean our horse Sam?"

"Yes," Amy went on, oblivious that she might be saying anything alarming. "Sam told me that he and Sarah were going to jump big jumps together. He says he wants to go to a horse show."

"Sam said that!" Ellen began to laugh. "Sam hates horse shows; he gets so nervous he won't even leave the trailer. He's a bit of a disaster."

"Well, that's what he said." Amy frowned. "He said that Sarah was his person and that he'd go if she went."

A prickle ran up my spine and I stared at Amy incredulously. Hadn't those been the very words I'd imagined Sam saying to me when we were out in the snow together? Was Amy some sort of psychic who could pick up on my thoughts, or was it just a really weird coincidence? I could only hope that Ellen thought it was funny rather than weird. I didn't want her reporting anything bad about Amy back to Cecily.

Amy and I thanked the Plekowski's about a million times before leaving. It had been a wonderful surprise.

Our house looked dark and forgotten after coming from the festive lights and decorations at the stable. Cecily must still be in her studio working on that project. I winced thinking about how cold it would be inside until I got a fire lit.

"Aunt Cecily looks like she's forgotten about Christmas," Seth said, frowning at the lack of decorations.

"*Aunt* Cecily?" I asked in surprise. "I didn't know you were related."

"She's my big sister," Ellen said with a laugh. "Although, sometimes I think I'm the eldest. Cecily's a bit of a dreamer and I've always been more practical than creative."

Like me and Amy, I thought, *I bet she'll be an artist, too, when she grows up.*

"You girls want us to come inside and wait with you until Cecily is done out in her shop? It's no trouble."

"No, that's fine," I said quickly. "She'll probably be in to check on us soon."

"Uh-huh," Ellen said, not sounding convinced. "Well, here's my number just in case you need anything. You two can call anytime, okay? Even if it's just to talk."

"Thanks," I said, quickly pocketing the slip of paper.

The house was as cold as I'd expected. We kept our coats and scarves on, and I made Amy sit on the couch wrapped in a blanket while I got the fire going. It didn't take long for the wood to start crackling and we huddled next to it while Amy told me once again the highlights of her ride on Powderpuff.

An hour went by, and then another, and Cecily still hadn't come inside.

"You stay here, Amy, I'm going to go check on her."

"I'm not staying in here by myself. I'm coming, too."

"Fine, but then you really have to get to bed. Tomorrow, Dee's going to pick us up so we can go to town for some Christmas shopping. We need to be up extra early."

We tramped down the well-worn path to Cecily's studio, Amy picking up speed until she was far ahead of me.

"I'm cantering on Powderpuff!" she called over

her shoulder. "Now I'm galloping, now watch me jump!"

I should have been watching. As she made her final leap, she reached the studio door and knocked it wide open, tripping and then rolling inside. There were two loud screams, and then the sound of something, many things, shattering.

My heart lurched to a stop and I closed my eyes for just a second before stepping through the open door. It was a disaster. Cups and plates littered the floor along with shards of broken pottery, but the worst part was the piece that Cecily had been working on desperately since we arrived had hit the floor and split right up the middle in a sharp, jagged line.

My sister sat still amid the wreckage, her face drained of all colour as she surveyed the chaos around her. "I broke it," she whispered, sounding near hysteria. "Sarah, I broke it. I wrecked it all."

Cecily stood in stunned silence, hands over her mouth and eyes wide with shock as she surveyed the room. "Get out," she said finally, nearly choking on her words.

"Cecily," I said, then stopped when she shot me a gaze so full of anguish that I couldn't go on. It was clear that the damage was irreparable.

"Take your sister and go," she said woodenly. "I'll speak with you later."

"Come on, Amy," I whispered, trying to pull her to her feet. When she didn't move, I knelt and picked her up like she was a little kid.

"I broke it," she whispered again softly in my ear and then she began to wail.

I carried her all the way back to the house and upstairs to her bed, dressed her in her pajamas and put her to bed and still she didn't stop sobbing.

"It will be okay, Amy," I told her, even though I wanted to throw up. The plan to get Cecily to take Amy on until I could take care of her myself had had a serious setback. I wasn't sure what Cecily would do now. I would have to talk to Dee in the morning and see if she could smooth things over.

"She hates me," Amy wailed. "She's going to send us both away now. I wrecked it for you, Sarah."

"No, you didn't, Amy. It was just an accident; it could have happened to anyone."

"No, it couldn't! I'm stupid and I wreck everything. Now you have to go away and you can't ride Sam like he wanted and it's all my fault."

"Amy, Sam doesn't care who rides him; he has a great family to take care of him and we...well, I guess we will have to keep looking for our family. It will happen, you'll see."

Finally, her sobs slowed and she hiccupped a few times before drifting off to sleep.

I sighed and wiped the few tears that had gathered behind my own eyes and wearily went down the stairs to check the fire.

To my surprise, Cecily was seated at the big

dining room table, the two halves of the piece she'd been working on laid out in front of her. She pushed them slowly together until the broken pieces made a large grey oblong disk; the edges twisted organically like they were part of some living thing. In the middle was a black outline of a horse that looked a lot like Sam. He stood, poised with one foreleg raised, ears pricked as if he were listening to something. The break ran right up the center of the horse, splitting the piece in half from top to bottom.

Cecily had her elbows on the table, chin resting on her bent hands as she glumly surveyed the damage.

I tried to back-track out of the room before she saw me.

"Come on in, Sarah," she said tiredly. "You're not disturbing me."

"Cecily," I said, wringing my hands together. "I am so sorry that Amy wrecked your stuff. She feels awful; she would have never done that on purpose."

"No, I know," she said, sighing heavily, "She's a little kid and kids break stuff. But it makes me seriously wonder if my sister was right. Maybe I'm not the right person to take care of anyone."

Damn it, I thought, *I knew that Ellen would stick her nose into things. I should have never trusted her.*

"We like living here," I said, gathering my courage. "It's better than any of the places we've stayed so far. We'd like to stay if you'll have us."

"Well, you're no trouble at all, Sarah. Ellen's already going on about how she'd like you to come up and help exercise the horses when her older girl goes back to university after Christmas. You've been nothing but helpful and quiet since you arrived. But your sister is so young, and so, well, excitable. I'm not sure that this is the right place for her."

The hope that had risen up when she'd said I could stay came crashing down to earth with a bang, shattering just as hard as the clay sculpture in front of me.

"Oh, why couldn't you want her instead?" I said, my voice coming out in a sharp cry. "I can take care of myself, but Amy *needs* you. She needs a real house and a real family. I'm not going to be able to protect her much longer once I'm not in foster care. I just need a place for her for a few years until I'm old enough to take care of her myself. Please." I was mortified to hear the desperation in my voice.

Cecily stared at me open-mouthed and I knew she regretted the moment she'd taken either of us in. We'd been nothing but trouble for her.

"Okay," I said, taking a deep breath to settle myself. "I totally get that it's not going to work out. Could we stay just until after Christmas, though? I'd like to give Amy just one good Christmas, if possible."

Cecily stared at me for so long I didn't think she

would answer. "Sarah, of course you can stay until after Christmas. I'm not about to kick you two out on the street tonight. I just have to think about if we're a good fit for each other. There might be a better family much better suited to the two of you."

"Yeah, there was," I said, not able to keep the bitterness out of my tone. "Our own parents. But they seem to be unavailable right now."

"Oh," Cecily looked back down at the table, "you must miss them terribly. Well, let's just sleep on the question, shall we? Dee will be here in the morning so we can discuss making arrangements then. Good night."

"Good night," I said, climbing the stairs numbly. I crept into my room and burrowed right under the covers without getting undressed, pulling them over my head so I was wrapped in a protective cave of blankets. How had my carefully laid plans gone so wrong? I was sure that Cecily had been falling for Amy, how had she come to like me better instead?

I was too scared to even cry. I just lay there staring at the ceiling until I fell into an uneasy sleep.

* * *

The morning light streaming across my bed woke me and I stretched aching limbs luxuriously, thinking of my fantastic ride on Lexington before I remembered the rest of the events of the night before.

Amy, I thought, wincing as my bare feet hit the cold floor. I pulled on my woolly socks and tiptoed from my room to my sister's. She was still asleep, burrowed under the covers just like I had been, and I decided to let her sleep.

Voices rose up the stairs and the smell of fresh coffee filled the air, so I hesitantly went the rest of the way downstairs to face the music. Cecily and Dee were seated at the table and both smiled when I entered the kitchen.

"Sarah, it's so good to see you," Dee said. "I've been hearing great things about you from Cecily here. She says you've been a real help around the farm."

"Um, thanks," I said, feeling awkward. "I don't really do anything. I just take care of Amy and make dinner and stuff."

"And tidy up after my messy self, and make sure the fire's going, and that I manage to eat at least once a day. Plus, you're a hero the way you rescued Sam. Ellen and Arthur think you're miraculous."

At that, I had to laugh. That was the first time anyone had ever called me a miracle. Bossy, stubborn, protective maybe, but never a miracle. I moved to the kitchen to grab some coffee and froze when I saw the large sculpture sitting on the counter.

"Wow," I said, stepping back to study it. Cecily

had fixed the two broken halves on a wooden base so they stood upright about an inch apart, the jagged break running through the horse looking like it was put there on purpose. It was perfect.

"Wonderful, isn't it?" Cecily said, beaming. "I'd say it was the result of an extremely fortunate accident. Some of the best things that happen in life are unplanned; I'd nearly forgotten that."

"So, here's the thing, Sarah. I thought about what you said last night and I'm willing to give it a try. We'll do a six-month trial for you and Amy to stay here, and if it doesn't work out then we'll take the time to find a place that works for the both of you, okay? I think Amy needs you in her life, Sarah, and it would be a real shame to split you two up. I can't pretend to be a real parent to her; I think that's your job at this point. But I can make sure she's fed and clothed and has a roof over her head, and is allowed to have a normal childhood."

"Seriously?" I stood stock-still, unable to process what I'd heard. That was not how I'd thought this morning would go. I was sure we'd be packing our bags. Had she really said what I thought she'd said? Could we really stay?

A strange buzzing noise sounded in my head and a sudden wave of nausea churned in my stomach. I felt strange; afraid and cold at the same time. It didn't make sense.

Sarah, a soft voice said in my head. *Sarah, you have to come. Amy is in trouble.*

"Sarah, dear, are you all right? I know it must be quite a shock...."

I spun on my heel, ran up the stairs to Amy's room and barged inside. Yanking back the bed covers revealed only her pillow and her stuffed bear.

"Amy?" I cried, spinning around, "where are you?"

Hurry, Sarah.

"Sam?" I said out loud. I ran down the stairs again to grab my coat.

"Sarah? What's going on?"

"Amy's run away," I said, stuffing my feet into boots. "I think she's in trouble."

"But how...?"

I was already out the door and running down the path to the barn. I flew inside, but Sam's stall door hung open and there was no sign of the horse or my sister.

"Amy!" I screamed, running back outside. "Amy, where are you?"

There was only silence. The front door slammed as Cecily and Dee hurried outside.

"Sam," I whispered under my breath. "Or whatever you are, please tell me where to find Amy. I need to find her."

Into the woods, Sarah, we're in the woods.

"What woods?" I spun around, seeing trees in every direction. "It's *all* woods!"

But there was no answer.

Calm down, I told myself sternly, *Do not panic.*

I forced myself to walk slowly back to the barn door and scan the ground. It had snowed yesterday and there was only one fresh set of hoof prints that led from the barn. They turned left abruptly and headed alongside the driveway and to the road.

"Oh, Amy," I whispered, as I caught sight of a few small child-sized footprints at the edge of a snow drift. "What were you doing? Where were you going?"

The footprints never made it to the road, instead, they turned left again onto a narrow, snow-filled path that led deep into the forest. I hurried along it, but the path slanted steeply downhill and my feet slipped out from under me more than once.

Sarah, hurry, the soft voice was in my head again and I scrambled onwards, not minding the icy branches slapping at my face or the cold snow biting my fingers.

Finally, there up ahead was Sam, his blue coat bright against the icy ground. He nickered as soon as he saw me and then dropped his head to nose something half-buried in the snow. Amy.

My heart shuddered to a stop, seized painfully in my chest, and then started again as I flung myself down the bank to where my sister lay.

"Amy," I sobbed. "Oh, Amy, wake up."

Her eyelashes were jet black against her pale face and she was so motionless that I was sure that she was already gone. Only Sam's soft nose, nudging gently against my shoulder kept me from falling apart completely.

I pressed my fingers against her throat and could just make out the faint flutter of her pulse.

"Amy, you've got to wake up now, sweetie. It's time to go home."

"Sarah?" Her eyes fluttered open and as soon as she saw me she burst into tears. "I got lost," she cried, "and I was so cold, and Sam found me and I could hear him calling you. He told me everything would be okay."

"That's right," I said, lifting her gently to her feet. "Everything is going to be just fine, Amy. Can you walk?"

"Okay." She took a step forward and then collapsed into the snow. "I can't!" she wailed, "my feet hurt, Sarah."

"That's fine, don't worry, I'm going to carry you. Can you hold on if I give you a piggy-back ride?"

She sniffled and then nodded as I knelt, but when she should have been climbing onto my back she didn't do anything; just stood there and cried with her head hanging and her tears dripping into the snow.

"I can't mooove," she wailed.

"Amy," I said sternly. "You can't stay out here, we need to get home. You have to help me a little."

Sam butted me in the arm; hard. I turned to

find him staring at me expectantly like he wanted me to figure something out.

"Amy," I said suddenly, "I'm going to lift you onto Sam, okay? He's going to carry you, but you need to hang on very tightly to his mane, you can't fall off. Understand?"

"Okay," she nodded.

You take care of my sister, Sam, I thought, *don't drop her and don't run away with her.*

There was no answer, but his eyes were soft when I lifted Amy onto his broad back, and when I moved forward he walked gently beside me as if he were walking on egg shells. Gradually, Amy's sobs quieted and she leaned forward to wrap her arms around Sam's neck. I grabbed her coat so she wouldn't slip off, but she lay there motionless; sound asleep.

"Sarah! Amy! Over here." Cecily ran up with her coat half-unbuttoned, her face tight with worry. "Thank goodness, we've been scared sick. I nearly called the police. Why didn't you tell us where you were going, Sarah?"

"I didn't know where they were," I said honestly. "I'm sorry, I just knew I had to find Amy."

"Well, you should have waited for us. You could have been lost, too." She paused then swept me into a tight hug that nearly choked me half to death, and then patted Sam on his shoulder so hard that he flattened his ears and side-stepped away.

Amy slept all the way to the hospital and I had to keep checking her pulse to make sure she was still breathing. I was so scared I could hardly take my eyes off her. Cecily held my hand when the doctors took my sister away, but even so, I couldn't hold back the tears that were running down my cheeks. What if she was hurt or lost her legs to frostbite? I should have protected her somehow; I should have known that she was gone. My parents would be so disappointed if they knew I hadn't looked after her properly.

I felt a gentle hand on my shoulder and found Ellen looking down at me sympathetically. "You look like you need a cup of strong coffee," she said, pushing a paper cup into my reluctant hands. "You know," she said, sitting down beside me, "I've spent more hours in this hospital than I can count."

"You have?" I said, wiping my eyes with my sleeve. "How come?"

"Oh, broken bones, cuts, concussions, things like that. You don't raise eight kids without having them injure themselves on a steady basis. Cecily, do you remember the time AJ ate the laundry soap pods? He used a step ladder to get up to the cupboard and ate not just one, mind you, but six or seven. He just started and didn't stop until he was rolling around on the floor in pain."

"He was okay?" I asked in a small voice.

"Right as rain. Had to have his stomach pumped and spent a night in the hospital for observation. I think I felt worse about it than he did. And my oldest daughter was a devil on the cross-country course. She had no fear and would jump anything even if it meant a fall. She didn't even care if she broke bones; she'd list off her injuries like it was an honor roll. She probably gave me at least half the white hairs on my head. Even Seth nearly drowned at the lake one summer.

"The thing is, Sarah, you can't live their lives for them. You just have to do the best you can and then pray that they turn out okay. Every mom feels that way. And Amy is a wonderful little girl; your parents would be so proud of what good care you've taken of her."

That did it. Something inside of me that had been bottled up for so long burst and I broke into heavy sobs. I couldn't stop them and Ellen just put an arm around me on one side, and Cecily did the same on the other side, and then let me cry until I had nothing left. And, even though it should have felt awful, it was actually a little wonderful, too. Afterward, I felt lighter, as if a heavy weight had been lifted off my shoulders.

In the end, Amy was fine. She didn't even have to stay overnight like the soap-eating AJ. We bundled her up in the car under strict instructions to keep her warm and rested, and headed for home.

After installing Amy on the couch with hot chocolate and cookies, Cecily went down to the basement, and she and Arthur brought up box after box of decorations. Arthur and Seth hung lights on the outside of the house while AJ and his sister Janie went and chopped down an actual living pine tree from somewhere in the woods and dragged it back home. They set it up in a stand, and me and all the little Plekowski's worked together to hang up all the ornaments while Amy directed us in a commanding voice from the couch.

It took all day, but by the time the sun sank below the horizon, our house was decorated from top to bottom. It looked like a Christmas wonderland.

Later that night, when I finally felt like I could leave Amy's side without panicking, I snuck out to the barn to see Sam. To my surprise, Seth was already there, leaning over the stall door, talking to Sam.

"Sorry," I said. "I didn't mean to interrupt. Are you...are you talking to Sam?"

He frowned and then laughed self-consciously. "Yeah, I do that sometimes. I mean, I talk to all the horses, but there's something about this big guy that makes me think that he understands, you know?"

He lifted a thermos off the hay bale at his feet and poured the contents into two metal cups he'd had waiting. "Hot chocolate," he said, handing one to me.

"Thanks." I wrapped my hands around the warm metal and came to lean on the door beside him, so close that our sleeves almost touched. "You know, something weird happened the first time I found Sam and again when Amy was lost. I almost thought I heard him...." I paused, knowing it sounded too ridiculous for me to go on.

"Heard him what?" Seth prompted, looking at me with interest.

I opened my mouth, but in the end I couldn't do it. "Nothing," I said, shaking my head, "it's stupid."

He was silent for a long time, and then he turned to me with a soft smile. "You know, Sarah, once you hang out with me long enough, you'll learn that I'm a good guy to share secrets with. I'd never make fun of you."

"Huh," I said, considering. "I'll keep it in mind. I guess I'll have to stick around long enough to find out."

"Here's to sticking around," he said, clinking his cup against mine. "You know my mom's dead set on you coming up to help us exercise the horses. I don't think she's going to take no for an answer."

Maybe I really will get to ride Sam, I thought, *maybe it will be just like Amy said.*

Sam nickered low under his breath and then turned to give Seth a gentle nudge that jostled us closer together.

"You stop that, Sam," I said laughing, feeling the strange, solid warmth of Seth's shoulder pressing against mine. This time I didn't move away.

The End

Afterword

A note from the Author:

Thank you for reading our collection: *Beneath the Mistletoe.*

I hope you enjoyed reading The Horses of Winter as much as I enjoyed writing it. If you'd like to share your feedback I'd love if you'd take a moment to write a short review on Amazon or Goodreads. Be sure to check out my full-length novel, Defining Gravity, the first book in a fantastic new horse-themed trilogy.

You can stay updated on new releases, contests and freebies by joining my fun newsletter list, All About Books. Or visit my website at www.genevievemckay.com, follow on Twitter @Geners_Mckay, or join my Facebook Author Page

Happy Reading!

Genevieve

A Highland Ghost for Christmas by Jo-Ann Carson

~*~*~

Jilted by her fiancé, librarian Maddy Jacobson is nursing a broken heart, when her best friend gives her an early Christmas present. Intended to be a fun, psychic reading in a spooky, tea house, the gift turns out to be life changing. Maddy becomes haunted by a mischievous, Highland ghost.

Ruggedly handsome, Cullen Macfie, the

Highlander, has been dead for over three centuries, and never in all those years has he been so attracted to a woman, as he is to Maddy. He falls hopelessly in love and decides to woo her.

Can there be a future for a librarian and a naughty, Highland ghost?

A Highland Ghost for Christmas is a sweet, romantic comedy guaranteed to warm the cockles of your heart, make you laugh out loud and leave you craving a man in a kilt ... and shortbread, of course.

One — Santa Clause is Coming... for Tea

December 19th

Madison Jacobson questioned her sanity as she followed her best friend Ellie inside the notorious tea house, which had a wicked reputation for all things supernatural. A wiry woman with piercing, blue eyes and white hair pulled into a loose knot on the top of her head stood beside the reservation desk. Her thin lips turned into a faint smile as she looked at them, over a pair of tortoise-shell reading glasses perched precariously on her narrow, ski-jump nose. For a moment Maddy felt like a new sales item in a Christmas catalogue. Around the woman's neck hung a magnificent, agate pendant, a talisman believed to have strong metaphysical power.

"You must be my eleven," the woman said with an exotic accent.

The smell of Earl Grey tea and freshly, baked scones mingled in the air, almost masking another odor. Maddy concentrated on the odd smell. Mold, moth balls and a whiff of cigar smoke? The hair on the nape of Maddy's neck rose. Perhaps the ghost stories were true.

"She is," said Ellie pushing Maddy forward towards the hostess. "She's your eleven."

Maddy wondered for the hundredth time why she had agreed to come here. It hadn't been easy for Ellie to talk her into it. She had wined her and dined her and when that didn't work, she reminded her of their blood oath taken at the age of eight. "It's destined," Ellie had said as she closed the deal the night before. "And it's my Christmas present to you."

It had to be the most unusual Christmas gift in the world.

Destiny, my foot. Maddy fidgeted as she looked closely at the older woman. A well-educated reference librarian at the local university, Maddy believed in facts, not destiny, psychics or any form of hocus-pocus. How anyone could believe a pile of tea leaves on the bottom of a porcelain cup could predict the future amazed her. They needed their heads checked. And haunted houses? They belonged in Halloween books.

Maddy twisted her neck to relieve tension and focused on the woman with the pendant. "My friend thinks I need your help."

The woman's eyes twinkled. "Indeed you do. Follow me."

The woman led them down a narrow hallway. Faded photographs in old, wooden frames lined the walls, covered in pink flower wallpaper. Pictures of people from years and years ago, probably long forgotten. A chill started at the base of her spine and rose slowly, pushing her creep-meter off its scale. Sheesh. How long would she have to stay in this place to honor her agreement with Ellie? Maddy bit the inside of her mouth.

The woman stopped at the second doorway and turned towards them. She gestured towards it. "This is Lilith's room." The old wooden floor boards creaked beneath their feet as they walked to the large table set for two in the middle of the room. Smaller tables surrounded their table, but they were not set.

The room had its own charm. Sunlight streamed through a large bay window, giving a natural glow to everything inside. A plump, black cat lay on the window seat, looking supremely comfortable as only a cat can. Maddy's eyes stayed on the cat for a moment, envying his contentment, until it began to shimmer in the light, as if it was a picture out of focus. She blinked and looked again. The cat looked normal. It had to be a trick of the light.

Faded, pink floral wallpaper covered the walls. A mahogany and glass cabinet, filled with well-displayed china hugged the wall opposite the window. It seemed the perfect place for a tea party. If only her stomach would stop twisting.

Weird smells, shimmering cats and an old woman whose behavior made Maddy feel as if she were a demon's main course. She sniffed. No matter how creepy she felt, she could get through an hour of this. It was a Christmas present after all.

Maddy took a seat on the far side of the table and focused on enjoying the warmth of the sunshine on her skin and the generosity of her friend for taking her out on an adventure. She needed to forget, at least for the time it took to drink a cup of tea, the real reason they had come.

Ellie sat opposite in her crisp, white blouse, unruffled by the strangeness of the place. She had pulled her long, blonde hair into a high pony revealing her perfect skin and high cheekbones. She looked, as always, cover-picture perfect. If they weren't such good friends, Maddy would have strangled her long ago.

The older woman stood at the end of the table. "I am Madame Azalea and this is my tea-house. Welcome." She pulled a small, silver bell from her pocket and rang it.

A few seconds later a college-aged waitress with a nose ring, wearing a French maid's outfit, appeared with a tea tray.

She placed a three-tiered china serving plate, filled with tea sandwiches, scones and squares, in the middle of their table. A china tea cup and saucer and a small plate setting had already been placed in front of each of them. The delicate, green flower design on the dishes looked regal and the food scrumptious.

Azalea poured the tea and then gave Maddy a knowing look. "Drink. I will return shortly."

Once Azalea had left the room, Maddy put down her cup. "What have you got us into?"

Ellie made mewing sounds as she nibbled on a tiny cucumber and cream cheese sandwich. "You need to try new things."

"I can do *new*. This is something else entirely."

As if in response to her comment, a loud chorus of laughter erupted from the other side of the wall. "That's a good one," a man said. And they laughed some more. "I'll raise you," said another.

Raise? Maddy looked at her friend. "Are they playing poker in a tea house?"

Ellie shrugged. "Try a cucumber sandwich. They're really good."

Maddy reached for a chocolate-covered square instead. "How did you get us a reservation so quickly? I heard you have to book months ahead."

The way her friend's face flushed made her feel cold all over. She knew that look. Ellie was hiding something.

"Oh, I guess I got lucky. I phoned and Madam Azalea answered and she said . . . " Ellie dabbed at her mouth with the white linen napkin.

"What did she say?"

"Okay. All right. It was odd."

"Ellie, what did she say?"

Her friend looked at the ceiling for a long moment. "That she had been expecting my call and that we were booked for eleven."

"Uh-huh." Of course. That made perfect sense. The woman was a psychic after all.

More laughter made Maddy choke on her square. But that did not diminish its rich flavor. Its gooey middle rocked. She leaned back in her chair and wondered how many calories she had just inhaled and how they would look on her hips. But why should she care? She had sworn off men. "You're an awful liar, Ellie."

Her friend laughed. "Would you have come if I had told you Madame Azalea expected us?"

Maddy was about to say an emphatic "no," when more laughter came from the other room. Louder this time. Then came the sound of squeaky door hinges turning slowly. "Shush," a woman said. It sounded like Azalea. "I have a client."

Silence, and then the door squeaked open again and softly clicked closed.

A minute later Azalea reentered their room. "Have you finished a cup of tea yet?" Her blue eyes twinkled like stars.

Maddy finished the last of her tea in one gulp. "Yes."

"Good. Then let us begin." Azalea sat in a chair at the end of the table and stared at Maddy. "Turn the cup upside down, place it on its saucer, and turn it three times in a clock-wise direction.

Trying not to hurt the fine china cup, Maddy followed her instructions carefully. Despite not believing in this whole supernatural ritual, excitement brewed inside her. Maybe the tea house mold had creeped into her brain.

"Now flip it up again and hand it to me." Azalea raised one finger to slow Maddy down. "And make a wish that's just for you."

Looking into the cup, Maddy saw wet tea leaves scattered in an odd design on the bottom. It kind of looked like a dragon when she squinted and tilted her head. She didn't bother making a wish, because this whole thing was nothing more than a soggy tea leaf sham, and besides her wishes never came true.

As she passed the cup to Azalea, and they both had their hands on it, the wish bubbled up on its own: true love. She wished for true love.

Azalea looked intently in the cup, looked up at her, and then she looked back into the cup. "I see," she said. "It may . . ." –she hesitated– "be possible."

Maddy's stomach cramped. "Let me guess. Tall, dark and handsome."

One side of the seer's mouth hitched up. "Not exactly."

The tone in her voice held a coldness that reached right into Maddy's mind and grabbed at her, leaving her with a cold and empty feeling. What the heck? She had agreed to come here to please Ellie, not to get bad news. The whole point of this fortune telling trip was to give her hope. Wasn't it?

Hope for Christmas, the perfect gift for the season.

Ellie grabbed Maddy's hand and held it tightly. "I'm sure it can't be that bad."

Azalea looked at the cup again and sat back. "Your heart is broken."

Why did Ellie have to go and tell the woman about that? Maddy gave Ellie an angry stare, but she shook her head.

Maddy folded her arms across her chest and nodded. "Yeah, my handsome prince turned out to be a horny toad. You know, the usual story."

Azalea's finely manicured eyebrows rose. Clearly she wanted details.

"A month ago I found Kevin, my lawyer boyfriend of five years, on our sofa kissing a cheerleader for the local football team. I threw him out. Two weeks ago he sent me a text from Hawaii telling me he was sorry, but he had found his true calling as a surfing instructor. Later that day I discovered he financed his trip with the money we saved in a joint account for our wedding. When I sent him a scorching text, he replied. 'Babe, I got to live my dream.'"

Azalea wiggled her nose. "No matter how awful you feel right now, my dear, know this: he is the fool. Not you. You are better off without him."

Many people had said this or something similar since the break-up, but Azalea's deep voice had a resonating quality that made her words sound truly wise, and well . . . prophetic. Despite not wanting to believe in the woman, Maddy warmed to her words.

"So do you see another man in my future?"

The woman toggled her head from side to side. "Two actually, and that's what gives me pause. You look like a woman who would prefer one."

"Well yes. That's exactly what I want, one true love to spend the rest of my life with." Was that too much to ask?

Azalea looked at the china cup again. Her blue eyes glazed over. "Spirits, speak to me." Her voice sounded other-worldly now, as if it came from a distance, from beyond. The table shook.

Ellie's eyes widened and she tightened her grip on Maddy's hand. Maddy's mouth went dry.

"You signed up with a dating service."

"Yes, I signed up for MeetYourMatch dot com," Maddy said as she nervously popped another chocolate square into her mouth.

Azalea nodded. "The first man is charming."

"Is he the one?"

Azalea's head tilted.

Laughter erupted in the next room again and she grumbled. "Oh, I do apologize. My brother has his friends over to play poker and sometimes they get carried away."

"The man. The one in my cup. Tell me about him."

"Well, you like him because he's fun and kind and treats you with respect."

Sounded good.

"But there is this other man who lights you on fire. You know what I mean. He literally takes your breath away and you wonder how you ever could have lived without him."

"I'll settle for respect if the first guy is faithful." She didn't need to lose her head over a guy with good moves. Never again. Nu-uh.

"Yes, well both men are intriguing in their own way. And handsome."

"How handsome?" Ellie said, putting down her napkin.

"Give me a second." She closed her eyes. "I can't get a clear fix on them for some reason." The table rumbled again. She opened her eyes, looked in the cup and tilted her head as if the angle helped her read the tea leaves.

"I don't really need a hot guy," Maddy lied. She

actually had never had hot, because hot wasn't safe. But she had dreamed of hot. Hell, yeah, she had dreamed of hot. And two hot men! Her chest swelled with excitement. Now that was something to imagine.

Azalea smiled at her. "Broad shoulders, six pack abs, slender waists and one wears a kilt."

"A kilt?" Maddy choked on her chocolate dessert. She loved historical romances.

"Yes, a kilt, but I should warn you, a man can appear differently in this realm than in real life. He may just have Scottish heritage."

"Is he *the* one? The Scottish guy?" The words flew out of Maddy's mouth, demonstrating once again that even at her mature age of twenty-five, she still believed in white knights and fairy tale endings.

Wait. Wait just one minute. She firmed her lips. Holy tamole, hadn't she just decided that she could live the rest of her life quite contentedly without a man? They complicated everything. Her plan was to live with her dog for the rest of her life. They could take nice walks.

After a long minute, Azalea said, "They will love you like no other man has ever loved you."

"Yes."

"They will go to the ends of the earth for you."

"Yes."

She waved her finger in the air. "But you will have to choose one."

"So he is the one."

The table jumped and the china on top of it rattled. What in the world?

Azalea sighed. "You need to be careful . . ."

Bang. A gun shot sounded from the next room. Azalea flew out the door. Ellie and Maddy grabbed their purses and ran for the car. What kind of tea house has a gun fight?

Two — All I Want for Christmas is ... Maddy

Cullen Macfie, the Highland ghost, hadn't missed a poker game at the tea house since they started holding them five years ago. That was the day after Rufus, the guy who used to own the place, was shot dead with an ace up his sleeve.

Six of the regulars had gathered, and he sat beside his best friend Antonio, the artist from Michelangelo's Florence, who loved to gamble as much as he did. They played with poker chips and the biggest loser of this game had to spend a night haunting Leroy Rankin, the local politician who planned to close the town's one and only casino.

Cullen felt lucky. If he could have tasted even one sip of the whisky in the glass, the day would have been perfect. This round they played five-card stud. He looked at his cards, grimaced and folded. No point in playing a bad hand.

His friend leaned his way. "Highlander, did you see the women in the next room?" His Italian accent made the words flow together like music.

"No. I came late."

"Go have a look. You won't regret it."

Cullen grinned. "Aye, I might do just that. It might bring me good luck."

"That it might, and there's no law on heaven or earth that can stop a man from looking at a *bella donna*."

Cullen strode through the wall into the adjoining room. There sat three women: Azalea, the sister of his host, a blonde who looked as though she ate starch for breakfast and a curvy brunette. A very curvy brunette.

He stood for a moment beside their table, ignoring the get-away hand gesture Azalea made in his direction, which was her attempt to dismiss him like an unwanted pet. Unable to hold himself back he leaned towards the brunette to take a closer look and to smell her earthly charm.

She had delicate features and full red lips. Her peaches-and-cream complexion glowed. And her curves! They were the kind he dreamed of.

Mesmerized by the sadness in her beautiful eyes, he listened to her tea-leaf reading.

How could any man treat this woman badly? If her horny toad were in the room, he'd run him through with his sword. Imagining the man in a pool of his own blood made him smile. Of course his shrink CeeCee wouldn't be happy. Only this morning she had reminded him he needed to behave himself if he ever wanted to climb the stairway to heaven.

But something about this woman tugged on his heart. Her hair smelled of sunshine and citrus and her lips looked so kissable he wanted desperately to capture them with his own. Why had fate brought her to him now? He stomped his ghostly foot at the unfairness of life and death, and everything in between, and the table rattled with his energy.

Time to break a few rules.

Three — A Wicked, Holly Christmas

When Maddy got home after the tea-leaf reading, she grabbed a bucket of caramel ripple ice-cream out of the freezer and headed for the sofa in the living room, armed with a big spoon and followed by her chocolate Lab, Booker. Within a couple minutes the opening credits for her favorite series came on, a romance with a Highlander. Comfort food. Check. Comfort TV. Check. Good company. Check. A woman had to know how to fight back in this cruel world.

She laughed at herself for her mental

checkmarks. A tea-leaf reading! Of all the crazy ideas in the world. How did she ever let herself get talked into it in the first place? Then she remembered the wine and the blood oath and grinned.

It had been, if nothing else, the most intriguing Christmas present she had ever been given.

Booker nudged the side of her leg. She scratched behind his ears and he gave her a soulful look of pure love. If only men could be as faithful and loving as puppies, then the world would be a perfect place.

She checked her Twitter feed, but no mention of the mysterious shooting at the tea house appeared. Should she tweet it?

Knock. Knock. Knock.

Is that my door? She wasn't expecting anyone. With a sigh, Maddy put the ice-cream bucket on the table and went to check out her visitor. She couldn't see anyone through the peep hole, so she put the safety chain on and opened the door a couple inches. Peering through the small space she still couldn't see anyone. Hmm. She could unhook the safety lock and open the door fully. But would that be wise?

Oh what the heck. Her life couldn't get more messed up. She slipped the lock and opened the door wide. Nobody. She could see nothing but a beautiful sky filled with sparkling stars and a full moon. A cool breeze made the skin on her face tingle and she inhaled the night air.

As she exhaled slowly relishing the moment, a feeling that someone had entered her home crossed her consciousness like a dark shadow. She shook herself, trying to break the hold of the feeling, but it didn't let go and it didn't make sense. Stepping out onto her small, wooden porch she looked around once more. Nothing. Just her vivid imagination. Visiting a psychic had spooked her. That's all.

***

Cullen could have walked through the door, her windows or any of her walls, but it seemed more proper to knock on a lady's door. He used a rock. Unfortunately, she couldn't see him, but he could see her. And he liked what he saw. Oh yes, he most definitely liked everything he saw. He followed her back into the house and took a seat beside her on the sofa, which faced the TV.

Maddy pushed her long hair behind her shoulders. It looked silky and soft. Cullen wanted to touch it, to run his hands through it, to smell it up close.

Maybe coming here hadn't been a good idea.

Maddy's eyes focused on the TV. The brown mutt who had been busy chewing a bone in the kitchen when Cullen came in, now joined them. He jumped up between them staring at Cullen. He barked, but being a wee pup, he sounded cute, more than menacing.

"Booker, get down," Maddy said.

The dog kept barking.

"Booker, down." Maddy's voice deepened. Cullen liked the weight of it. "Good dogs don't jump on the furniture."

The Booker dog kept barking.

"Be quiet," Maddy said. But the stupid mutt wouldn't shut up. "Shh, they're just about to kiss. Don't ruin it. Oh. Oh my. He's pulling her closer."

The dog kept barking.

"What's the matter with you?"

Booker growled and spit at Cullen.

"That's enough of that." Maddy paused the film and picked up the dog. Cullen followed as she walked into her bedroom with the mutt in her arms. He kept barking, even when she placed him in his kennel. "Settle down, sweetheart." Maddy said.

She calls a dog sweetheart? She definitely needs a man. Cullen shook his head as he followed her back to the TV.

***

After the intimate love scene, the main characters took to their horses to chase English soldiers. Maddy yawned and scrolled through her phone messages to see if anyone had responded to her profile on the dating site. "Woo hoo," she called out. "I've got a hit." She scrolled some more. "I've got three hits." Her profile had only been up for six hours and already three men wanted to meet her. "I love this site."

Cullen tilted his head. Who did she think she was talking to? And who were these strange men courting her through the tiny phone?

While the show continued, Maddy texted back and forth with her suitors. It felt wonderful to be appreciated. They all seemed nice, but the fitness instructor named Hank stood out. He had a wicked sense of humor and seemed like a genuinely nice guy, while the others spent most of their time telling her how cool they were. She set up a coffee date for the next day with him and hit send.

Grumbling, Cullen slid to the kitchen and pulled out the cutlery drawer. It fell to the ground with a loud smash. He had never been one to rattle chains.

Maddy jumped a foot off the couch. That sound couldn't be her imagination. With her phone in her hand she ran to the kitchen. Knives, forks and spoons sprawled all over the floor. What the heck?

Cullen smiled.

Her pulse raced. That drawer had been closed and she knew there was nothing wrong with it because she had cleaned it two days ago, grumbling the whole time that it was a stupid thing for a single woman to be doing on a Saturday night.

Maddy swallowed and walked around her house turning on every light, inspecting every corner looking for an answer and found none. First the knocking on the door, then that feeling of someone entering her house and now knives and forks strewn everywhere . . . It seemed as if . . . A ghost? No, that couldn't be.

Cullen followed her around the house blowing on her neck every few feet.

When she got back to the kitchen, rubbing her neck, she considered her options while she picked up the cutlery from the floor. Methodically she put it in the sink for washing. What could she do? Phone for help? 911 would not appreciate a call about this. What could she say to an emergency operator? "I need help: my spoons fell down." She laughed at her own joke. She could phone Ellie, but she didn't want to sound silly. Who else was there? Her parents had retired to Florida and she didn't want to bother them on their bowling night. No, she had to deal with this herself.

She looked at her sink. The knives and forks had not jumped onto the floor by themselves. She swallowed again, but that didn't help. Could there have been a minor earthquake? She checked her phone. No seismic activity in the area. Maybe a magnetic anomaly? What the heck? Talk about her imagination running wild.

After cleaning the cutlery and returning it to

the drawer she paced the kitchen.

Cullen followed her enjoying the view of her back-side.

Okay, so she couldn't come up with a logical reason for the cutlery being on the floor.

"A ghost?" she said out loud. "Have I picked up a ghost from the haunted tea-house?" Other people pick up common colds; trust her to attract a more exotic malady.

Cullen smiled.

What was she thinking? She didn't believe in anything undead. Besides, she had lived in this house for two years and never experienced anything unusual before. "I don't believe in ghosts," she said out loud.

Cullen tossed her coffee tin onto the floor.

Four — He Better Watch Out . . .

Feeling proud of his antics, Cullen folded his arms across his chest and smirked. *Let her try to explain that one.* But a cool touch on his shoulder chilled his good mood.

"Macfie —return to me." The unmistakable, shrill voice of his shrink filled his head with dread. Why couldn't he enjoy an evening with a pretty lass? Her words sucked his essence out of Maddy's kitchen and spit it into the counselor's office in a dank cave in the land before heaven. "You stubborn, Scottish idiot," she hissed.

Ouch that hurt. It was one thing to insult him, but to insult his country took things too far.

"CeeCee, I'm busy."

"What do you think you're doing?" She stood in front of him with blazing eyes. Literally blazing, as in shooting flames. CeeCee was a ten-foot-tall, white angel with supernatural abilities, charged with helping souls like Cullen mend their ways and find their way to heaven. She could be dramatic when angered.

Cullen considered his options. Telling the truth not being one of them. "I wanted to help the lass. She seems lost."

"You're lying."

He stood his ground. "The woman has a broken heart. I thought the company of a good man would cheer her up, give her a new perspective on life."

Her eye-flames simmered down a bit and he could see her powder, baby blues returning. "Ha. And you, Highlander Macfie think you're the man for that job?"

"Why not? In fact, who would be better? I understand women."

"No you don't."

"I had many lovers in my twenty-five years on earth. None of them complained."

"Of course not. You're so bullheaded, you wouldn't listen."

Ouch. "Are you saying they weren't happy?"

"Cullen, there is more to making a woman happy than sweet kisses."

"I happen to be very good at kissing."

"Oh, I'm sure you were stellar, but that's not enough to keep a woman happy."

Cullen exhaled slowly. "If I didn't know better, I'd say you have PMS."

CeeCee doubled over with laughter. At least it returned her eyes to normal. "Good one, but no, I'm not in a state of hormonal overload. I'm suffering a state of Macfie overload. You don't understand women. You like them. But you don't understand them."

"So knock me dead." Cullen grinned at her. It was one of his favorite retorts to her attempts to shrink him into an acceptable candidate for paradise. He had no intention of letting her do that while there was still a lot of fun to be had on earth.

CeeCee sighed. "I called you back when I learned you chased that woman home. At first I didn't want you interfering in her life, but now I'm wondering. Maybe it wouldn't be such a bad thing for both of you. She might benefit from your company, if you don't cross any lines. You could be a caring presence to comfort her in her time of pain. You can listen to her laments and learn first-hand how a woman feels when a man lets her down."

"How a woman feels?" CeeCee was so full of angelic trash. "Are you saying lasses have different feelings than men?"

CeeCee's smile reminded him of a rabid cat he

once knew. "I'm just saying we see the world differently, and modern women aren't afraid of saying so."

"And you think she'll be good for me."

CeeCee cast him a wary glance.

"Then I'll make you a deal."

"I don't do deals." Her tone took an icy edge meant to scare Cullen, but it only prodded him on.

"If I can make her happy before Christmas, you will stop trying to shrink wrap me for the next six months."

"What does that mean?"

"You'll stop complaining when I don't arrive for our weekly meetings on time, stop nagging me about cheating at my poker games and stop telling me how I should think and feel."

"For half a year."

"Yes." That seemed like a reasonable bet.

"But what do I get out of this?"

"A happy mortal woman and a happy ghost. A win-win."

CeeCee's eyes frosted over. "No, that's not good enough. I'll wager you this: if you succeed you get a six-month pardon from counseling, but if you don't succeed, if the woman remains inconsolable, or if by chance you finally understand the depths of one single woman, then I get to send you to the big guy."

A chill ran up his ghostly skeleton. What were the odds? Twenty to one in his favor, at least. He knew he could make her happy, and as for him, he wouldn't change. He had known many women over hundreds of years and despite his bragging, he knew in his heart, he had never understood one, but that wasn't his fault. Women were beyond understanding. So he didn't expect to understand Maddy. "Okay. Deal."

She gave him that rabid cat smile again.

"But how will we assess who wins?"

"By Christmas. That gives you five days to make her happy. If she's not smiling, or if you've seen the light, then I win."

The thought of spending five uninterrupted-by-CeeCee days with the pretty lass made his ghostly heart sigh. And following that with six months of not being nagged was a dream come true. What could go wrong?

"Deal," he said.

"Deal."

Five — The Most Confusing Time of the Year

Maddy looked at her French Roast coffee beans spilled all over her kitchen floor. How could that have happened?

No . . . it couldn't be. But there was no other rational explanation for what had happened. The coffee container had flown through the air right after she declared out loud that ghosts don't exist. It fell from the counter, as if, as if . . . a ghost was answering her.

Now what?

After sweeping the beans into a dust pan and throwing them into the garbage, she took another look around. She appeared to be alone.

"I don't believe in ghosts," she said for the second time.

Cullen leaned towards her and blew a warm breath on her neck just under her left ear. Her sweet spot. Heat instantly rolled through her body. "Stop that," she said without even thinking. "I don't know you."

Cullen wanted to do anything but stop. He liked the way her cheeks blushed and her eyes widened. He loved her smell. So womanly. Oh, if only she could feel his touch. He went to the kitchen window and drew up the Venetian blinds. They made a dramatic clattering sound in the silence of the room. Moon-light shone in creating an eerie ambiance.

Maddy blinked. What the heck? Okay, whether she liked it or not, something was there. She opened her cutlery drawer and took out a spoon. "If you are a ghost, use this spoon to tap once." She put it down on the counter and watched it travel up into the air and then down to the surface of the table to tap once.

"Oh, my goodness." Her heart slammed into her throat. She sat down at the kitchen table and put her head in her hands. This couldn't be happening. Good librarians weren't haunted by ghosts. She lifted her head. "Tap once if you're a woman."

Cullen smiled as he lifted the spoon and tapped twice.

"Newly dead?"

Again he tapped twice.

"Are you here to hurt me?"

Again he hit the table twice.

"So you're an old, male ghost who doesn't want to hurt me."

One tap.

Cullen felt pleased with himself. Already the woman was thinking of something other than her last boyfriend. He'd make her happy and prove CeeCee wrong.

"So what do you want?" said Maddy.

And there it was. The real question. What did he want from Maddy Jacobson?

A familiar jingle played on Maddy's phone. "It's a text message from Ellie," she said as if conversing with an old friend. "She says . . . Oh dear . . . She says she asked around about Azalea's brother and it turns out he's been dead for five years. That means that either Azalea was lying about the poker game or her brother and his guests were all . . ."

Cullen tapped once.

Maddy put the phone down. "You followed me home."

One tap.

The memories of her tea-leaf reading came flooding back to her. Surely he hadn't heard all of that. "You know that I have a broken heart?" The words tumbled out of her mouth and she gasped.

One tap.

"Are you trying to get to heaven or get a merit badge or something?"

No taps.

"Hmm. How old are you? Are you over one hundred."

Tap.

"Two?"

Tap.

"Holy hell. Tap your years in hundreds."

He tapped three times.

"You're over three hundred years old?"

One tap.

"Can I see you? Wait, that's a stupid question. I can't. Is there something I can do to see you?"

Cullen spotted a pen and a pad of paper on the far side of the counter. He brought them both back to the table and started writing.

"I am no *deamhan*. My name is Cullen Macfie, of the clan Macfie. I was born in 1720 in the Highlands of Scotland, though my ancestral home is the Inner Hebrides. You need not fear me. I am your friend."

Maddy watched as the pen flew over the paper. A Highland ghost! A friendly, Highland ghost.

"Do you wear a kilt?"

"*Aye, mo nighean dubh*, my brown-haired lass, I do," he said as he wrote, "with nothing underneath but my manhood." CeeCee hadn't said he had to behave.

"A man in a kilt." That was something to dream about. "Did you die in battle?"

The page turned and the word, "No," appeared. "A man caught me kissing his bride."

She laughed. "You are a bad boy, then."

He shrugged, but she couldn't see that.

"Why are you still here?"

After a few seconds he wrote, "My shrink says I'm not ready for the big guy."

She laughed.

"But that's okay. I like it here. I play poker every day."

"Did they play poker in eighteenth-century Scotland?"

"I've always been a betting man. I picked up the card game later in America where I was banished for poor behavior."

"I see."

Silence.

"Well, you've certainly taken my mind off of my problems."

"I would like to run your horny toad through with a sword for hurting you."

She giggled. "But you wouldn't."

He wrote nothing.

"He's not that bad a guy. We had fun, especially

in the beginning."

"How long did you know him?" He didn't really want to know about a man who was stupid enough to let this woman go, but he wanted to keep her talking and he wanted even more for her to get over Kevin. As in, well over.

"Five years. We met at the university. We both liked watching film noir and playing tennis. We spent almost all our free time together. When we started our careers we had less play time, but we worked hard to maintain our relationship and planned to be married this spring."

Worked hard on their relationship? That sounded odd. "What did you like about him?"

"Kevin's good looking."

He shouldn't have asked.

"And witty."

He hated him.

"And," she sighed.

"Sexy?" he wrote.

"Yes, well, to look at."

Sexy to look at? What did that mean? "I don't understand?"

"He's drool-worthy cute when he wears a suit, but not so great beyond that."

"I *dunna* understand."

"When he kisses me, the magic just isn't there. You know. I used to think it would come with time, but it never did. I decided he was a practical choice for a husband. Together we could afford to own a home and raise a family. I want that more than anything. But, truth be told, he was more a buddy than a . . ."

"Lover? Then it's you who should be running. You don't want to marry your buddy even if he has the right equipment."

"That's not a problem now."

"Tell me what happened."

She sighed and tears welled in her eyes. "We had planned to have dinner at his place. I got off early to surprise him. But boy oh boy was I surprised. I found him lying on the sofa with a blonde-haired bimbo all over him."

"I see."

Tears rolled down her face. "She's not even pretty."

He said nothing.

"Why would he do that?"

"*Mo maise*, my beauty, he's an idiot. No man in his right mind would cheat on you. He's not worthy to breathe the same air as you."

Maddy smiled. Was it wrong to take counsel from a ghost? Maybe a little odd. But one thing for sure, Cullen made her feel better than she had felt for a long time.

"Is it really true Highland warriors wear nothing under their kilts?" Her cheeks heated as she spoke, but it was something she had always been curious about. "Or were you just teasing me?"

Before he had a chance to answer, someone

pounded on her front door.

"Let me in, Maddy. We have to talk." The sound of Kevin's voice pierced her heart with a sliver of ice.

"Kevin!"

"I'll take care of him," wrote Cullen. Then he flew out of the room, went through the door and eyed the toad. The last thing he would call this maggot was drool-worthy. In one hand the toad held a dozen red roses. In the other a bottle of wine.

Cullen grabbed the wine and hit him on the head with it. The man went down like a sack of potatoes, wine flowed down his face and the roses spilled across Maddy's porch.

Six — Peace in her World

Maddy opened the door and burst into laughter. There sat Kevin the toad looking dazed, with red wine dripping off his chin.

"What the hell?" he mumbled.

"Serves you right," she said between laughs.

He rubbed his head and looked around, trying to make sense of what had happened. "I came to apologize. I made a mistake." He squinted with wine-soaked eyelashes. "Several mistakes."

"Yes you did, but an apology won't make that right. No words will ever erase the image of you and that . . . that woman on our sofa."

"I know it was wrong." He stood up slowly.

"Uh, yeah."

"I didn't mean for it to happen."

That's what they all say. "You couldn't keep it zipped, eh?" The night before he had told her he was too tired and that doubled the hurt.

"No. Listen. You need to let me come in to explain it all. Give me a chance. Then if you want to throw me out, you can."

Maddy eyed him narrowly. They had been together for five years. The wedding had been set for May. They had monogramed napkins for the reception and she had in her closet the wedding dress of her dreams. Shouldn't she at least listen to him? "Okay, come in."

Kevin rubbed his head one more time and collected the smashed roses. As he entered the house he handed her a bunch of broken, long-stemmed flowers missing petals.

She put them directly into the garbage, which now smelled of coffee and roses. Cullen took the door from Kevin's hand and slammed it shut.

"What the?"

"Never mind the door. It does that sometimes. Wind currents or something."

"Since when?"

"What did you want to tell me?"

"Oh. That. The day you walked in on me with the other woman . . . it had been a horrible day at the office. I lost a big account and Jenkins threatened to . . ."

The fruit bowl on the counter turned upside down, emptying all the apples. It then floated through the air to the sink. Kevin stopped talking and watched. His Adam's apple went up and then down. The tap turned on, the bowl filled with water and then it headed through the air to him.

Kevin ran from the house screaming, with the bowl following a foot behind his head. He didn't look back

Seven — Angels and Highlanders

"Well you certainly got rid of him."

Cullen strutted to the kitchen and picked up the pen on the counter. "There is no excuse for what he did. If you forgave him, he would only do it again. You don't need him."

"Will you let me see you now?"

He frowned. "I am what they call a 2B—a class two—benevolent ghost. I can't appear whenever I want to."

"They classify you?" Unbelievable. But then everything about this night was beyond her imagination.

"Aye, they do. Class ones appear anytime they

want, anywhere they want, but class two's have less talent. I can only appear in the pre-dawn light for thirteen minutes and then I fade away. *Ye ken?* But I can move things around with my ghostly energy any time I want."

She nodded. "Will you appear for me?"

"Aye, if you would like to see me."

Maddy smiled. "But I can't touch you."

"No, *mo maise*, if you try to touch me you will feel only air. I no longer have a body, but I still have a heart."

"And a mischievous spirit." She winked. Conversing with air felt awkward.

"Aye."

"What do you want with me?" She had to ask.

Cullen hesitated before answering. Was it too much to ask a lady for her company? Things had changed over the centuries. How men and women interacted had changed. Not the best stuff, of course, but the dance before it. Ach, it gave him nightmares. He didn't want to scare her away and being a man of honor, he didn't want to lie to her. "Just your company."

"Okay."

If he still had lips, he would have kissed her right then, but he didn't, so he flew over to her wind chime and made it ring.

She laughed. "You can stay the night. I would love to get to know you and you can tell me all about your ghostly realm and your ancestral home.

And then, when the sun peaks over the horizon, I will finally meet you."

Cullen picked up the spoon from the table, the pen and the pad of paper with his writing on it and moved them all to the table in the living room. Maddy followed and sat on the sofa opposite the Christmas tree. She curled her legs underneath her.

What a sight she was to behold. He found himself locked on her full lips wondering how they would taste, and then he realized they were moving.

"Cullen? Cullen? Are you still there?"

He tapped once with the spoon.

"Tell me about your life. Were you married? What was it like to live in the eighteenth century?"

Cullen wrote a paragraph at a time, telling her about his uncle's castle in the Highlands. She had many questions and he enjoyed the conversation, until she asked, "Why were you kissing a married woman?"

Not even CeeCee had asked him that. He took a minute to think about how to explain himself. "Bronwyn was my childhood sweetheart. I loved her as long as I can remember. But she was betrothed to an Englishman. Many people thought intermarriage was the way to bring peace to the land, in those days. She obeyed her father, but I know her heart was always mine."

"So the Englishman killed you."

"Yes, he killed me and, as I lay bleeding out on the ground, he killed her."

"Oh, my. Both of you. Is she also a ghost?"

"Ach, no. Bronwyn was always pure of heart. She passed directly to heaven."

"And you have a black heart? I find that hard to believe."

"With my dying breath I cursed the Englishman and swore to all that was holy and unholy that I would avenge Bronwyn's murder. That hatred has kept my spirit alive."

"What happened to him?"

"I'd rather talk about you. Do you have plans for Christmas?"

Maddy couldn't remember enjoying a man's company as much as she enjoyed Cullen's. He was so easy to talk to. Granted, she couldn't see his expression, and for all she knew he could be sticking his tongue out at her, but their conversation was so darn comfortable and interesting, the way she had always thought it should be between a man and a woman. He didn't interrupt her once. She sighed. "Christmas. I love everything about the season." She told him about her plans to drive north to visit with her family.

"I haven't finished my tree yet," she said. "Would you like to help me with the decorations?"

One tap.

Two unopened boxes of tinsel lay on the quilted skirt beneath the tree. She picked up the first box and he took it from her. She laughed as the tinsel came out of the container and flew on to the tree. She had always thought tinsel magical, the way it reflects light and gives the tree a shimmering look. Decorating with a ghost made it all the more magical.

"Are you getting tired?" he wrote. "You can go to sleep. I'll stay here until morning, in case the toad pops up again."

The thought of him saying "toad" in a thick Scottish brogue started her giggling. Yes, she was tired. "But I don't want to miss seeing you in the morning light."

"I'll wake you," he wrote.

Eight — Christmas in her Kitchen

Maddy woke to the sound of her alarm clock. She had missed the dawn. Scrambling as fast as her feet would take her, she ran to the living room. On the table, Cullen had left a note.

"*Mo Luaidh*, I will see you tonight. You looked so beautiful sleeping, I couldn't wake you." Maddy googled the Gaelic, because he didn't translate it for her this time. It meant, "my darling." The warm feeling of friendship he had ignited in her heart the day before notched up a few degrees. Oh poop. It was just her luck to fall for a ghost. *Wonder what he looks like.* She threw on some clothes and walked Booker around the block, thinking of nothing but the Highlander.

On the way to work she called Ellie. "I have to thank you. Thank you. Thank you, for the best Christmas present ever."

"A bad tea-leaf reading in a house with gamblers, guns and ghosts?"

"You gave me a Highland ghost."

"What?"

Maddy told her all about the night she spent with Cullen.

"Well, at least you can't get pregnant." Ellie, ever the thoughtful friend, always saw the bright side. "And I like that he clobbered Kevin with the flowers." She laughed. "But a ghost? Really? You might want to think twice about getting involved with one of them."

After work Maddy went straight home, eager to spend time with Cullen. On her kitchen table sat an enormous vase of large pink peonies. Her breath caught in her throat. She had mentioned they were her favorite flowers and he had remembered.

Booker lay amicably under the kitchen table, chewing a long piece of rawhide. Obviously the boys had bonded.

Cullen turned on the tap and poured water into the kettle. He was making her tea. Could he be any more thoughtful? They chatted about her day and his poker game. Apparently the pirate had won most of the games so, unlike the day before, she didn't shoot anyone. Cullen said he didn't mind losing because he had tonight to look forward to.

"I was planning on baking shortbread," said Maddy. "I always take home a few cookie tins filled with my favorites. Would you like to help me?"

"I remember the taste of shortbread," Cullen wrote. "I would love to. Do you have an apron I could wear? That way, you'll know where I am."

"Great idea, but I only have one, and I don't think you're going to like it."

"Did you want to wear it?"

"No, no. I wasn't planning to, but I don't think you'll like it." Heat rose to her cheeks and she bit her lip. "It was a gift from Kevin."

"Ach, the toad. I'll do my best to stain it. Maybe I can even light it on fire."

What the heck. She pulled it out of her drawer and handed it to him. When he unfolded it, she expected him to decline. But not Cullen. He put it on and flew around the room.

Her mind reeled with the image of a Highlander in a kilt underneath the pink apron covered with tiny, red hearts. And the best part was the saying on the bodice: "Caution. Extremely Hot." She laughed. Hanging out with Cullen rocked.

After he had circled her a few times, he stopped by the table and wrote: "I like hot."

Maddy sighed. Why couldn't she find a guy like him? Of course it would be better if he breathed. "Guess we should get started." She pulled the butter out of the fridge and put it on the counter.

Cullen opened every cupboard in the kitchen and dirtied all her spoons. He was more a menace than a help, but she didn't care. Flour flew through the air more than once and by the time the dough was complete, she had flour in her hair and all over her face. Cullen's playfulness knew no bounds. After the pie plates filled with batter went into the oven, she turned towards her ghost in the pink apron.

"That was fun."

"Aye. You deserve to be with a man who makes you happy. What's the saying? A man who makes a mess of your lipstick, not your mascara?"

"Ever thought of writing for a greeting card company?"

"Maddy, sweet Maddy, you know in your heart I'm right. Kevin is a scoundrel. He's not just black hearted. He's stone-stupid. You deserve much better."

She exhaled slowly. "Yes, you're right. I should have ended it long before I found him in another woman's arms. But I didn't . . . I don't . . . want to be alone."

"A woman as beautiful and kind and charming as you will never be alone for long."

"Most men don't notice me the way you do."

"But you don't want most men. You want a real man who knows how to treat his woman."

She nodded. "That would be a dream come true."

"So find him."

"Will you let me see you in the morning?"

Cullen took a step back. Did he dare? Her eyes shone with hopefulness and, damn, he didn't want to disappoint her. She had had enough of that. "In the pre-dawn light," he wrote.

Nine —Not so Merrily on High

"In the pre-dawn light?" CeeCee hissed in his ear. "What are you doing, Highlander?" She said all of this as she sucked his spirit, with her supernatural, vacuum lips, back to her office between realms.

"The lass wants to know what I look like."

"Madison Jacobson is falling for you, hard, and you know it, you stupid old Scot."

Cullen sighed. "What if she is. She needs a good man."

CeeCee stared at him.

"Okay, maybe I'm not so good. But you know what I mean. I would never break her heart by cheating on her. I will bring her flowers. Hell, I even baked cookies with her."

CeeCee continued to stare.

"We have fun together."

Her eyes glowed red.

"It's been good for her to have me around. She's smiling again."

Steam flowed from CeeCee's ears.

Cullen put his hand to his chin. Perhaps he hadn't really thought this through. He rambled around the shrink's sterile office filled with the latest books on ghost therapy. CeeCee's steam warmed the room to an uncomfortable level and gave it a sulfur smell, which reminded him of the preview he'd been given of the lower world. He paced.

His life had never been fair, and he wasn't ready to give Maddy up. Not his Maddy, so beautiful in spirit and in body. In the three hundred years he had been a ghost he had never been so attracted to a woman. And he had met plenty.

He stopped in front of CeeCee whose black bushy brows locked in an inverted V above her burning eyes. "When people love each other that's all that matters," he said. His words sounded lame even to himself.

"And what exactly do you think will happen when she sees you?"

"She'll fall more in love with me."

"Then?"

"We can . . ."

"Not even kiss," said CeeCee. "The woman needs a real man. One with lips that can kiss, arms that can hold her tight and a real heart she can hear beat when she rests her head upon his chest. You, my haggis-eating sap don't make the cut."

"But I . . . I love her."

The fire in CeeCee's eyes dimmed. "Aah, so you have learned to love again. This is good news Cullen. Good news. A real breakthrough." She went to her door and opened it for him to leave.

That was it? "What should I do?"

"Drop a ghostly pair."

"What?"

"Man up."

And as her powers flew him back to Maddy's kitchen he heard her say, "Listen to your heart."

Ten - Maddy's Hallelujah Chorus

Maddy had not missed Cullen. The way the realms work makes time insignificant. He returned to her side to watch the shortbread bake. The kitchen smelled of butter and sugar baking in perfect harmony.

"The smell of Christmas cookies baking takes us all back to our childhood," she said. "Do you agree."

"Aye, it does. Especially when it's a Scottish treat." For Cullen, it brought back memories of his youth in the Highlands and of Bronwyn, the two being permanently entwined.

He was thirteen the first time he kissed her and it had been Christmas Eve. After all these years, the taste of her still lingered on his lips. It was the most perfect moment in his life, one that nothing could change or erase.

He looked at Maddy. She deserved that kind of moment and he couldn't give it to her. Not now. Not ever.

Maddy pulled out the pies and cut the cookies into triangular pieces. Cullen watched her beautiful hands at work, so delicate and soft looking. What would it feel like to have her fingers touch his face? He groaned loud and long enough to be heard.

"Cullen?" She laughed. "You made a ghost sound."

He made it again, because she clearly liked it. They did enjoy one another's company. It was the simple things they did that made them both feel happier. But what kind of future did they have, if all he could do for her was make her laugh with groans? After she died of course . . . But that would be a long time from now, or so he hoped.

Hope. Yes, he hoped she had a good, long life, filled with the love of a good man and children. He could see her with lots of children. She really didn't need him.

They talked through the night about their lives. Maddy told him about her family and about their

Christmas traditions. Her pure heart shone through her words.

"Cullen, you're awfully quiet," she said.

"The light is coming," he wrote.

"You're going to let me see you?"

It was the least he could do. Right? It was only fair. Right? CeeCee said it would make Maddy fall more in love with him, but that was just nonsense. It would just bring them closer.

He lay down on the rug in front of her Christmas tree, adjusted his kilt and pushed back his unruly, red hair.

Maddy opened the blinds and waited. It seemed to take forever, but finally the predawn light danced on the horizon giving a warm rosy glow to the sky. She looked around and there he was, Cullen Macfie under the Christmas tree.

"Oh, my," she said.

"Do you like what you see?" he said out loud in a thick Scottish brogue.

"Aye." She laughed. Her face heated and she found it difficult to swallow. He was the most perfect specimen of a Highland warrior she had seen, and she had looked at a lot of romance covers. His chest was bare. She swallowed. He had broad shoulders and muscled arms. His finely sculpted abdomen was covered with red hair. Her eyes traveled lower. She had to look, after all. His red and green tartan kilt hung low on lean hips and beneath he had well-toned legs and long bare feet.

Her warrior. Her eyes travelled back to his face. Her heart pumped faster than the last time she ran a marathon.

He had crystal blue eyes, a generous mouth set in a wicked grin and long, wavy red hair, which fell back behind his shoulders. Oh my, he was gorgeous. "Did you just talk?"

"Aye," he said and laughed out loud. "I can talk only in the pre-dawn light and only for thirteen minutes." His thick accent made it hard for her to get everything he said, but there was no mistaking the amorous look in his eyes.

"Cullen you have made me so happy these last two days." If they only had a few minutes, there was no point in beating around the bush.

"And you me, *mo nihean dubh.*"

"My brown-haired lass. I know that one, but the way you say it . . ." *makes me hot and bothered from the tips of my toes to the top of my head*, but she didn't say that.

Cullen stood and walked towards her. Maddy stopped breathing. He looked down at her. His eyes softened and his lips trembled.

"If I could only kiss you."

She swallowed. "I'm not sure I could handle that." And that was the truth. He was the hottest man she had ever seen, so well built, so handsome and so sweet to boot.

"Oh, I think you could, lass." His deep voice was undoing her.

Okay, she could die now and go to heaven. Cullen was even more than she expected. He wasn't just sexy. He was hot, hot, hot. So freaking hot.

"You're making me blush," she said.

"Aye, your beautiful cheeks are a rosy red and I would like nothing more than to see what other parts of you are blushing."

Desire spiraled through Maddy's body and pooled in her nether regions. But he was a ghost. She was just about to suggest the equivalent of phone sex, when he started to disappear, as if he were mist on a sunny day. "Nooooo," she cried. But he was gone.

The pen on the table began to move again. "I am still here *mo maise*. I have not left you."

Disappointment flooded her senses, icing out the lust that had possessed her only moments before. "I need sleep."

"Of course," he wrote. "If it's all right with you, I will lie by your side."

"Okay, I have a few minutes before I have to get ready for work." She lay down in her bed and imagined him at her side. It was a comforting thought, but it was, after all, only a thought.

On the way to work, she received a text from Hank. "I know I shouldn't chase a woman who stood me up, but I can't help myself. I thought we connected."

Hank? Oh fudge. She had forgotten their coffee date. "I'm so sorry. I didn't mean to stand you up."

No answer.

"Let me make it up to you today."

After a second's pause: "Tell me where and when and I . . . will . . . be . . . there."

Eleven- Jingle Bells Rock for Coffee

The next night Maddy and Cullen made gingerbread. Maddy wanted to make ghosts with the cookie dough, but Cullen wouldn't let her. He wanted traditional Christmas cookies, so they cut out men, women, children and reindeer. The smell of fresh gingerbread baking in the oven flowed through the house, and white flour flew through the air.

Cookies that became deformed were given to Booker, who contentedly watched from underneath the table, as if a ghost and a human were a normal thing in his pack.

"What are you doing?" Maddy said as a scant handful of flour flew towards her.

"Trying to make you laugh," he wrote.

She pulled flour through her hair and stared at the empty-looking apron. "Oh yeah." She grabbed a handful and threw it at him. A few minutes later the floor had a good covering.

"Enough," she said through laughter.

He wished he could grab her and tickle her. Actually there were a lot of things he wanted to do with her. "You seem different tonight," he wrote.

Damn. It must show. "I just need more sleep tonight."

"Okay. Is that all?"

She grabbed a broom and started sweeping. "Of course." He read her easily. She had never been able to manage two boyfriends at once, but she thought if one were a ghost, it might just work.

Cullen put the dust pan in place to scoop up the flour. They worked so well as a team. "Have I done something wrong?"

"No, no. I love spending time with you."

"And I with you, my darling." He took a fresh towel from the drawer and wetted it under the tap. Gently he washed her face with it. The warmth of the water and the softness of the touching made her heart flutter. She had read about that reaction in books, but had never experienced it first-hand. A gentle touch can mean so much. A few drops of the water trickled down her neck inside her blouse to her cleavage. Her pulse kicked up.

"Will you let me see you tonight?"

"Of course, but let me wash your hair and watch you sleep first."

He woke her hours later before his coming-out time. As the predawn light rose above the horizon Cullen's ghostly figure appeared by the Christmas tree once again. This time he had flour in his hair.

"I've waited all night for this," he said out loud.

Maddy wanted to throw her arms around him, but of course she couldn't, so she edged towards him. Close up he looked even more drool worthy than at a distance. His cheekbones were chiseled perfectly and the stubble on his cheeks made him look as though he had just rolled out of bed. *Yeah right. Give your head a shake.* That facial hair had been in place for hundreds of years.

"What's wrong?"

Damn, her face must have given her away again. "I just wish I could kiss you."

He nodded. "Just one kiss, and I would be happy forever."

Her eyes filled with tears and she wasn't even sure why. "Our time together has been so wonderful. You've helped me heal. You've made me happy. But ..."

"Aye. It is bittersweet." His figure dissolved into nothingness.

As Maddy dressed for work, she wrestled with her feelings. Never had she been involved with two men before and she didn't like the weight of guilt seeping into her heart. She decided to tell Cullen about Hank that night.

Twelve — More Rocking

After work she met Hank for the second time. She expected the spark between them to be diminished after her baking adventure with Cullen, sort of drowned by the flour of her supernatural, ghostly affair, but she was wrong. So wrong. The spark between her and Hank grew.

He told her funny stories about his childhood claiming that his feet were always too large and that explained his clumsiness, but he didn't look klutzy to her. He looked pretty darn perfect, like a blonde Ken doll with a sexy dimple that came out when he smiled at her, a mega-watt smile, which made her feel like the only woman in the room. Hell . . . in the universe. Butterflies began propagating in her stomach. When she left the coffee shop he brushed her cheek with a kiss that made them dance.

"I know there are only two days left before Christmas, and that you're probably really busy, but I'd love to see you again."

Without even thinking, she nodded. "Tomorrow's my last day at work. Let's meet again, same time, same place."

Thirteen — Frosty the Snow Fight

After dinner Maddy and Cullen baked sugar cookies in the shape of Christmas trees using white, red and green icing to decorate them. He managed to get the sticky icing over everything, but their cookies were miniature masterpieces of art and tasted divine, and that was what mattered. They put them away in tins for Christmas.

Booker ate his quota as well.

Afterwards Maddy and Cullen sat on the sofa by the Christmas tree. She sighed. "That was fun. I couldn't have baked so many cookies without your help."

"So you forgive me for making a mess."

"I forgave you the moment you picked up the mop."

"Uh-huh. So what's wrong?"

"Wrong? Nothing."

Cullen continued to write. "Something's got into you. I can feel it. I hope you haven't been talking to Kevin."

Maddy looked out the window, trying to think of a way to explain Hank. It had started snowing. Large, fluffy, white flakes floated to the ground. "Look!" She pointed. "It's snowing."

"How about a snowball fight?" Cullen said.

"Seriously?"

"I love the snow."

"Okay, but you have to wear a hat, so I know where you are."

"That's fair."

And so they went out at ten o'clock and played in the snow. Cullen made large grunting sounds as if he were being hit.

The soft snow, the perfect kind for making snowballs, fell around them. Maddy made four balls and searched for Cullen. He looked stationary, so she started throwing. No grunts. Hmm.

And then she felt him lift her into the air and gently lay her down on the ground blanketed by the newly fallen snow. His cold breath touched her face.

"I gotcha," he said, but he knew she couldn't hear him. He traced her face with a snowball.

"I'm cold," said Maddy. "Let's go in. I'd like a hot chocolate by the fireplace with you at my side." Cullen complied, but he ached inside to hold her. She fell asleep on the couch and he watched her. Her cheeks were a ruddy red from the cold.

In the predawn light Cullen appeared in front of Maddy. They held each other with their eyes and for thirteen minutes everything in the world felt right.

Fourteen —
It's
Beginning to
Look Messy

After work, Maddy met with Hank for their third coffee date. This time they went to her favorite place a few blocks from her home. Christmas tunes played over the speakers, as the snow continued to fall outside in large flakes. A Christmas tree decorated with children's crafts and cookies sat in the corner. Gingerbread men hung from ribbons over the large, picture window. The air smelled of cinnamon and ginger. A bowl of candy canes sat beside the cash register. Shoppers laden with bags strolled in, along with the regulars from the neighborhood. With only two days left until Christmas, the place buzzed with holiday cheer.

Hank gave her is full attention making her feel as if she were the only woman in the world. They talked about their families and about Christmas.

When it came time for them to part, he kissed her lips gently, and she felt transported to another world. Her entire body melted like snow. She looked up at him. "Tomorrow I'm leaving to be with my family for the holidays. I'll be back in a week and we can get together then."

Gently he brushed a strand of her hair away from her face. His fingers lingered on her cheek. "I'm not sure I can wait that long." He gave her a sad smile that made her feel missed already.

Fifteen- I'll be Home for You

When Maddy opened the front door of her home, the smell of roast beef cooking in her oven almost knocked her over. Good thing she hadn't started early on her New Year's resolution to go vegan. "I'm home."

The candle-lit table was set with her best dishes, and a bluesy Christmas song played over her speakers. The room was set for love.

After dinner, they watched her favorite Christmas movie, Love Actually is ..., with Booker sitting between them. When she got up to dance to the music, Cullen joined her wearing the throw blanket so she could see him. He didn't even make fun of her when she cried at the sentimental parts. She fell asleep on the sofa before the credits finished. Four late nights had taken their toll.

She awoke to Cullen in his full body singing in his deep, rich voice. *Oh my*. There could not a more perfect man. He held her with his eyes and she felt caressed by his heart. Thirteen minutes passed quickly.

"*Mo maise*, it is time for me to go."

"I want you to hold me."

"I canna do that, Maddy, or at least not so that you would feel it."

"Kiss me?"

He shook his head. "At best it would feel like kissing a dead fish. At worst, a Popsicle. But mostly it would feel like kissing dead air."

"What are we to do?"

"I could bathe you with a warm washcloth." His right brow rose. "Like I did last time."

Heat rose to Maddy's cheeks, but it didn't seem right at all. She didn't want a washcloth love affair. "Am I being selfish keeping you here? Is there something I can do to help you, you know, go upstairs?"

"To heaven, ya mean?"

She nodded.

Cullen shrugged. "I've never been what you would call angel material, lass."

"But you're good, and kind, and caring. You may like cheating at cards, booze and women, but your heart is made of the stuff of angels."

His rumbling laughter had a deep bawdy tone that made her laugh. "My head-shrinker tells me I can make it, if I put some effort into it, but I don't know that I want to. Can you imagine me with wings?"

"I bet heaven is a beautiful place and Bronwyn would be there."

His face darkened. "Aye, I would go for her, but there is no guarantee she will be there and no guarantee that she would want to see my sorry arse. I did get her killed."

"Oh, I bet she wants to see you."

Cullen stepped closer to Maddy and vanished with the dawn. Too tired to talk any more, she picked up her cell phone and headed upstairs. She had time to get a couple hours sleep before she set out on her road trip.

But her heart felt heavy. She had feelings for Cullen, deep feelings she couldn't deny, and it wasn't right to spend time with another man. Pulling out her cell phone, she thought about how much fun the last four days had been, hanging out with him.

Maddy typed: *Hey Hank I have to cancel our date next week. I like you.* She stopped typing. Hell, that was weak. Hank was hot and funny and when he touched her, he made her world tilt off its axis. *I don't want to lead you on. I'm involved with someone else. I wish you all the very best that life has to offer.*

Merry Christmas, Maddy. Hank deserved to find a woman devoted to him She hit the send button, rolled over and went to sleep.

***

Cullen stood by the side of her bed. Maddy looked so peaceful when she slept. But what kind of life could they share? He loved her. Oh how he loved her. With every morsel of his ghostly heart, he loved her. Adored her. Worshiped her. Never since Bronwyn had he met such a goodhearted woman. She brought him so much joy.

But what could he give her?

He picked up her cell phone to put it on the table and hesitated. Who had she been writing to before she went to sleep? *Not the horny toad.* He opened it and read her text message to Hank. With a sinking heart, he scrolled to read more of their conversations.

There was another man, a man with flesh and blood, who wanted to be with her. Cullen cursed in Gaelic, then in English and then in Gaelic again.

Outside the snow storm kicked up, but it was toasty warm in her room. How he longed to cuddle up with her under the large duvet and make love. A tear trickled from his eye. He hadn't cried for hundreds of years, but he knew what he had to do.

He opened Maddy's phone and using a pen to apply pressure he typed a message to Hank. *Hank, if you care for Maddy, come over right now and claim her with a kiss. A big, earth-moving kiss. Address: 235*

Bumbleberry Road. My best regrds, Culle, a friend of Maddy's. Ps. She likes posies.

Sixteen —
Here Comes
Santa

Twenty minutes later there came a knock on the front door. Maddy was too deeply asleep to hear it, so Cullen answered.

Hank did not disappoint him. A good looking man, he stood tall and proud, with regular enough features and some muscles. In his hand he held a bouquet of pink posies.

"Maddy?" Hank called.

Cullen grabbed the arm of his jacket and pulled him inside.

"What the ...?"

Cullen closed the door and turned on the lights.

"Maddy? Maddy are you here?" Hank called out louder looking around.

***

Maddy woke to the sound of Hank calling her name from the first floor of her home. That made no sense at all. She stretched and shook her head, but still, she could hear him calling her name.

"Maddy?"

Grabbing her silk robe, which had been left on the edge of her bed, she flew down the stairs. In her front foyer stood Hank. Snow covered the top of his blue toque and his cheeks were red from the cold. In his right hand he held her favorite flowers.

But she had just told him to go away. "Hank?" She slowed as she reached him and stopped in front of him. "What are you doing here?"

Hank's eyes softened as she neared, just like in the romance movies. Without a word he lifted her chin and kissed her, lightly at first and then deeper and deeper and deeper. So deep and hot a kiss, she thought the world had stopped.

Seventeen — Oh Come all ye Highlanders

CeeCee sang Hallelujah, off-key, as she sucked Cullen back into her office. "You've done the right thing, Cullen Macfie."

"Aye," he said feeling the tears wet on her cheeks. "I love her with all my heart and I want her to be happy."

A door opened before them, to a staircase of shimmering light. "It's your time, Cullen."

Epilogue

One year and one day later, first-class angels Cullen and Bronwyn visited the house on Bumbleberry Road. In a pretty, little basinet sitting beside a brilliantly lit Christmas tree lay a newborn baby boy. Stitched onto his blue blanket was the name, "Cullen," Booker, now double his puppy size, sat on guard beside the child's bed.

Hank and Maddy sat holding hands on the sofa, blissfully happy and in love. An engagement and wedding ring adorned Maddy's left hand, and on the wall hung a picture of their celebration.

And the angels sang.

The End

About
Jo-Ann
Carson

Jo-Ann Carson's stories are a saucy mix of fantasy, adventure and romance. Her latest stories are in the Gambling Ghosts Series: *A Highland Ghost for Christmas*, *A Viking Ghost for Valentine's Day*, *Confessions of a Pirate Ghost* and *The Biker Ghost Meets his Match*. She also wrote the Mata Hari and Vancouver Blues series. Currently she's working on a spin-off series from the ghost stories.

Once a school teacher, she loves watching sunrises, playing Mah Jong and drinking coffee. Jo-Ann loves to interact with readers on social media: www.jo-anncarson.com/newsletter

Monsters for Christmas
by M. A. Reitsma

~*~*~

James and Sally had moved out of town with their mother to an old house that had originally belonged to their grandparents. Their Dad was gone and James knew that something malicious was trying to get into their house. His older sister thinks he's being a big baby and his mom just gets irritated with him. What is he going to do?

Dedication

This story is dedicated to:
my sister and niece; thanks for the encouragement
and the kick in the butt.
DR, LR & LJR; the best family I could hope for.
and
In memory of my Mom, sorry I didn't finish it
sooner.

A short story
- Monsters
for
Christmas

Shadows everywhere! They moved stealthily around his room. Something sinister scratched and banged on his bedroom window. James knew it was only a matter of time before whatever was trying to get in would succeed and he'd be lost. He hated it here. Why did they have to move to the outskirts of town? It was so dark here. And the house was old and creaky and cold. It smelled like mildew and mothballs. He'd liked the townhouse they rented. This old house had been his grandparent's before they died. Although it now belonged to his mother, no one had lived here in years. He shivered under his quilt. The noises were growing louder.

James kept his bedding tightly wrapped around his head to hide from the shadows and block out the noises. His hand ached from the death grip he kept on his flashlight under his covers. He held it in a grip that turned his knuckles white. If only he could fall asleep. When he was asleep his anxieties and fears didn't bother him, aside from the occasional nightmare. He thought his mom would be mad if she knew he was hiding under his covers scared. She didn't believe him; thought he was being a baby. She told him he was being childish and to grow up. Sally, his sister, wasn't scared. But she was older and had their cat, Golda.

Now it was 5:30 and Mom still wasn't home and James was hiding under his covers. They were supposed to decorate the Christmas tree she'd brought home the night before but now she wasn't even here. He'd asked her if he could go with her, but she'd said no.

"But Mom, that's not fair," he whined. "I don't want to stay here. I don't like it here. I want to see Dad".

"James, stop whining," Mom snapped. "I don't have time for this behavior today. I have a million things to take care of and I want to be home before it gets too late. Sally will start dinner and we can quickly eat and then start decorating the tree when

I get home."

It wasn't fair. Making them move. Being away from Dad. James missed his father so much. Dad always understood; why couldn't they go home. Dad always made everything better. His breath-stealing bear hugs, belly laughs and crazy talk created a warm, safe haven that chased monsters away. The 'anti-monster' spray his dad gave him was all gone. He needed to see his dad. It was all Mom's fault. If she'd asked him not to go, he wouldn't have gone.

James peeked out from under his covers. It was so dark, but he could see something moving outside his window again. And he was sure he could hear a soft wailing sound along with the incessant scratching noises at his window. Pulling out his flashlight, he shone it slowly over every surface in his room. Everything was still. Too still. He couldn't even hear his sister's Christmas music playing anymore. Sweat began to form under his hair at the nape of his neck and he felt colder still. He trained the light from one item to the next—bed, nightstand, dresser, wardrobe, bookcase and desk. He paused just before moving the light across the window frame. Bit by bit, he slid the beam of light across the frame over the blackness of his window. Six glowing yellow orbs with black centers appeared beyond the glass. His scream pierced the darkness.

**

Down the hall, in another bedroom, Sally sat on her bed watching the shadows and twinkling lights play across her bedroom walls. Golda sat on her lap, purring softly. They'd had a busy day. Sally spent a long time digging through boxes looking for her Barbie Dolls and Christmas ornaments. Sally certainly didn't care if everything seemed to be going insane around her. It was getting close to Christmas and she was going to continue with her traditions.

Every December, for as long as she could remember, Sally decorated her bedroom for Christmas. Too old to play with Barbies, she still dug them out every December. Years ago, when she was a little girl, her great-uncle made her a large dollhouse. It was amazing—a miniature life-like log cabin. It even had a deck with a fence around it and a roof that hinged in the center to access the inside. She also had a beautiful 2-foot white Christmas tree that Nanny bought her. Together, the Barbies, dollhouse and Christmas tree created a wonderful holiday scene.

Dad usually helped her carry everything up to her room while teasing her about being too old to play with dolls. He'd make her eggnog and pop in at regular intervals to check the progress of her Christmas masterpiece. This year, Sally hauled everything to her room alone. Her brother pouted in his room with his video games and who knows what her mom was doing. She'd said she had errands and would be home later, leaving a lasagna for Sally to put in the oven for dinner.

Playing 'Elvis' Christmas Album', over and over, Sally worked. Her first step was to lay down the white batting for snow, layering it in places to resemble snowbanks. Thinly-stretched batting and baby powder sprinkled over the roof and deck gave the look of fresh fallen snow. Sally's Barbies were dressed in their finest and her tree decorated with tiny twinkling multicolor lights and mini silver, gold, red, green and blue round Christmas balls. Every once in a while, Sally had to push Golda away, as she tried to bat a ball off the Christmas tree or roll in the batting and baby powder.

Finding the stash of wrapping paper, Sally proceeded to use the scraps her mom always saved to wrap tiny presents to put under the tree. After being pushed away several times, Golda left the room. A few minutes later, she returned with something in her mouth and rubbed up against Sally. Giving her a quick rub, Sally pushed her out of the way again. Golda dropped what she'd been carrying on the floor, while Sally continued her work.

"All finished, girl", she said. "What do you think?"

With her paw, Golda batted whatever she'd been carrying over to Sally. Picking it up, Sally saw it was a leaf broken off her mom's Christmas cactus and tossed it in the garbage. Golda's ears went back and she lunged at the small trash can, knocking it over. She picked up the leaf and carried it to the Christmas tree and laid it down among the other presents and looked at Sally.

Sweeping Golda up in her arms, Sally said, "Oh, thank you for the present. You beautiful cat."

Reaching across her bed to the dresser to start Elvis again, she heard a bloodcurdling scream.

***

Sally's heart stopped as she jumped up, dumping Golda unceremoniously on the floor, and sprinted out of her room. Like the rest of the house, the long narrow hallway was covered with wall-to-wall moss-green shag carpet and pallid yellow walls. Sally shuddered in spite of herself; her brother's incessant keening wafted toward her down the hall. Running into James' room, Sally was greeted by a quivering ball, wrapped in a dinosaur-themed quilt, wedged into the space between his bed and night stand.

Sally asked, "What are you doing? I thought you were dying or something."

James poked his head out and stammered, "The monsters are back. They're trying to get into the house. I saw their eyes in the window. When will Mom be home? I want Dad!"

Sally looked at his tear-stained, white face with his huge blue eyes and dark circles. This had been so hard on everyone, most of all James, and she felt a rare wave of sympathy for her little brother.

Looking around his messy room with its weird orange and yellow flower-patterned wallpaper.

She sighed, "James, there are no monsters. You probably saw somebody's headlights." She walked toward his window, "Why did you take down the sheet Mom put up? You can't see out the window with the sheet up. Our new blinds should be here in January and Mom said we'd paint over the holidays. Things won't seem as creepy once we've redecorated." Sally picked up the dark blue sheet and scrounged on James' desk for the pushpins that had been holding it up. "Bring me the chair to stand on. I can't reach the top of the window."

Still whimpering, James struggled to untangle himself from his quilt and pulled himself to his feet.

Glaring at Sally, he muttered "paint doesn't keep the monsters away. Only Dad can keep them away. I hate it here. I don't want the sheet up. I can't see what's trying to get in the house with the sheet up." Despite his protests, James lifted the box labelled 'Christmas Books' off of his chair and pushed it toward his sister. Stopping several feet short of the window, James said "I'm not going any closer to the window. They might crash through and grab me."

"Oh, but it's fine if they grab me," Sally muttered.

Exasperated she marched over to her brother and yanked the chair out of his hands. "Seriously, you are being ridiculous." Sally carried it to the window and stepped up, taking a moment to check her balance. She hoped the chair would hold her; it was old and rickety. "This chair better not break. If I fall and hurt myself, you are toast." Sally took one end of the sheet and rammed a pushpin through the corner and reached up to push it into the molding around the window. It broke.

"Crap! Go get me some more pins from Mom's desk. And hurry up."

James ran from the room as Sally tried again with the other pin she held in her hand. Her sympathy for her brother was fast dissolving. Trying again, she rammed the unbroken pin through the corner of the sheet and pressed it, with more care, into the molding. Arriving back with a fist full of pins, James shoved them at her.

"Well, bring them over to me," Sally barked at him. "I can't reach them from there."

With reluctance, James stepped close enough to Sally to drop the pins in her hand. As Sally put another pin through the top of the sheet and started to push it into the molding, something appeared outside the window. Stepping backward instinctively, she screamed as down she went with malevolent glowing orbs watching and scratching on the window.

***

Sally lay on the floor, the now broken chair beneath her. With the wind knocked out of her, she felt confused for a moment. It was James' screams that brought her back to her senses. Hauling James into her arms, she screamed along with him while spinning them around to run from the room. Daphne, their mother, had just arrived home only to hear screaming coming from her children and in a panic, raced toward the bedrooms. The three of them converged in a head-on collision ending with all three on the floor in a confused heap of screams and crying.

"What in the name of Heaven is going on?" Daphne asked once she was back on her feet.

Sally explained the preceding minutes to her mother in a frantic voice, "Mom, I know nothing could be there—but something WAS THERE! James is right, something is trying to break into the house, and it's not something wanting to wish us peace on earth and merry Christmas!"

"You probably saw a dog or cat walking through the yard. There's nothing out here to be afraid of. I grew up here." Daphne turned and walked into James' room, sighing as she saw the broken chair. Stepping over the chair, Daphne repinned the sheet to the window frame.

"Gather up the pieces of this chair; I don't think it's worth trying to fix. Just put the pieces in the garage for now. It smells like dinner should be ready. Let's go eat, then we'll start decorating the tree. That will take you mind off of all this silliness."

Cutting off the expected objections, Daphne added, "Tomorrow morning we'll go outside and scout all around the house. You'll see that there is nothing around to cause alarm. There could be some branches hitting the house from the big storm the other night. That might be what you hear."

The kitchen at one time would have been considered fresh and cheery. A more apt description now would be shabby with a side of garish. The walls were covered with large, bright orange flowers with yellow centers and large yellow flowers with pink and orange centers on a background of pale yellow with moss-green swirls. In one corner was a dining nook with built-in rust-coloured benches and a silver-topped chrome table. Harvest gold appliances and moldy-looking wood cabinets completed the look. The drab appearance of the kitchen, however, didn't diminish the delicious aroma of the homemade lasagna and garlic bread. The three of them, hungry despite the drama of the last few minutes, sat down to eat.

"Wait," yelled Sally. "We need some Christmas music. I made something that we can all enjoy." Sally grabbed a USB stick off of the counter beside their computer and held it up, smiling. "I compiled songs that each of us like, so we don't have to argue over what to play." Popping the USB into the mini-stereo, the first song up was Ella Fitzgerald's

"Sleigh Ride" followed by James' favourite, "Feliz Navidad". The cheerful music, along with the hot comfort food, provided them with some much needed relief from the earlier panic. By the time they finished their meal, packed away the leftovers and cleaned up the kitchen, all of them were singing along—at full volume—to the Barenaked Ladies' "Jingle Bells".

***

James refused to get as close to the outdoors as the porch, so it was up to Daphne and Sally to haul in the Christmas tree. It was a challenging exercise to say the least. The bushy seven-foot Douglas fir, with soft blue-green needles, was not easy to navigate through the door and around the corner into the main part of the house. But, with only one broken branch, and a lot of needles on the floor, they made it to the living room where James was waiting with the tree stand and a bucket of water.

"Okay, kids," mom said, "let's get the tree up and the lights on and then we'll finish decorating tomorrow."

"But mom!" Sally and James shouted in unison, ready to harangue their mother until she changed her mind.

Knowing what was coming; Daphne sighed, rubbed her hand over her forehead and stated, "No buts about it! We finish it tomorrow. It's been a long day and we're all tired. Sally, why don't you bring your Christmas music in here so we can hear it better?"

Working together, they lifted the tree into the tree-stand and filled it with water. James held it in place while Daphne and Sally wrapped the rope around the center of the tree and stood on small stools to attach it to the sturdy hook high up on the wall next to the large window. It was absolutely required to have the tree secured to the wall, so that when Golda decided to climb it, she would not topple the entire thing. They'd lost a lot of ornaments over the years from the cat. Daphne almost looked defeated as she began to pull the mass of lights from the torn box.

"James, come and help me untangled these." The tiny colourful Christmas lights were a knotted into a huge snarl and Daphne sighed. "This is going to take a while. Remind me to wrap the lights around a piece of cardboard when we're putting them away next time."

Finding one end and working their way along, it took them just over half an hour to untangle the messy mass of lights and replace the three bulbs that weren't working. Maybe we should switch to LED lights—I don't think they burn out." With the tree up, secured and adorned with lights, even without all the other decorations, it looked beautiful.

Sally sat on the floor sorting through all their Christmas books and putting them into a wicker basket that sat on the floor next to the fireplace.

Every year a new book was added to the collection and Sally made sure she read each one every Christmas. Usually Sally and James were allowed to haul the books out of the storage room on November 1, right after Halloween, which gave them two months to read all of them. This year, because of their move, they'd have to read fast or skip some because on December 31 they would all be packed up and put away for another year.

Sally held out James' favourite book to him and noticed that he looked scared and dejected. "What's wrong, James?" she asked.

Daphne had gone back into the kitchen to make hot chocolate and James whispered to Sally, "I keep hearing things. I don't want to go to bed. Something's going to get us in the night if we're not all together." His eyes were shining with tears; the memory of the glowing orbs and screeching noises stuck in his head.

Sally gave him a rare hug and said, "Everything will be alright. I have an idea." And she ran into the kitchen to tell their mom her idea.

Soon they were sitting on the floor in front of the cozy fireplace with their steaming hot chocolate. They'd pulled out their camping mats, sleeping bags and pillows and were going to sleep together by the tree and cozy fireplace.

Daphne grabbed one of the favourite books saying, "I know you guys say you're too old to be read to, but it's almost Christmas and I want to read you a story." The three of them snuggled up together while Daphne read.

Soon Golda was curled up with them, as well, and they all drifted off to sleep.

***

It was still dark when Daphne woke up. Sally wriggled around as Golda began her early morning demand for food. The Christmas music was still playing, over and over again. She'd asked Sally to put it on repeat because every time they tried to shut it off, James began to whimper in his sleep. She lay there wondering how there could only be few days left until Christmas, and still so much to do. Normally they all loved Christmas, and December was full of excitement. They'd decorate the house on the first weekend in December and listen to Christmas music constantly. "Well we have the Christmas music 'playing constantly' down anyway," she mumbled as "Silent Night" began playing for the umpteenth time. She stretched her arm out but couldn't quite reach the stereo from where she was lying and decided to get up.

"Come on, Golda" she said, climbing out of her sleeping bag and snapping off the stereo as she walked into the kitchen. "Let's get you fed and then make some pancakes so we can get outside to find out where the monsters are hiding."

With breakfast finished and the kitchen tidied, they put on their boots, warm jackets and mitts and headed outside—James with his baseball bat in tow. There had been another heavy snowfall last night and the air was crisp, cold, and so quiet. It didn't often snow here, and this would be considered a new record snowfall. Kids would be out en masse again today, to build snowmen and find hills that they could slide down.

"Okay guys," Daphne said, "we've circled the house twice and haven't seen any footprints."

"No paw prints, either, Mom!" James scowled at Daphne. "Maybe the monsters fly and don't leave footprints."

"You got me there, kid" Daphne exclaimed. "Let's go once more around to see if we can find any other evidence."

. Sally looked put out, "Mom, this is silly. I want to get on with the decorating and baking cookies. You promised we'd bake today."

"I know. Just once more around and a quick walk down to the creek to see if it's frozen over," Daphne smiled and jostled Sally's toque. "Let's go."

This time Daphne looked closer at the sides of the old house. The siding could definitely use re-painting—maybe next summer. Coming up to James' bedroom window, Daphne leaned in to look closely. There were some scratches on the wood trim around the window and it looked like something had been spilled over the trim and down the siding—greenish, congealed lumps of goo. Daphne reached out to see if she could tell what it was and realized that some of the siding was loose. On closer inspection, it looked as if something has tried to pull the siding away from house.

"I hope it's not rats," Daphne shuddered. "Okay let's head down to the creek."

The yard was long and sloped down toward the slow-moving creek, which saw a large number of paddleboards and kayaks in the nice weather. There were a variety of large trees running down the sides of the yard and a collection of shrubs going down to the water. The snow drifts were so deep in places, higher than James' knees, and he fell over laughing a few times. The water along the edges of the creek was frozen, but it was still running in the center.

"Make sure you don't go anywhere near that ice," Daphne cautioned Sally and James. "It's not going to be very thick and I don't want any accidents. And stay off the fallen trees."

Three trees of varying sizes had fallen over in the storm. Two of them lay across the yard and one had fallen into the creek. Broken branches were scattered everywhere. James moved closer to the creek and examined one of the trees. He suddenly jumped backwards and shrieked.

"Mom! There's something in the bushes."

"Yes, James," Daphne said with more patience than she felt, "it's probably somebody's cat or a squirrel."

Daphne bent down to examine the area around James. Farther along she noticed a fair number of tracks, of varying sizes. They were small, almost like a child's hands—five long toes. She leaned closer and heard chittering followed by a low growl. She backed away as the sunlight came out from behind a cloud and shone on something in the bushes that glowed.

"Mom. Mom. Let's go. Back to the house. Back to the house," James shrieked and grabbed at Daphne's coat.

"Mom," Sally whispered. "What's going on?"

"Oh kids; it's okay. It really is," Daphne laughed. "I think the storm destroyed someone's house," she said pointing to the tree lying in the creek.

Hidden amongst the branches was a hole that looked large enough to be used as a den. "I think that tree was someone's home. I would guess the paw prints by the creek belong to a family of raccoons. They're likely cold and hungry. I bet they were wishing they could get inside where it was warm the last couple of nights."

Sally and James just stood there staring at their mother. She went on, "James, any idea what that stuff is on the outside trim of your window and down the siding?"

"Uh oh! Busted!" Sally declared, grinning at James. "I knew she'd figure it out sooner or later."

"Figure what out?" Daphne asked, already a knowing look on her face.

James looked sheepish and gazing down at his feet, mumbled, "It might be pea soup. I couldn't flush it down the toilet because Sally was taking too long in the bathroom and you'd said I had to finish it by the time you got back from putting the laundry in the dryer."

"So, our MONSTERS are hungry raccoons after my delicious pea soup and someplace warm to sleep. Hmm! Imagine that!" Daphne proclaimed. Daphne fell over in the snow laughing and laughing. Sally and James were so delighted to hear her laugh that they plopped down in the snow giggling as well.

"What do you say we gather up some of the broken branches and make a little den the raccoons can use for now? The snow will likely be gone in a few days and then they can go on their way."

"Really, you're awesome, Mom!" both cried in unison, throwing their arms around her.

***

The next couple of hours were spent happily creating a small shelter for the raccoons. Trudging around through the snow, James and Sally gathered up branches and cedar boughs while Daphne went in search of sturdy string and a bag of leaves from the garden shed. Daphne's mom always bagged leaves and added them periodically to her compost bin. Her mom loved to garden and creating her own compost was an important part of the whole process.

Pushing some of the debris aside, they were able to find a spot near the fallen tree that had several solid branches. They began by layering a two-foot-by-two-foot area next to the tree trunk with cedar boughs and leaves. Then, using the broken branches they collected, small pieces of firewood and string, they constructed a nice little cozy den, leaving only a very small opening of about 8 inches—just big enough for the raccoons to squeeze through. To complete their undertaking, they covered the whole thing with more cedar boughs, both to disguise the shelter and to keep the wind out.

Sally snapped pictures of their project with her iPhone while James stood preening. Daphne looked on, contented and full of love for them.

"Wait!" James cried out as they started back toward the house. "What are they going to eat?"

"You know we don't feed wild animals, James," Daphne stated. "It's not good for them. They become a nuisance and get into trouble when people give them food. It's much better for them to forage on their own."

"But it's cold. And there's so much snow. They're going to be so hungry," he pleaded. "They'll keep coming to the house to trying and get the food off the wall."

"Uh, uh," Daphne shook her head. "You are

going out with a brush, and hot, soapy vinegar and water to scrub the mess off the siding."

Looking defeated, James started stomping back up the yard toward the house. Sally thought she'd give it a try.

"Mom, what if we throw a few things down by the creek? Just this once? It'd be like a Christmas present for them. They deserve something, too. Some bread and cereal?"

James, hearing Sally's entreaty, turned around and was looking hopefully at his mother. Daphne just stood there for a minute looking at her two amazing children and finally threw up her hands in defeat.

"Okay. Just this once. The food goes right down by the creek. Spread some leaves over it so they at least have to do a little work. No bread. No cereal." Sally and James were vibrating with happiness and excitement.

"They need real food. You can take a couple of handfuls of nuts, some frozen berries from the freezer and a can of sardines."

"Yuck! Sardines?" Sally grimaced.

"Yes! They're not vegetarians. Sardines are full of good nutrition." Daphne said.

"Well better them than us!" Sally declared as they all laughed and headed back to the house.

As they reached their back door, they heard the crunching of tires on the driveway out front. They walked around to the font of the house as the car came to a stop. Sally and James stood in stunned silence for a minute. And then the screaming began.

"Dad!" bellowed James, launching himself into David's arms.

"Dad!" yelled Sally as she ran and threw her arms around her dad and brother. Daphne stood back watching, somewhat incredulously. David had tears on his face as he disengaged from the children and walked toward her.

"I'm so sorry," he said. "I'm not going. I turned down the position." He stood staring at her. Waiting, hoping, for a positive response.

"Why," she asked, her voice barely above a whisper.

"This is where I want to be. No job is worth moving across the country and away from my family."

Standing still, looking apprehensive, James and Sally waited for their mom's response. They were beginning to think she'd turned to stone, when the façade cracked and a single tear of happiness ran down her cheek as she smiled.

"Welcome home, David. Let's go decorate the tree—after a huge group hug, of course."

James grabbed Sally's toque and ran to the house yelling, "The monsters are gone, and this is going to be the best Christmas—EVER!"

The End

Afterword

A note from M.A. Reitsma

Thank you for reading our box collection – *Beneath the Mistletoe*.

And... thank you so much for reading my story, *Monsters for Christmas*.

It was a lot of fun to write and I hope you found it enjoyable. If so, would you please take a few minutes and leave an honest review. Writers enjoy hearing that readers like their stories, and hopefully, others will read your words and choose to read it as well.

A Scary Christmas by Wendy J. Merritt

~*~*~

Change is scary...

It's frightening to move to a different place and go to a new school, where you have no friends. Just when things start to brighten up, Christina's black lab, Mia, the star of the Christmas pageant goes missing. Will Christina get Mia back before Christmas?

Dedication

This story is dedicated to my granddaughter, S. J. Merritt.

A short story
- A Scary
Christmas

"Dad, Dad!"

Christina almost tripped on the lip of the concrete floor as she ran into the barn. Mia got there just ahead of her.

"How was school today? Did you learn anything?" he asked her, the white milk making zinging noises as it hit the sides of the pail between his knees.

"Of course, but Daddy, I need to tell you something," she said, bouncing back and forth, the pink pompoms on her boots bobbing.

"Okay. Shoot." He moved the pail of milk out from under the Jersey.

"Miss Gregory said I could bring Mia to the Christmas play at school. She can be a reindeer."

Her father frowned. "Now, wait just a minute."

"Don't say no, Dad," Christina pleaded, her whole body vibrating with excitement. "The whole class thought it was a great idea."

"How is a black lab going to be a reindeer?"

"Easy," she said with a shrug. "You make him antlers. I'll teach him the rest. Please, Daddy, please."

Christina's dad stood shaking his head as the snow started to fall heavier and the wind picked up. He turned and walked toward the big house without saying a word. There would be no talking about it right now. She hung her head, kicking at the snow.

Christina followed in her dad's footsteps as they walked to the house. The Christmas lights twinkling on the house looked so pretty, but her dad was not answering her which wasn't a good sign. Why did he always take so long to decide? *If I was a boy he'd probably let me,* she thought. She lifted her chin and changed her walk to a defiant little stomp.

As they were finishing their stew and hot biscuits, Christina couldn't wait any longer.

Dad, what did you decide?"

Her dad looked at her, starting to shake his head. "I don't think it's a good idea, Pipsqueak."

"I am not a pipsqueak. I am nine years old. Why

not?"

Christina's mom had started to clear the plates off the table. She frowned. "What's up guys?"

Christina began to tell her mom the idea for the Christmas play at school and how everyone wanted Mia to be the reindeer. As her mom started to get excited about the idea, her dad pushed back his chair and stood up.

"No. It will be too hard on the dog. It just won't work." He strode off to the family room.

Christina looked up at her mom with tears in her eyes. "It was my idea. They never like what I say but they liked this." She stood up and carried her dishes into the kitchen.

Her mom gave her a big hug and said, "Let me try." Christina brightened up. "No promises but I'll talk to him," her mom added.

***

"Morning, Christina. How are you this morning?" Her mom was making pancakes.

Christina shrugged. "I feel sick. I don't know if I can go to school today." She'd heard her parents talking last night but couldn't make out what they were saying. She had rolled around her bed for what felt like forever.

Her mom turned around from the stove, smiling. "It's a go."

Christina let out a big breath and fell across the table. Then she ran to her mom and hugged her.

"Thanks, Mom. Thanks so much. I was so

scared."

"Do you think that you will be able to go to school?"

"Oh, yes. I think I can eat four pancakes, too." She was all grins while she set the table.

* * *

The night of the big Christmas dress rehearsal arrived. "I'm so nervous." Christina was pacing the kitchen when her dad came in and handed her the carved antlers. "Oh, Daddy, they are the best. They aren't heavy. Oh, Daddy. I never even imaged they could look so good." She rushed to her dad and threw her arms around his neck as he squatted for her assault. "Thank you, Dad."

"No problem, Pipsqueak. I'm still not sure this is a good idea." He tweaked her freckled nose.

Christina didn't correct him this time. She looked up as her mom came in with something wrapped in white tissue paper.

"What's that, Mom?"

Her mom held out the package and Christina ripped off the paper. Her brow furrowed as she held up the blotchy brown material. "I don't get it." She looked at her mom questioningly.

"Reindeer aren't black. So, I made Mia a costume."

The dog danced around wondering what these crazy people were doing as they tried the outfit on her.

"It is so cool, Mom. You made holes for her

legs and her tail. It's great. She will look like a real reindeer tonight at the dress rehearsal. Should we get going?" Christina was jumping up and down, her aqua eyes shone.

Her dad said, "How about some supper first?"

When they arrived at the school, it was wild. Kids were everywhere with teachers trying to restore some order but when Mia entered everyone stopped and went quiet. They started yelling and saying how great a reindeer Mia made. Christina stood tall and answered questions and felt important. "Mom, they never even talk to me. Isn't this great?"

At that moment, Christina's mom looked at her with some concern. "Is there something I should know about, sweetheart?"

"Oh, no Mom, everything is just perfect now."

Then everyone was called to the gym to get the practice rehearsal started. Her parents left and Christina tied Mia up by the back door. "See you soon, Mia. Be a good girl."

It was a while before the teacher said, "Okay, Reindeer Elf, go get your reindeer."

Christina, with her curled-up elf shoes, pointed ears and a tilted elf hat, ran off to get Mia.

The dog was gone.

The whole group was stunned when she returned without her dog. A couple of the teachers made a search of the school and another couple went outside. No Mia.

"Who would take my dog?" Tears streamed down Christina's face as she hung out of the window of the truck.

Her dad had driven down every street of town at least five times, and now he turned the truck towards home.

"No, Dad. We can't go home."

Her dad's voice was firm. "This storm is getting worse and you have school in the morning. I said from the beginning this wasn't a good idea. We are calling it a night. Now buckle up and close the window."

"Please Daddy, drive slowly and I'll see if she is in the ditch somewhere on the way home." She watched her parents exchange looks.

"Honey," her mom added, "maybe Mia is at home, sitting on the porch wondering where we are."

Her voice sounded discouraged, "I'll still watch."

Mia wasn't on the porch when they got home. Christina went to bed but could not sleep. Who would have taken her dog? She went over anyone who she thought might. Who? Who? What if she was out in this storm? It was frigid outside. Mia might die in this cold. Christina started to cry even more. Then she heard a noise outside. She ran over to the window and saw their truck backing out of the garage. Where was her dad going? The wind was blowing snow against the window and the floor was cold on her feet. Jumping back into her bed, she rolled on her side content in the knowledge her dad was still looking for Mia. She drifted into a restless sleep.

She awoke when she heard the truck come back. She said a little prayer as she waited for her dad and Mia to come in. But her dad walked by her door without a sound. No Mia. There was no more sleep for Christina.

Her dad looked up as she entered the kitchen still in pajamas. He raised an eyebrow. "The bus will be here in about fifteen minutes. You'd better get a move on."

"I can't go to school. I feel sick."

"You are not sick. You are upset. We all are. You are going to school so go and get dressed. Hurry." He returned his focus to the paper he had been reading. He waited a few seconds then said, "Now. Get going."

As she turned, she mumbled, "you don't even care about Mia."

"Pardon me?"

"Nothing."

The school bus was almost full when Christina got on. She hated the bus ride. No one talked to her and if they did, it wasn't anything nice. It was snickers and them laughing at her. She kept her eyes down. The last seat was at the end, of course. But today was different. Right away they started talking, all at the same time, asking about Mia.

"Is she home?"

"Did you find her?"

"Who is going to be the reindeer now?"

They seemed sorry as Christina shook her head and her eyes filled with tears. Some of the kids reached out and touched her arm as she walked to the back of the bus. On top of everything else, she had to share a seat with the meanest kid in the school.

"So, you lost your stupid dog," he sneered.

Christina just sat looking at her lap.

"She probably hated you. Got tired of being with you. Who dresses a dog up as a reindeer? Stupid." He rolled his eyes.

Gary turned around from two seats in front and said, "Shut up, Darcy. You only wish you had a dog. Leave her alone."

"Who's going to make me?" Darcy started to get out of his seat.

Christina looked at Gary and shook her head. She didn't want a fight on the bus. They'd all be in trouble.

"No one is, Darcy. Take a chill pill." Gary turned to face the front of the bus.

Darcy sat back and crossed his arms, scowling. Christina heard the hiss from him, meant only for her, "You think you are so smart. You get what you deserve." The big yellow school bus turned into the schoolyard.

At recess, some of the kids came over to

Christina and asked her to go with them so they could check the town.

"Thanks, guys. I don't think that would be a good idea."

Gary joined the small group. "No time. We need to go at noon."

"We aren't allowed to leave the school grounds. My dad drove all over town last night," Christina said.

Gary shrugged. "Up to you. We just need a few of us. The teachers won't even miss us. You can't see anything driving around in the dark and it was snowing hard last night. She may have been going up one street while your dad was driving down another. It's up to you." He turned and went off to a group of boys in the corner of the schoolyard.

At noon in the cafeteria Christina always sat by herself. As she packed up her uneaten sandwich she made up her mind and went over to the table where Gary sat with his friends. Looking right at Gary she lowered her voice and asked, "Did you mean it? Go and look for Mia?"

He looked at his friends around the table and they were all nodding in agreement.

"Can I come?"

He shook his head. "We move faster, no offence. They will be watching for you to leave. If you stay here, they won't miss the four of us." He looked at his friends who were nodding in agreement.

"Okay. Please find her."

Gary smiled, "we'll try."

A little while later the boys returned but there were no victory smiles. Gary shook his head and said, "no luck."

"You guys might be in trouble. Darcy saw you leave and went and told Mr. Hawthorn."

"Don't worry. This isn't the first time I've left at lunch. I'll just say we went and ate at Kyle's. Gary looked at Kyle who was nodding in agreement. "There's the bell." Everyone in the huddle got up to go to their classrooms and Gary said, "we need another plan. I'll see you at recess."

He was off and gone as Christina hurried to her own classroom. Gary was a year older and in grade four. *"I hope he has a plan by then,"* she thought.

The group was quite a bit bigger by afternoon break. Despite still wondering where Mia was, Christina had never been the centre of attention at school and it felt okay. Everyone was talking, asking questions, and then Darcy joined them.

"What's going on here? Still trying to console the new girl?" He looked at Christina and said, "Dog still missing? Too bad," He didn't look too sorry. "Maybe you should let a dog be a dog. She ran away because you dressed her in that stupid outfit and made her wear those dumb antlers. No wonder she took off."

Christina started to cry. "She loved it. What would you know? Why do you always try to start trouble? You're mean."

Several of the students told Darcy to get lost. He took his time turning away from the group. The bell rang and they had to go back in.

After school, they loaded into the bus to go home. Christina sat near the front this time as she was usually the first picked up and the first to be dropped off. She always sat by herself but today Gary dropped down in the seat beside her.

"I have an idea."

"What?"

"I think Kyle knows more about this than anyone."

"Why?"

"I didn't even see Darcy at the rehearsal."

Christina shrugged. "I'm not getting you." She shook her head.

Gary rolled his eyes. "I've known Kyle a long time. He's always in trouble. He doesn't even have a stick to play hockey with us. He always has an excuse not to do something with us."

"So what?"

"If he wasn't at the rehearsal how did he know your dog had a costume and antlers?"

Christina's mouth opened and then closed. She moved her head from side to side and the bus driver called out her stop. As she got up, Gary added, "meet me at the end of your driveway in half an hour; I have a plan."

Christina knew there was no way her mom

would let her go off with Gary and on a skidoo, no less. She sat eating a fresh baked peanut butter cookie, and having a drink. All of a sudden, she'd had it. She stuffed the cookie into her mouth and gulped down the milk. She ran to the porch, got into her boots and coat, grabbing her mitts and hat and yelled to her mom, "Paper guy is here, going to pick it up." She ran out the door. She heard her mom say something, but she kept moving.

She got to the end of the drive as Gary pulled up on the snowmobile, spraying snow all over her as he came to a stop. She glanced back at the house, then jumped on and they were off. She hoped they would be back before her mom missed her.

They headed back towards town, took a left and pulled up into what seemed like a dead end. There was a rundown old house with smoke coming out of the chimney and the barn doors were open. The driveway wasn't plowed but the snow sled had no trouble getting up to the back door."

Christine and Gary got off the machine and stopped to make a plan. She looked at Gary and said, "Now what?"

Without hesitation Gary said, "We ask to speak to Darcy. Simple."

The door was thrown open and at large man stood glaring at the two kids. "There's a 'no trespassing' sign posted. What are you doing here?"

It didn't look so simple to Christina and she felt herself start to shake but Gary stood tall, gulped and said, "Hi, Mr. Witherspoon, I am Gary and this," he gestured in her direction, "is Christina. We go to school with Darcy."

"So?" came the gruff reply. It was then that Christina noticed his missing half leg. She felt like she was staring and tried to focus on something behind him. She saw the cupboard full of dirty dishes. A pan on the stove was burning something that smelt awful.

"Well, we thought we come over and visit him."

"Yeah, why?" The look was menacing. "I don't see that machine big enough to hold three people."

"No, not for a ride." Gary faked a chuckle. "Just want to ask him about an assignment we had at school today." Gary beamed thinking this was clever.

Mr. Witherspoon pursed his lips and his face took on the suspicious look of someone being lied to. "Let me get this straight. You want to talk to my kid about a school assignment?" He grinned but it didn't reach his eyes. "You kids get out of here before I have to use this." He had reached over and grabbed a rifle.

Christina, pulling on Gary's arm, moved towards the snow mobile. "Mr. Witherspoon, I've lost my dog, Mia. She is in the Christmas pageant; she's the reindeer; now she's lost. She could be lying in a ditch somewhere dying. I need to know if your son has seen my dog. Or if you have seen my dog?" She added the last part as an afterthought. "If anyone has seen her." Tears in her eyes, she tugged at Gary's arm when Darcy's dad moved the big gun forward a little. She looked at the barn and saw Darcy framed in the opening to the run-down barn. He didn't move.

Gary got her back to the end of the drive as she saw her dad's truck backing out of the garage. "*Great, they know I've been gone,*" she thought. She jumped off and yelled over the noise. "Thanks. You'd better get going." Gary gunned the motor and took off home, snow flying everywhere.

Her dad pulled up alongside, rolled down the window and said, "Get in."

Her mom was shaking her head. "What's going on? Where have you been? What were you thinking? You could have been kidnapped or killed."

Her dad said, "We'll deal with this in the house, when I've finished the chores." Her dad went to the barn and Christina and her mom entered the kitchen through the garage door. Now her mom wasn't talking. That was worse than getting yelled at.

They didn't discuss it at the table. Her mom said they'd all have indigestion. Waiting was making her feel sick and no matter how she worded an explanation in her head, it sounded stupid. She pushed her food around her plate. She did the dishes as slow as possible. Her dad poked his head in the kitchen. "Get a move on. Then we'll see you in the family room."

As she entered the room she put on a smile and said. "The dishes are done." There was dead silence and she knew they had been talking about her. She sat on the edge of the love seat as close as she could get to the arm and waited.

Her dad began. "So now, things have settled down." He nodded towards her mom. "We would like to know just what happened after school."

She gulped. "All of it?"

"That's a thought." He kind of nodded, in ever-so-slight a way.

"Almost everyone, well, most people were worried about Mia."

He raised a questioning eyebrow. "Almost everyone?"

Christina sat a little higher and looked square at her parents. "You don't."

Her mom said, "what do you mean, we don't? Your dad was up driving around half the night looking for Mia. He made fliers and took them around town and to the post office."

Christina's bravado shrank. "I saw his truck leave in the night." She turned to her dad and in a very low voice said, "I'm sorry, Daddy."

He nodded and gave his girl a wink. "Okay, now the rest of the story?"

"The kids were great. Gary and his friends

snuck off the schoolyard and went around town, at noon, looking for Mia. Like they really care my dog is missing." She was unable to stop the shaky voice and tears.

Her mom echoed her words, "Who is Gary? Snuck off the schoolyard? They didn't have any lunch?"

"Oh, Mom, they went after they ate."

Her mom was nodding as her dad added, "So, they didn't find Mia either?"

"No."

"And..."

"There is this kid at school that's doesn't like me and is kind of mean."

"Yes?" Her dad sat up a little straighter at this news.

She shrugged and continued, "Gary thought that maybe Darcy had taken Mia."

It was her mom's turn. "For heaven's sake, why would he think that?"

Christina was excited as she answered, "Darcy wasn't at the pageant."

"So? You can't blame someone that wasn't even there."

"Gary knew he had been there because he knew about Mia and more important, her costume. The antlers."

At her parent's confused look, Christina continued. "So when I got off the bus, Gary said to meet him at the end of the drive. He had an idea."

She folded her hands in her lap and said, "so I did."

"You don't even know this boy." Her mom was looking at her and shaking her head.

"I go to school with him every day."

Her dad wanted to get at the root of this talk. "So, where did the two of you go?"

She looked down at her feet. "We went to Darcy's."

"Darcy is Jack Witherspoon's son." It was a statement.

Looking at her husband, Christina's mom asked. "Who is Jack Witherspoon?"

"He's got a place at the end of the road the Campbell's live on. He is a loner. He's a veteran who lost part of his leg in Afghanistan. He's pretty tough on his kid, I've heard. I understand they are not very well off."

Christina interjected, "That's for sure, and their place isn't very nice. He's really scary."

"Scary? How?"

Right then, the doorbell rang and they all jumped. Christina, not wanting to explain about the gun Mr. Witherspoon had had, jumped up and ran to the front door. "I'll get it," she yelled back. She caught her breath when she opened the door and there stood Mr. Witherspoon. Now he had two legs and he looked even bigger than he had that afternoon.

Her dad had come up behind her and put out his arm over her head, offering a hand to their visitor. "Hi, Jack Witherspoon, isn't it?"

Jack looked down and said, "Yes. I've come because my boy has something to return." He turned back towards his rusty old blue pickup and gave a signal.

Christina heard the door of the truck squeak as it opened and then a big black blob was racing toward her. It was Mia, her legs and snow flying everywhere. She slid across the porch and came to a stop just before knocking over Darcy's dad.

Darcy followed the dog, his head hanging, but at a tenth of the speed as though this was the last place he wanted to be. He increased his speed ever so slightly when his dad yelled out, "Get a move on." When he reached the door, he handed the paper bag he carried to Christina.

"You did steal my dog!" she exclaimed. She opened the bag with the reindeer costume and the antlers her dad had made.

Darcy responded, "I never stole your dog." He glared at her in defiance.

Christina's dad was quick to interject. "It's freezing. Come in and we can have hot chocolate and talk about this."

Mr. Witherspoon was shaking his head. "This won't take long."

"That's right, so come in and we'll get it done." Her dad opened the door wider and the two outside pretty much had to come in. Neither was very happy about it.

With the hot drink and some Christmas goodies, the story came out in full.

"I heard a noise outside my window and got up to see what it was. It was snowing and really hard to see, but it looked like something lying on the driveway." Now Darcy looked at his dad. "I knew you were asleep in the chair so I went outside to see what it was."

Turning to Christina, he said, "Soon as I saw that stupid costume I knew it must be your dog."

"It's not a stupid costume. My mom and dad made it. It's a great costume."

Darcy looked down and shrugged. "Anyway, I could see that she was in a bad way but I got her into the barn, made a bed in the straw and went back to the house to get a cover and something for the dog to eat. When I came back I lay beside her and wrapped us tight in the blanket."

Darcy's dad spoke up. "Where did you get a blanket? I never heard a thing."

"You were asleep and I went into that old closet where mom kept all her favourite things in and found the blanket." As an afterthought, he said in a low voice, "I knew she wouldn't mind."

Mr. Witherspoon looked off into space and said, "No, she wouldn't have. She'd have done the same thing." His voice was sad. He looked back at the people around the table and said to no one in particular, "My wife died last year. Finish the story, Darcy."

"Well, I fell asleep and then I was woken by a wet tongue licking my face. I knew she would be okay so I went back in the house and went to bed."

Mr. Witherspoon finished the story. "I don't go to the barn. Darcy does the chores. I didn't know we had a visitor in the barn. But after your daughter was there with her friend today I knew something was up because Darcy's been taking so long to do the chores." He looked at Christina. "I am sorry if I scared you today. I'm not used to people coming around."

Christina smiled at the sad man. "That's okay. I'm just glad Darcy took care of Mia." She turned to beam at Darcy whose face was red. "Thank you, Darcy."

"So are we." Christina's dad piped in. "Look, Darcy. It was a good thing you did. We are planning on letting Mia have pups in the spring and I, no all of us, would like you to have first pick of the litter. What do you say?" Christina and her mom were nodding in wholehearted agreement.

Darcy looked at his dad with pleading eyes. "Please, Dad."

Mr. Witherspoon started to shake his head, when Christina's dad jumped in, "Jack, may I call you that?" Darcy's dad nodded. "Jack, it's a ways away. What say you just think about it?"

Darcy looked up at his dad. "Please, Dad. I can take good care of a puppy."

His dad smiled down at him and said, "I see

that. Okay, we'll consider it. Now let's go home."
He pushed his chair back from the table and stood
up.

At the door, Christina said, "Oh, isn't this the
best Christmas for everyone?" She was kneeling
down rubbing Mia behind her ears. Mia turned
around and ran to Darcy and jumped up on him,
one paw on each shoulder, and gave him a big wet
kiss. Everyone laughed.

The End

Afterword

A note from the author, W.J. Merritt,

Thank you for reading our Christmas collection – Beneath the Mistletoe

And... thank you for reading my story – A Scary Christmas. What fun to developed it with the help of my granddaughter, her suggestions started the whole plot. I hope you will leave an honest review for us.

Come visit me: My website is http://wjmerritt.com. My blog 'Merrittsmuse'. Twitter- @writerwjmerritt

Mistletoe Kisses by Megan Riley

All Ellie wants for Christmas, is to go home...

When Ellie Harper misses the bus going back to Rockport, Maine, she's devastated. It's Christmas Eve, and all she wants is her flannel pajamas, and to sip hot cocoa in front of her parent's fireplace.

What she *gets* is Tanner Riggs.

The only plausible solution to her dilemma, is to get a ride back home with her brother's best friend. A guy who hasn't spoken to her since that fateful kiss under the mistletoe two years ago.

What could possibly go wrong?

Dedication

I loved every second of writing this story, but I couldn't have done it without the help of some pretty amazing people.

I want to dedicate this story to Meika Schauerte and Katie Doell who are my awesome beta readers, who give me the strength, and en*courage*ment to follow my dreams.

To my mom, for being pushy, insistent and not letting me give up. Thanks for being my cheerleader. I appreciate it more than you know.

And lastly, my hubby, who puts up with my mood swings when I'm upset with my characters—yes, I'm aware that they're fictional—and loves me anyway.

You are all awesome and I wouldn't trade you for anything...except maybe chocolate.

A short story
- Mistletoe
Kisses

Ellie took a deep breath, counted to ten, and tried again. "But I really need to get home."

"I'm sorry, Miss." The blond lady smiled sympathetically. "But you missed the last bus."

"I missed it," Ellie deadpanned. "But it's Christmas Eve. Surely you have another one going to Rockport."

"There isn't another bus until quarter to midnight."

Ellie glanced at the digital clock above the ticket booth. 8:03pm. Three hours and forty-five minutes was a long time to wait for another bus.

"Would you like me to print you a ticket?"

She stared incredulously at the lady, and then shook her head.

Why had she insisted on staying to finish the house she was decorating? She shouldn't have taken Jessica Noble on as a client at the last minute. The woman was demanding, rude and didn't care that Ellie had gone out of her way—which included an eight-hour bus trip—to take on her job.

She'd been here two weeks, at the busiest time of year, and working her butt off to meet all of Jessica's high expectations. Just so Jessica's house would look amazing for the Christmas party she was going to have there.

A party Ellie wasn't invited to, even though *she'd* done all the work!

Ellie didn't normally take jobs in the *Big Apple*, but she'd thought it would be a great opportunity to get her name out there. She and her best friend, Julie owned their own interior design store back in Rockport, Maine. They were good at what they did, and the residents that lived in their quaint, renaissance town knew and appreciated their work.

It hadn't exactly fazed her to take the bus here. Ellie didn't particularly enjoy driving, especially in the winter months. She'd thought this job would be a slam-dunk, and that she'd be in and out within the week. Ellie had ordered most things online, and had had them sitting there waiting for installation; only to have Jessica go and change her mind at the last minute.

About everything!

She wanted brass instead of brushed nickel; she'd changed her mind about the color of paint, she'd changed her mind about having a textured feature wall in the dining room, and the fabrics for the kitchen chairs weren't right. The furniture was all wrong, and of course, it was all Ellie's fault.

"I want to 'wow' them, Ellie." She'd said more than once, in that cool, condescending tone. *"Not bore them."*

The job had taken a lot longer than she'd hoped, and now it was too late. She'd missed the last reasonably timed bus, that would've taken her home. Feeling deflated and way too close to tears, she took a step back.

And collided with a solid wall of muscle.

She whipped around and locked eyes with Tanner Riggs, her brother's best friend. A guy she'd barely seen in the last two years. Not since *that* day, when she'd had one too many glasses of spiked eggnog, and impulsively kissed him under the mistletoe.

Rockport wasn't too big. With a population of only 3,330, it was hard not to bump into people you knew—people you'd known all your life. Unless they were studiously avoiding you, that is.

Tanner had barely said two words to her since that day, and he never came around her parent's place anymore to visit. Sure, he'd chalk it up to being busy with the family business, but it didn't take a genius to see that he'd just been steering clear of her.

Now, here he was with his muscled arms folded across his chest. At five feet eleven, he towered over her slender five-foot four frame. Without even trying to, he made her feel both delicate and feminine.

She knew that his construction business kept him very busy. Building houses had him on the go constantly; and she'd barely seen him since they'd shared that explosive kiss.

What are you doing here?" she blurted, hating the way her voice shook at his nearness.

Tanner shoved his hands in the pockets of his jeans and rocked back on his heels. "I was here for a construction consultation with a client. Your brother called me, said you were a damsel in distress, and that you needed a ride back home."

"And here you are, ready to rescue me."

He grinned. "Didn't you know that I moonlight as a knight-in-shining-honor when I'm not building houses?"

She snorted. "How did you know I was at the bus station?"

He smiled then, flashing those dimples that made her heart skitter. "Because I knew there was no way you would've driven seven-and-a-half hours alone on an icy highway. Oh, and Josh told me you took the bus here two weeks ago."

Ellie's eyes narrowed and she crossed her arms. "I don't like driving in the winter. A lot of people don't, and it's closer to an eight-hour drive."

His green eyes crinkled with another grin. "There's no way it takes eight hours to get back to Maine, Ellie. No way."

A line appeared between her brows. "Well, if I go with you, I think we should go slower, and head up through Albany."

He arched a dark brow at her. "Are you going to be navigating this trip?"

"You wouldn't want that. I'd probably navigate us right into the ocean."

The corner of his mouth twitched. "Then let me do it. I'll get you home safe. I promise."

"Why are you willing to give me a ride at all? You've barely said five words to me since..."

His jaw clenched and his eyes dropped to her mouth. "I've had my reasons for staying away from you, Ellie."

She blushed and averted her gaze. "But now you want to travel cooped-up in a car with me for hours?"

"I never said I wanted to," he said, his brows drawing together. "But I'm heading back home anyway, and I might as well take you with me."

"Are you sure? You don't exactly sound thrilled about it."

He blew out a sigh of frustration. "I wouldn't be

here if I wasn't okay with it. And for the record, I have a truck, not a car."

As if that made a difference, they'd still be trapped within the small, confined space and forced to breathe the same air.

Sounded like great fun.

*   *   *

Tanner Riggs took a deep breath and watched her walk across the parking lot, her hips swaying in an enticing way, of which she was obviously unaware.

Ellie Harper.

A girl he'd thought about way too often. Especially since that kiss two years ago, that had spooked the crap out of him.

He'd kissed many women throughout his thirty-three years but that one; that one had gone from chaste to carnal in a nanosecond, and he thought about it all the time.

Way too often.

She was Josh's little sister, which made her off-limits. It went against the Bro Code. Thou shalt not sleep with your bro's sister.

Not cool, man, he told himself. *Don't even think about it.*

He never should've let her kiss him in the first place. It didn't seem to matter how much time and distance he'd put between them either. He could still feel the jerk of the invisible chain that tethered him to her. Distance hadn't broken it, and he was starting to think nothing ever would.

He'd known she had a crush on him, and he never should've encouraged it. He'd been in no position to offer her anything. He didn't do relationships, not after the disaster of his parents' divorce. Moreover, Ellie still believed in happy-endings. She probably still believed in unicorns. She would pin her hopes and dreams on him, he'd end up breaking her heart, and Josh would probably break his nose.

It would cost him a friendship that meant far more to him than a quick roll in the hay. Even if it was with the one woman who always meant more to him than she should.

The snow was coming down heavy now, with big, thick snowflakes and the wind seemed to slice right through the jacket he wore. They both climbed inside his black F-150 and he started up the engine.

"Please, please turn on the heat."

He glanced over at her, she was huddled on the seat of his truck, her arms wrapped tightly around her middle, and her lips were turning an interesting shade of blue.

"It's warm enough in here," he said firmly. "You'll be fine in a minute."

She leaned forward and cranked it up to full blast. She opened the vents and pointed them at herself, sighing with pleasure when the hot air hit her splayed fingers.

He shook his head and steered the truck out of the parking lot. He turned left to head southeast on Steve Flanders Square toward Park Row. "You must hate winter."

"It's not that I hate winter," she said with a shiver. "I just hate being cold."

"Josh couldn't talk long on the phone. He didn't tell me what you were doing in New York," he said casually. "So, was it business or pleasure?"

"I was working. Not that it's any of your concern."

His eyes narrowed. "Friends can't ask about each other?"

"Sure, they can," she said sweetly. "Are we friends, Tanner? Because I don't think *friends* avoid each other for two whole years."

He studied her for a few seconds and then turned his attention back to the road. Only Ellie could go from vulnerable to annoying in no time flat. Which drove him crazy because the last thing he wanted was to be stuck with her for a handful of hours trading barbs.

Not when she kept blushing when she looked at him, worrying that lower lip, and making his mind go places it shouldn't.

"You don't have to take me with you," she said primly, her eyes narrowed. "I can wait for the next bus. It was Josh who asked you to pick me up, not me."

He knew that, and he had no idea why it

bothered him so much. Why *she* bothered him. Why she'd *always* bothered him. "Yes, he did ask me to, and I'm a good friend, so I said no problem."

"Hmm," she said. "Bet you're regretting that.

He frowned at her. "Maybe we shouldn't talk."

"Then don't."

"Fine."

"Fine!"

They both fell silent as he steered his truck down the winding road that led along the coastline. He liked silence. Silence was good. Apparently, she'd warmed up some because she'd stopped hugging herself, and now all her curves were right there, only inches away.

She was curvy and lush and touching her would be a colossal mistake. He knew that, and yet, that hadn't stopped him two years ago. It hadn't stopped that reckless, impulsive kiss from playing on repeat in his head like a stuck record ever since. He could still remember the smell of her skin, and the taste of her lips. How it had felt when she'd slipped those small hands into his hair, and held him tight, as if she never wanted to let him go.

December 22nd.

He'd stopped by to drop off a couple of chairs his dad had made for the Harper's front porch. Ellie had been home alone and invited him in. Instead of heeding the alarms going off in his brain, he'd followed her inside. They'd sat there and talked, drinking eggnog and catching up.

He should've known something was up when she'd walked him to the door. She'd had a small smile on her pretty face as she dropped her head back, and stared up at the mistletoe hanging in the open archway of the living room. He'd barely had time to think before she'd stepped up on tiptoe, grabbed hold of his shoulders and slanted those soft, pink lips against his.

He'd brought his hands up with every intention of pushing her away, but somehow the wires in his brain got crossed and he'd yanked her against him instead. She'd gasped and he'd kissed her the way he'd secretly been wanting to for a long time. Long and deep and wet. He'd pulled her against him, and rocked his hips into hers. She'd gasped again and that time, it did the trick, it brought reality back in stinging clarity.

Josh's little sister, dude. Off-limits. Like, way, way off-limits!

He remembered pushing her away from him a little too roughly, because she'd stumbled back a couple steps. She'd brought trembling fingers up to her lips, stood there staring at him, eyes wide and speechless. Which for Ellie, wasn't an easy feat.

He could still remember the hurt in her eyes when he'd left.

We shouldn't have done that, Ellie. Forget it ever happened.

Yeah, maybe he should practice what he

preached. He thought about that kiss, and about *her* all the time. He couldn't seem to forget the way she'd looked afterward—flushed and breathing heavy, with her eyes dazed and her lips red and swollen from his—she'd been his for those few intense minutes.

His.

He shook his head.

He *had* been avoiding her for the past 24 months. He'd needed to. It was the only way he'd keep his hands off her. He wasn't good at relationships. He never had been, and Ellie was a traditional girl all the way through. She was the kind of girl you took home to mama. The kind you dated, married, and promised forever to.

The kind he'd always stayed away from.

Clearly, she was still upset about the wide berth he'd been giving her. She was sitting over there with her arms crossed, staring out her window and not saying a word. He could smell the orange blossom lotion she'd been using since her teens. It teased his nostrils, and stoked the fire coursing through his veins.

She was wearing dark-blue skinny jeans with tall black boots that looked more stylish than practical. Her jacket was black, fitted, and hugged her body tight. She brought one leg up and crossed it over the other, drawing his attention to those sexy limbs, limbs that he'd imagined...

Eyes on the road, Riggs.

He forced his gaze away from her, clenched his jaw and tightened his hands on the steering wheel until his knuckles turned white. Maybe she bothered him because whenever he was in her presence, he couldn't seem to focus on anything else *but* her.

He shook his head to clear it.

"How's Riggs Construction?" she asked after a while. "Are you still loving it? Has your dad retired yet? What about Tristan and Teague? Have they moved back home to help you guys?"

Tanner sighed, long and loud. "You're going to talk all the way back to Rockport, aren't you?"

She blinked, tossed him a glare, and shut her mouth.

For a nanosecond.

"I guess I am," she said, tipping her chin up. "There's nothing wrong with a little conversation. It's a long drive. I love to talk."

"Lucky me," he muttered. "I thought you were mad at me."

"I am," she said firmly. "But we might as well talk about something."

Letting out another sigh, he glanced at her, and then back at the road. "Fine. About eight months ago, dad had a heart attack and he still isn't well enough to come back to work. Frankly, I don't know that he should at all. The twins moved back officially in November. It's been really good having them around again."

He stiffened when he felt her small hand on his forearm, giving him a gentle squeeze. "Oh, Tanner. That's awful about your dad. Did Josh know? He never mentioned it to me."

He nodded stiffly. "Yeah, I told him. Dad didn't want everyone knowing and fussing over him. He's fine. He hates being told what to do but, yeah, he's fine."

"Well, I'm glad your brothers came back to help run things. Running a business is a lot of work for just one person. Especially a construction business. I know how busy you guys are."

He shrugged. "I've got good workers. It's nice to have the boys back though, even if they are driving me crazy."

The corners of her hazel eyes crinkled. "Trust me, the feeling is probably mutual."

*　　　*　　　*

When Ellie woke up, it was snowing so hard and so thick that she could hardly see a thing. The windshield wipers were swiping furiously, but not really making much of a difference.

She sat up straighter in her seat and gripped the arm of the door.

"We're fine," Tanner told her reassuringly. "I've got winter tires on the truck. We'll be okay."

"When I checked the forecast earlier it said *light* snow," Ellie said, blowing out a sigh. "Not a blizzard."

Tanner shrugged and rubbed the back of his

neck. "Maybe you should write them a letter and complain."

Her eyes narrowed slightly. "I'm just *saying* it would've been nice to be prepared."

He laughed and shook his head. "Weather has always been unpredictable. You get up, it's sunny, and then three hours later it's black and raining. That's why you should always have a back-up plan."

"And I suppose you have one of those?" she asked him, arching one dark brow.

He flashed her a grin and Ellie felt her heart take a nose-dive. She didn't always like him, but lust? Oh, yeah! Just looking at him in those dark wash jeans with the ripped knees, and a black leather jacket, increased her heartrate.

His dark brown hair fell carelessly across his forehead and looked messy, like he'd raked his hands through it half a dozen times.

There were a lot of people travelling along the coast; heading home for the holidays. Quite a few more than she'd expected. Everyone was crawling along the road, and the cars were bumper to bumper.

"Maybe we should stop somewhere for the night and continue driving in the morning," Ellie suggested worriedly. "It's better to be safe than sorry, right?"

"It's Christmas in the morning," he pointed out.

As if she didn't know.

"Yes," she agreed. "And I'd like to be *alive* to enjoy my mom's turkey, thank you very much."

He rolled his eyes. "We're two and a half hours away. That's not very far. We can make it the rest of the way just fine."

"Tanner, this road is super icy," she stated impatiently. "I'd feel better travelling when the sun is up. We can get up early and be there before lunch."

"How would you know if it's icy or not?" he demanded with a scowl. "You've been snoring this whole time."

"Excuse me?" She crossed her arms again. "I do not snore."

He laughed. "You're right, you don't. You just breathe like Darth Vader."

Ellie glared at him, and pointed to a hotel coming up on their left. "Quit arguing with me and turn up there."

Tanner's smile slipped and he sighed as he flipped on the signal light; guiding his big truck into the left lane and then into the parking lot of a local B&B. The lot was jam-packed with snow-covered vehicles, which only seemed to make him grumpier.

"Where are we?" she asked him.

"Connecticut," he told her, frowning. "Hartford. Not far from home. Close enough that we could've kept going."

"A Bed and Breakfast sounds lovely," she said on a dreamy sigh, ignoring him.

He gave her a look as he parked the truck. "You've slept the whole way here. How can you possibly be tired?"

Ellie frowned at him. "I've been working from sunup to sundown for the past two weeks. Working for Cruella Deville. I'm exhausted."

"It's probably the weather," he muttered.

"Maybe it's the company," she said sweetly.

He shook his head as he opened his door and climbed out.

Ellie followed suit, scurrying behind him to get in out of the swirling snow and biting wind. She careened to a stop behind him, and brought her hands up to brace against his back. He stiffened at her touch and frowned at her over his shoulder.

"I bet you're on Santa's naughty list," she whispered. "It's Christmas for goodness sake. Maybe smile at the guy instead of scowling like Ebenezer Scrooge."

His eyes darkened but his lips twitched. Turning back around to face the flustered owner, he stepped closer to the desk. "I'd like to book two rooms please."

Ellie watched the blond man flap his hands helplessly and fidget under Tanner's tight smile. "I'm sorry, sir. This storm came out of nowhere, and a lot of people have stopped to book rooms."

"Isn't that what you want?" Tanner asked,

eyeing the guy up and down. "It's kinda bad for business if people *don't* book rooms."

Ellie smacked his shoulder and stepped in front of him. Glancing up at the man that didn't look much older than her, she gave him a smile and stepped closer to the desk.

His nametag said Tim.

"Do you have any rooms left, Tim?" she asked gently.

"There wasn't a no vacancy sign outside," Tanner pointed out tightly.

"We have one room left," he said, his Adams apple bobbing in his throat as he looked from Ellie to Tanner. "With a double bed."

"A double bed?" Tanner repeated incredulously, his eyes narrowing in irritation. "That's barely big enough for her. Where am I supposed to sleep? On the floor?"

Ellie fixed a bright smile on her face and opened her purse. "Ignore him. We'll take it please."

Tanner nudged her gently out of the way and slapped a couple of bills down on the desk in front of them. "How much for the room?"

"Umm, it'll be eighty dollars, sir," Tim said. "I just need some information from you."

After doing all the check-in procedures, Tim handed Tanner a key with a green keychain that said #6 on it.

"Thank you for your hospitality," Ellie told

him. "Merry Christmas."

Tim flashed her a grateful smile at being able to diffuse the situation, and reign in Tanner's temper. "Merry Christmas, ma'am."

Ellie rotated her stiff shoulders and stretched her neck from side to side, and front to back. She glanced around the room and smiled when she saw the brightly-lit tree in the corner by the front door. There was a tiny nativity scene on a table with a hot pot of coffee and a small stereo. She could hear Elvis singing 'Silent Night', but her smile slipped when her eyes snagged on mistletoe.

It was hanging down from a piece of red velvet ribbon above her. Her eyes slid to Tanner who glanced up as well, and then back down at her. His green eyes darkened, dropped to her lips and his jaw clenched. The fingers of his right hand tightened around the key he was holding.

"Mistletoe," Tim said ever-so-helpfully from the counter. "My wife loves the stuff, hangs it everywhere. She says no lady standing under mistletoe can refuse to be kissed."

"Perfect," Tanner muttered with a scowl. "Just perfect."

Ellie's eyes slid to his lips and of its own free will, her mind wandered and it wondered. *Was his kiss as good as she remembered it being? Would it feel the same?*

He shook his head. "Stop it."

"Stop what?"

"Looking at me like that," he growled.

"H...how am I looking at you?"

"Like you want me to do it," he said, his eyes glittering as he stared at her.

He took a step forward, so that barely an inch separated their bodies, and she had to tilt her head back to see his face. Just breathing caused them to touch; chest-to-chest, thigh-to-thigh, and everywhere in-between.

Ellie couldn't breathe and with effort, she cleared her throat. "I really don't. Want you to, that is."

"Yes, you do."

Oh, boy.

She did.

She so, *so* did.

*   *   *

Tanner stepped closer and slid his arms around her. At the warm, soft feel of her, his brain stuttered to a stop and completely flatlined. He tightened his arms instinctively; his mouth unbearably close to hers as their eyes locked and everything around them seemed to fade to black.

She whispered his name and it sounded like an invitation, one he desperately wanted to take. He closed his eyes and tried to recite all the million reasons why this was a bad idea. She wasn't the type of girl to do things for the sake of doing them. She was an ever-after kind of girl. She wanted a good guy with a nice office job, a nine-to-fiver who would give her a nice home, a minivan, and two kids.

That was so far from who he was, that he almost laughed.

"Tanner?"

He kept his eyes closed as he tried to get himself under control, realizing faintly that he'd always loved the way she said his name.

"Kiss me," she whispered softly. "You're right. I do want you to."

He opened his eyes slowly and stared at her. "This is a really bad idea, but for the life of me, I can't remember why."

He brought his hands up and he lifted her face, looking into her eyes for a long moment before lowering his mouth. He kissed one corner of her lips, then the other, and heard himself moan at the taste of her.

It should have been a simple, closed-mouth kiss, a quick meaningless peck. Only there was nothing simple about it. She revved his engine. He slid one hand up the side of her neck, brushing her dark-blond hair back over her shoulder, and stroked his thumb along her jaw as his mouth teased hers.

When he pulled back, she fisted his shirt and held on tight as if she didn't want to break the connection. A low moan escaped him, and then he was kissing her again. This time; long and slow, deep and wet, and took his sweet time doing so. He kissed her until a lack of oxygen forced them apart.

"I'm really starting to love mistletoe," she panted, sounding breathless.

Tanner didn't know what to think. Personally, he was starting to wonder if the stuff was trying to kill him.

*   *   *

They went back outside into the swirling snow and walked down to their room. Ellie, in boots not made for icy winter conditions, felt like her feet were going to come out from under her on the slippery, snow-covered walkway. She wanted to grab his had so that she didn't slip, but didn't dare. The walk was silent, charged with tension, and thankfully short. When they got to their room, Ellie impatiently tugged the key out of his hand, and unlocked the door.

The room was small, with dated furniture, and muted yellow walls. There was a thick embroidered quilt on the bed with a blue floral pattern. It sat against one wall, with nightstands on either side of it. A brown dresser was against the opposite wall with a TV sitting on it. There was a mini-fridge, a microwave, and a coffee machine. Two blue armchairs sat in front of the window that faced the parking lot.

"I should've asked for a cot," Tanner muttered, staring at the bed.

"That mattress is plenty big enough for both of us," she told him. "This isn't a hotel. They might not even have cots. We'll make do with what we got."

His eyes cut to hers and Ellie felt her stomach bottom out. With just one look, he made her heart race and her breathing shallow. He made her want to be reckless and daring which weren't words that belonged in her shy, inexperienced dictionary. Ellie was smart and practical. She made good choices, or at least she tried to.

Tanner Riggs looked like a beautiful mistake. He didn't date much if at all and he kept to himself. He rocked the dangerous bad-boy persona that intrigued every female on earth, and she was no exception. It certainly drew her in like a moth to a flame.

Did he ever think about her? About that kiss two years ago that had rocked her world?

"I'll sleep on the floor."

His words snapped her back to the present, and got her head out of the clouds.

"Tanner, you're being ridiculous," she sighed. "We can share the bed."

"Not a good idea."

"There's no mistletoe in here," she said with a smile. "I think we're safe."

When he didn't return her smile, Ellie rolled her eyes and tugged her little hard-shell suitcase over to the bed. She lifted it up onto the mattress and opened it. She pulled out her toiletry bag and the red plaid pajamas.

"You're going to melt in those," Tanner told her, amusement lacing his words. "What is that? Fleece?"

"Flannel," Ellie said, glancing up at him.

His lips twitched. "Not much better. You, me and flannel. You're going to cook."

Ellie felt her cheeks heat. "I could always sleep in my underwear and the shirt."

Those intense green eyes darkened. "Not if you want me to keep my hands to myself."

Ellie's eyes rounded and she made a hasty retreat to the bathroom. She changed and splashed cold water on her face. She glanced up and her reflection stared back, looking wide-eyed and flushed.

Holy moly.

She distracted herself by washing her face and brushing her teeth, taking a little longer than necessary, but she could barely breathe with apprehension.

She opened the bathroom door and stopped cold. Tanner was sitting on the end of the bed. He'd taken the coverlet off, leaving only the thin beige blanket and crisp white sheet.

The room was chilly and she shivered; but as she looked across at him, she realized it was more than just the temperature in the room that was giving her goosebumps. Her body vibrated with nerves, her skin felt stretched tight, and her blood was hot in her veins. Looking at all that tanned skin made *her* skin tingle. Her eyes brushed his pecs, traced the lines of his obliques, and lingered on his washboard abs.

Good grief.

Who knew that building houses would give a guy muscles like that?

He was wearing a grey pair of sweats, sitting precariously low on his hips. She managed to avert her gaze; but not before her retinas had scanned his chest and stomach muscles, taking a mental picture, and imprinting the image on her brain so she'd never forget.

Good golly, Miss Molly.

Taking a deep breath, she walked across to the bed and climbed in. He didn't say a word to her, but he flipped off the light, and shrouded them in darkness.

Ellie's heart pounded hard when he climbed in behind her, slid his big hand over her hip, and across her abdomen. He pulled her back against him, and she could feel the heat of those long, strong fingers like a brand. Her back was plastered to his front, and the knowledge of that made her feel lightheaded.

"Breathe, El," he said with a soft laugh. "I'm just holding you until you warm up."

She felt her face heat and took a deep, shuddery breath. Of course, he was. He wasn't holding her because he wanted to. It was on the tip of her tongue to tell him that she wasn't cold—that in fact, she was very hot—but she couldn't find the words.

His breath stirred the tendrils of hair at her nape, making her shiver and his hand fisted in her shirt as if he was having trouble keeping it there, and needed the material to hold him in place.

Now or never, girl.

Taking a fortifying breath, she twisted around to face him and slid her hand up his muscled bicep to the back of his neck. She tangled her fingers in the hair at his nape, and tugged him in a little closer.

"Ellie." There was a warning in his tone, and his body was strung tight with tension. "Turn around."

She shook her head as she put her head on his pillow, and lined up their mouths.

"I knew I should've asked for a cot," he whispered on a sigh. "That you, me, and a bed was a bad idea."

"Tanner."

"Your brother is going to kick my..."

"Please kiss me again," she whispered softly. "*Please.*"

He swore under his breath and shifted closer, his lips mere inches from hers as he spoke in a low tone. "Tell me no, El. Tell me *hell* no."

"Yes."

"*Ellie.*"

She slid her hand down to his chest. She could

feel his heart beating hard and fast beneath her palm. Before she knew what was happening, she closed that last little bit of distance, and placed her mouth on his.

Tanner immediately took charge; sliding his big body on top of hers, he pinned her to the mattress. His arms came up, caging her in, and with his hands cupping her face, he wound his tongue around hers. He licked the top of her mouth, bit her upper lip, and sucked on her lower one.

Ellie arched against him, wrapping her arms around his neck. He slid a muscled thigh between hers, his hands moved down to her waist, and skimmed her sides.

The kiss grew hotter and more intense with every breath, and when he rocked his hips into hers, she let out a needy little whimper. When he slid a hand up under her shirt, along her back, and stroked her bare skin, Ellie shivered.

"*Tanner.*"

"I know," he said against her lips, sounding just as breathless as she was. "Be sure, Ellie."

"I am."

"Really, *really* sure," he said through his teeth.

The lighting in the room was dim. She couldn't make out his eyes, but she reached up and grabbed the back of his neck, and pulled him back down on top of her. She raked her hand through his thick hair, brushing it away from his eyes only to watch it fall back into place.

That seemed to be all the reassurance he needed. He whispered her name before he dropped his mouth back down to hers. They kissed and kissed, over and over, barely coming up for air. They kissed until they were breathing heavy, and kisses were no longer enough.

*   *   *

Tanner woke up tangled in her.

Her satiny-soft legs were entwined with his, her head was on his chest, and her hair was everywhere. She looked so darn cute that he gave in and kissed the tip of her up-turned nose. He watched her eyelids flutter open as she woke up. It surprised him to notice that those hazel eyes of hers, were more green than brown. They caught and held his, and Tanner felt something shift in his chest.

"Merry Christmas," she whispered with a shy, sleepy smile.

"Merry Christmas," he whispered back.

She flushed and he watched, fascinated as it slid down her neck, along her bare shoulders, and across her chest.

She pulled back slowly and he noticed that his arms were reluctant to let her go. He immediately missed her warmth. It was dangerous just how much he liked waking up with her like this, like he could do it every day for the rest of his life.

They'd crossed over into unchartered waters last night but he couldn't bring himself to regret it.

He'd kinda always known it would happen one day, he just hadn't expected it to affect him so deeply. He wasn't an emotional guy, but he suddenly felt the urge to spout poetry, and he knew that it was all her fault.

With a frown, he sat up. "We should probably get dressed and hit the road again."

Ellie nodded and slipped out of bed, taking the sheet with her. He watched her walk into the bathroom.

He loved her.

The realization seemed to rise and wallop him in the face, and it was a good thing he was sitting down, because the knowledge knocked the air out of his lungs.

She messed with his head, and made him want things he'd never wanted before.

*   *   *

Tim and his wife, Lily, had made everyone peach-cobbler along with bacon and eggs for breakfast. It was delicious and Ellie had eaten way too much, while Tanner hardly ate anything at all.

They'd slept in too late and by the time they each grabbed a coffee to go, it was mid-morning.

That's what happens when you wake up in the arms of the man you love and you don't want to move, she thought on a dreamy sigh.

Oh, crap.

Somewhere along the way, her teenage crush had turned into love.

She settled into the passenger seat and stared wide-eyed out the windshield as he drove. He wasn't a morning person and seemed to be lost in his own thoughts. That was fine, she was okay with him being completely unaware of her internal dilemma. Last night had been perfect. He'd been perfect. Loving and gentle but it was messing with her head, as well as her heart.

Probably because you've always loved him and you have no idea how he's feeling.

Inhaling deeply, she glanced out the passenger window and willed her heart to come back down from the stratosphere.

The highway was quiet, but then again, it was Christmas day and everyone else was probably already at home with their families. Being joyous and happy. Looking in their stockings, having breakfast, and opening presents. Displaying love, laughter, and happiness. Reminiscing about the year before and setting goals for the year coming up.

"Do we need to talk about last night?"

Her eyes jerked over to his and she shook her head, her cheeks flushing.

He glanced over at her, his gaze hot and intense. "It was the best Christmas Eve I've ever had, Ellie."

A slow smile shaped her lips. "Me, too."

She peeked at him beneath her lashes and noticed that his shoulders had relaxed and there was a slight smile on is lips. It was then she knew it didn't matter to her if he was broody and scowling, if he barked orders or drove her crazy sometimes.

She loved him anyway.

By the time they made it back to Rockport, and her parents' home on Summer Street, Ellie was feeling anxious to see her family. She loved this old white house, with the big landscaped yard, and all the snow-covered trees. She couldn't understand how anyone could ever leave this place. There was just something about Maine, it didn't matter what time of year it was, there was no place she'd rather be.

There was something about the big Christmas tree in the heart of downtown, and the strings of multi-colored lights that decorated the boats moored in the marina. There was something about the ocean, the salt air, and life always being better at the beach.

Meet me where the sky touches the sea, she thought with a whimsical smile.

There was something about this house, a house that had been reconstructed over the years, and re-imagined by all the wives that had put their own personal touches on it. The open staircase was original and hand-carved, along with the built-in bookcases and fireplace mantels. There was a carriage house with a three-car heated garage and workshop that her dad tinkered in. There were two beautiful gardens that her mom lovingly tended to in the spring, just steps away from the harbor.

"I've always loved this house."

She turned to him in surprise. "You have?"

He nodded. "I was here more often than I was ever at my own house."

That was true, she supposed. He'd always been here; eating her mom's food and raising hell with her brother. Ellie was the same age as Tristan and Teague, seven years younger than Tanner and Josh. The three of them had always managed to get into their own amount of trouble. Especially when the twins would switch places in school. Ellie was usually a co-conspirator, or at least knew about the ruse, and therefore guilty by association.

"You wanted to be around Josh. I get it," she said with a smile. "He has a way with people."

"I didn't just come here to be around Josh, El," he said seriously, his eyes on hers. "One day I looked and you didn't have pigtails anymore. You grew up without me even realizing it, and in that moment, everything changed. You've always tempted me."

Ellie felt her mouth drop open in surprise but before she could say anything, he unbuckled his seatbelt and opened his door. She climbed out too, and walked around the truck, his words playing over and over in her head. *Did he mean them?*

The house was completely lit up. Christmas lights were everywhere; on the house, on the trees in the yard, and each one was a different colour. Green, red, blue, green and yellow. It was beautiful and festive and made Ellie's heart feel full.

When it started snowing lightly, she felt a grin tip up the corner of her mouth and she closed her eyes. She tipped her head back and felt the flakes melt against her heated skin.

She loved this time of year. There was just something about this place at Christmastime.

"Your dad went all out again," Tanner said wryly. "He is aware that no one else in town decorates as much as he does, right?"

Ellie swatted his shoulder with a frown. "He likes it. Leave him alone."

Tanner laughed. "I'm joking. It looks good. It always does."

"I think *your* dad is here."

Tanner craned his neck and furrowed his brow. "Teague's R8 is here, too."

"I imagine they came together. Tristan is probably here, too."

"Nobody tells me anything," he said, rolling his eyes.

"My mom probably invited you all over for Christmas. As you know, it's a whole day affair," Ellie said with a smile. "She's probably made enough food to feed the Army."

Tanner moaned. "Your mom is the best. I can guarantee that the Riggs men would have been eating frozen pizza for Christmas dinner."

Ellie laughed. "Well, we can't have that."

He smiled at her and grabbed her luggage out

of the back. He carried it in for her, and the two of them walked carefully up the icy path to the deck.

Upon opening the door, they were swallowed up by family. Ellie could smell the turkey cooking, and it made her mouth water.

Her mom squealed upon seeing her and hugged her so tight, Ellie felt her eyes bug-out. Tanner and Josh hugged each other and exchanged words that Ellie was curious about because her brother frowned, braced his feet apart, and crossed his arms. Looking every bit, the tough cop she knew him to be. She watched Tanner greet his brothers, his dad, and then slip out of his shoes.

He came back into the foyer, shrugging out of his leather jacket, and his eyes touched hers as he hung it up in the closet. When she was done taking off her coat and scarf, he held out his hand. Ellie set her purse down, took off her coat and unwound her scarf before passing them to him.

She took a quick glance up, but didn't see any of the smooth-edged, evergreen leaves with the clusters of small white berries. She didn't know whether to be relieved or disappointed.

Memories of last night flooded her mind; the smell of his skin, the taste of his lips, and the feel of his hands. She'd loved waking up with him this morning, and could see herself doing it again and again. She could envision them being woken up early in the morning by young children with boundless energy, wanting pancakes and cartoons.

Redirecting her thought process, she glanced around her childhood home. Much like the outside, the inside of the house was decorated, too. Green garland was wrapped around the hand-carved banister of the open staircase. There was the little village of figurines and tiny houses that her mom set up every year on a table in the foyer.

Jane Harper had a fascination with snowmen and every year she would buy herself something to do with them. Everywhere you looked, you saw them. Ellie couldn't help but shake her head as she unzipped her boots and took them off.

She walked into the living room and into her dad's open arms. He hugged her tight and swayed her from side to side. She took a deep breath of Old Spice and let out a sigh.

"She's getting worse," she said with a laugh. "It looks like a snowman sneezed in here."

Henry Harper threw his head back and laughed. "I've tried to reign her in. She will not be tamed. She's even got them in the bathroom."

Ellie giggled.

"Merry Christmas, Ellie-girl?" he said with a dimpled grin. "I'm glad you guys stopped and waited out the storm last night. It was a doozy. We got another 16 centimeters."

"Merry Christmas, dad," she said with a smile. "I'm glad we stopped, too. It got bad fast."

"We could've made it," Tanner said, shrugging one shoulder.

"Not worth it when you have precious cargo."

Tanner's green eyes dropped to Ellie's. "She's definitely that."

"I bet it killed you to stop," Tyler Riggs said, smirking at his eldest son. "Once you get driving, you drive all night."

Tanner shrugged. "The road was icy and Ellie didn't feel comfortable travelling on it in the dark. I probably would've kept driving if I'd been by myself, but keeping her safe was more important."

The twins exchanged knowing looks and grinned. Josh folded his arms and fixed Tanner with a thoughtful, assessing look.

The Christmas tree was real and smelled so good, fresh and earthy, like home and hearth. It was decorated to the nines. Everything from hand-made ornaments she and Josh had made growing up, to big glass bulbs and sparkly red ribbon, that was wound all the way around it. There was a red and gold angel holding torches that sat on the top.

Her parents had gone overboard on the presents again this year. Every gift had been perfectly wrapped and placed just so. Ellie always wondered why people made such a big deal out of presents looking so good, when the paper just got ripped up and recycled anyway.

"How was the trip?" Jane Harper asked, interrupting her thoughts.

Ellie's eyes shot to Tanner's and she felt her face get all blotchy. "Fine."

"Hmm," Jane said thoughtfully, glancing between them.

"We stopped at this cute little B&B in Hartford."

Her mom wrapped an arm around her shoulders and steered her toward the kitchen, where they could be alone and have a well-needed mother-daughter heart to heart.

"So, what happened in Hartford?"

"Things got a little complicated."

Her mother raised a fist in the air. "Praise the lord!"

"Mom!" Ellie said with a laugh. "Shh. They'll hear you."

"Not those guys," she said dryly. "They're probably out there talking sports. They won't hear us. We're safe in here, so give me the nitty gritty."

Ellie shook her head at her. "We encountered some mistletoe."

Jane smiled. "That seems to be your thing with Tanner. So, the two of you kissed or what?"

"Or what."

"I see," Jane said softly. "He's always had a soft spot for you."

Ellie snorted. "He's barely acknowledged my existence for the past two years."

Jane's eyes softened on her face. "He watched you grow up and turn into a beautiful young woman. He probably told himself he was too old for you or some such nonsense. I imagine it has more to do with your brother than anything else. Josh's approval will matter most to him."

"Do you approve?"

"I've always known you'd end up with him, Ellie. A mother knows best. He's a good man, with a successful business," she shrugged. "Of course, I approve. He's always been a tad moody but you can handle him."

"Mom," Ellie said with a laugh. "I know you love 'Tangled', but the *mom* in that movie is controlling and creepy."

"Fine. She's creepy," Jane reluctantly agreed. "What I'm trying to say is that I've always had a feeling that the two of you would fall for each other eventually."

"He's not all that easy to read," Ellie whispered. "I don't know how he feels."

"I think you do. Plus, you told me that the two of you..."

"I did not!"

"You didn't have to, baby," Jane said with a laugh. "Your face told me everything I needed to know."

*   *   *

Tanner watched Ellie put on the diamond earrings her parents got her, and hug Josh tight for giving her a gift certificate to one of the local spas. She looked beautiful and happy. He couldn't seem to stop looking at her like she was the only other person in the room, only she wasn't, and he was drawing attention to himself. The twins were giving him weird looks, and his dad was smirking at him.

"You got it bad, don't you?" Teague asked him, bumping his shoulder with his own.

He frowned. "I do not."

Teague laughed. "Dude, it's written all over your face."

Tanner frowned. *Well, that's awesome.*

"What are we talking about?" Josh asked as he stepped into the semi-circle.

"Nothing," Tanner said, glaring at the twins.

They just grinned back at him, the jerks.

"Tanner's got the hots for your sister," Tristan blurted, pointing a finger at him.

Josh's eyes shot to Tanner's. "Is that so?"

Tanner shook his head. "Ignore him. He was dropped as a child."

Tristan rolled his eyes, and shook his head.

Josh folded his arms across his chest. "Is it true? Do you have a thing for Ellie?"

Tanner blew out a sigh. "It's complicated."

"Always is when it involves a woman," Teague muttered.

Tristan chuckled softly, earning him a glare from his look-alike. They shared one of their creepy *twin-tuition* looks. The one where they appeared to read each other's thoughts, which usually meant they were up to no good.

That look had always freaked Tanner out.

"Did something happen between you two?" Josh asked him. "At this *cute* little B&B?"

He didn't sound angry, but he had that intense stare going on. The one Tanner had seen him make countless times growing up. The one that had given him a reputation for being a tough cop, a cop that was good at his job.

"What was the question again?"

Josh's eyes narrowed. "Have you made a move on my sister?"

"Define *move*," Tanner said cautiously.

Tristan whistled low. "Wrong answer, big brother."

"Fine," Tanner said tightly. "If we're going to stand here and gossip like a couple of old ladies, then, yeah, last night..."

Josh held up his hands and slammed his eyes shut. "Never mind, forget I asked."

Tristan burst out laughing. "This is the best Christmas to date. Tanner looks like he's about to have a stroke. Getting all hung up over a girl. A girl that used to run around in mud-caked overalls, and follow him around like a lost puppy."

Tanner shoved him, knocking him into Teague who in turn, shoved him back. They got all up in each other's faces.

"Boys!" Tyler Riggs barked, his bushy white brows narrowed as he stared at them. "Knock it off. What are you, twelve?"

Teague smirked, stood up straight, and gave

their dad a salute. "Yes, sir."

Dad rolled his eyes, but a grin tugged at his lips.

"Do you have feelings for her?" Josh demanded. "Or are you just using her?"

Tanner glared at him. "Of course, I have feelings for her. I'd never use her and you know it."

They both stood there staring at each other for a long, measurable moment and then Josh's fierce expression slipped, and he grinned.

"I know you wouldn't. I'm just messing with you."

Tanner frowned at him. "You're messing with me?"

Josh's broad shoulders shook as he laughed. "It was fun. You should've seen your face."

"I almost had a heart attack," Tanner muttered on a groan, closing his eyes and pinching the bridge of his nose with his thumb and forefinger. "You had your cop-face on, I thought you were going to shoot me."

Josh smirked and shook his head. "Too much paperwork. I hate paperwork. I can take it out and point it at you though. If that'll make you feel better."

Tanner let out a sigh but it didn't do anything to alleviate the pressure at the back of his skull. "I'll pass, thanks."

Josh shook his head, a grin still on his face. "You've always been easy to rile. How long has this been going on?"

"Nothings really been going on. I've stayed away from her the last two years."

Josh frowned at him. "I may be a little slow on the uptake, but even I noticed you stopped coming around here as much as you used to."

"That's when I kissed her for the first time. Two Christmases ago."

"So, that's why you stopped coming around. I thought you just got busy with clients, building houses, and didn't have time to hang out. Little did I know you were just running scared."

Tanner rolled his eyes at his friend and blew out a sigh. "I wasn't running."

"Have you told her how you feel yet?" Teague asked him. "Just do it, man. Rip the Band-Aid off. You'll feel better," he frowned slightly. "...or worse...depending how you look at it."

Tanner shook his head. "Been denying it a long time, and I'm not all that good with words."

"So, don't tell her," Tristan shrugged. He dipped his hand into the candy dish on the coffee table, tossed some red and green peanut M&M's into his mouth, and chewed loudly. "Show her."

Tanner glanced across the room, Ellie looked up at him, and time seemed to stand still. She was wearing one of those Christmas sweaters, bright red with a white poinsettia pattern all over it. It was cheesy and ridiculous, but she looked so dang cute that he couldn't hold it against her. Suddenly, he couldn't remember why he'd fought this for so long, how he felt about her.

"Go talk to her, man," Teague said. "She's been crushing on you her whole life. Since we were kids."

"Tanner," Josh clapped a hand to his shoulder and squeezed. "You know I don't object, right? She's been in love with you forever, and I've seen the way you look at her even though you're good at hiding it. Just make her happy, dude."

His eyes shot to his best friend. "You're seriously okay with me dating her?"

Josh shrugged. "She could do worse."

Tanner laughed. "Gee, thanks, I think."

"I've always thought of you as a brother, Tan," Josh said seriously. "If you play your cards right, that could become a reality."

She's been crushing on you her whole life.

She's been in love with you forever.

Did he love her back?

The answer was simple.

He always had.

The room seemed to spin, his vision blurred, and he swayed on his feet. He grabbed a hold of Teague's shoulders, and held him tightly. The air was sawing in and out of his lungs, and he felt lightheaded. His heart was jackhammering against his ribs in a steady rhythm. *Thud, thud, thud.*

"What's the matter with him?" Tristan asked warily, taking a step back like whatever it was, might be contagious. "He looks like he's going to pass out. If he pukes, I'm out of here."

"He's in love," Josh said, stepping forward and slapping Tanner hard on the back. "Breathe, man. I don't think it's fatal."

Tristan took another step back, eyes wide and wary. "Love does that? Gives a dude an anxiety attack? Sounds like fun."

"Only love can make a guy that unsteady," Teague muttered. "Tanner, breathe. You're fine. Just go talk to her."

Ellie must have noticed him wigging out, because she crossed the room and reached for him. "Are you okay? Do you need to sit down? What's the matter?"

He shook his head, brought his hands up, and slid his fingers into her hair. He pulled her forward until her body brushed his, dropped his forehead to hers, and inhaled her orange blossom scent. He stood there for a few silent moments, holding her to him. Just like that, his vision cleared, and his heartrate went back to normal. He lifted his head, and his eyes snagged on hers.

She anchored him.

Ellie's hazel eyes rounded. "I do?"

Crap.

He hadn't meant to say that out loud, but it was the truth. She did something to him, and she always had.

"Can I talk to you?" he asked her. "Alone?"

"Of course, you can, love," Jane said, standing

up and snapping her fingers.

With a smile, she ushered everyone else out of the room so they could have some privacy. Josh grinned at him, Teague winked, and Tristan grabbed more M&M's and made kissy faces at him. Jane was the last to leave, and she smiled over her shoulder as she went.

He cupped Ellie's face in his hands, and watched her eyes dilate, and the pulse in her throat jump. He watched his thumb stroke lazily back and forth across her jaw.

"What are you doing?" she asked, her eyes searching his. "There's no mistletoe in here."

Tanner smiled. "I don't need mistletoe as a reason to kiss you, El."

"You don't?"

He shook his head. "I never have. I kissed you two years ago because I realized I wanted you. I kissed you last night because I realized I love you. Pretty sure I always have."

Her eyes seemed to melt. "You love me?"

He nodded. "I do."

"I love you, too," she whispered. "The mistletoe kisses only made me love you more."

Slipping an arm around her waist, he pulled her against him, and slanted his mouth across hers. She kissed him back, slipping her fingers into the hair at the back of his neck, and drawing him closer. When she let out a little whimper, he was lost. He slid his hand up her back, and pulled her flush against him.

Tanner meant to keep it light, but like always, Ellie scattered his braincells. He kissed her deep, biting down on her bottom lip before relaxing his hold. He slid his hands down her arms to her elbows and took a tiny step back.

Tristan opened the door to the kitchen, and poked his head out into the living room. "Hurry up and pour your heart out, Tan, I'm starving."

Teague smacked the back of his head, yanked him back in, and shut the door.

"Those two," Ellie said with a laugh. "How do you put up with them?"

"No idea," Tanner muttered. "I remember asking for a brother when I was a kid. I guess be careful what you wish for. I didn't know they came in two's. Maybe they're like gremlins, Teague got wet, and multiplied."

Ellie burst out laughing. "They're not *that* bad. You make them sound like devil spawn."

"Not Teague," Tanner said with sly grin. "But Tristan? Definitely."

Ellie laughed again.

Tanner sobered and stroked his thumb across her cheek.

"Can you forgive me for being an idiot and wasting so much time?" he asked her, tucking her hair behind her ear. "And for not making you mine years ago?"

She smiled up at him, looking so darn happy

that his heart rolled over and exposed its tender underbelly. His chest felt so tight. Like his heart had swelled up behind his ribs, was pushing up against his lungs, and making it hard for him to breathe.

"I've always been yours," she said softly. "I'll stay that way so long as you keep kissing me."

Tanner grinned. "Sounds good to me."

The End

Afterword

A note from the author, Megan Riley

Thanks for reading our box collection – Beneath the Mistletoe

And... thank you so very much for reading my short story, **Mistletoe Kisses.**

I hope you enjoyed reading it, as much as I enjoyed writing it. I'm a sucker for happy-endings and I hope you are, too.

If you liked my story, please take a few minutes to leave a review. Your feedback is greatly appreciated.

Sincerely, Megan

Give me a shout:
Write to me, I'd love to hear from you.
My email: RileyWrites@hotmail.com

Dark to Dawn by Sandra Hunter

~*~*~

Haunted by bad nightmares, Jake is forced to deal with his demons so his family can enjoy their first Christmas together in four years.

A short story
- Dark to
Dawn

Jake let the night air chill the sweat off him. Drawing deeply on his cigarette, he massaged at the pounding ache in his chest. With a grimace, he clenched his hands between his knees and hung his head.

Same friggin' nightmare every time.

They're in the LAV-25, patrolling in the Brown Zone when it happens. The explosion, blowing them apart—a god-awful ear-splitting crack, and then a sensation of flying through a hot, soundless tunnel toward a distant light. This is it, he thinks, and then somebody's screaming … he can

hear that even over the ringing in his bloody ears.
Ammo's cooking off … oh-my-God! I gotta help …

Gusting a smoky exhale, Jake levered upright
and paced the knotted wood planks of his back deck.
He scrubbed at sweat in the bristles of his hair. Jody
was crying—she'd wanted to put some coffee on and
come sit with him.

"No,*"* he'd said.

He didn't mean to be abrupt—she ached to
help.

But she can't understand what it was like.
Jake shrugged a shoulder. *Anyway, she's always gotta
get up early with Ryan in the morning.*

The corner of his mouth quirked upward.
She's putting her heart and soul into Christmas.

"This is extra special, Jake," she'd said, "the
first time in four years we've been able to be together
for Christmas."

Christmas. Jake rested his shoulder against
the porch post. Last Christmas all he could dream
about was being home—Lord God how he'd missed
them.

Now here I am—and I just can't connect, not
with family, not with friends, or the familiar folks in
town.

I'm hurting them, he thought. *The people I
love the most.* Chaplain says, '…it'll get better with
time…'

Hooah.

Father McDowell said to pray. Okay for *him* to say—he's got a direct line. *Do I even remember how?* The other night he had stood in the hall by his son's room and heard Ryan at prayer with his mother, ".... and God bless daddy and make him not be 'stressed'."

Jake coughed into his fist and stood there a moment with his eyes squeezed shut, as he fought down the urge to bawl like a baby. *Weak, that's what.*

He twisted his cigarette butt into the root ball of the Christmas pine, and then flicked it out into the dark.

***

Jody listened to Jake pacing the length of the cedar deck that ran the width of the house. Back and forth, pausing now and then. He loved her and Ryan—he'd been doing so much better the last couple of months, but now it's like he's distancing himself again. The nightmare, and he was back to sometimes just sitting and staring off—he doesn't even hear Ryan trying to get his attention.

It broke her heart to see her small son subside, staring at his dad's expressionless face—but then he'd shuffle closer to his daddy's chair and sit leaning against Jake's leg as if to keep him company. She felt so helpless to know what to do.

Jake used to be such a vibrant guy—he had a smile to die for. Her mouth curved.

He'd seemed more like the old Jake today—putting up the Christmas lights, and playing ball with Ryan. Then it was like a switch went off.

"That's enough, son," he'd said, and turned to come into the house. He'd dropped into his chair in front of the TV, and turned on TSN.

Drying the dishes, Jody watched him as she walked back and forth, opening and closing the cupboards. His eyes weren't even on the screen, he was doing that thing—what did Dax call it, '*the thousand-yard stare*'.

Jody sighed. Maybe Dax'll come and visit again soon. Jake *talks* to him—they went to battle school together, and had been on the same tour for a while.

***

Ryan thumped the ball into his mitt thoughtfully, and then brightening, he sprinted into the house and down the hall to his bedroom. He yanked his camouflage patterned comforter off the bed onto the floor, where he mounded the material and shaped it just so.

It's gotta look like the desert where they're patrolling.

Then he got his box of Army Combat Soldiers, and their armored vehicles down off the shelf. He placed his favorite army guy, Buddy, in the recon vehicle ... *daddy always used to be Mike, my second favorite guy. Mike can drive the Humvee.*

When everything looked right, Jake went into the TV room.

"Daddy. I need you to come."

"Not now, Ryan."

"I really need to show you something." Ryan tugged on his dad's hand until at last his dad stood, and Ryan pulled him into the hallway and toward his room. Letting go of his hand at the doorway. Ryan dropped to knees at the edge of his contoured comforter *badlands*. With an inviting glance at his dad, he started moving the recon Lav-25 around a low "hill". He rumbled in his throat, a well-practiced Detroit-Diesel engine sound, and then as he completed the turn he made M4 carbine gunfire noise: "ratta-ratta-ratta" and then "buhboom!" explosion.

Ryan looked up at his dad where he leaned against the doorjamb, his wide smile revealed where his top front baby teeth had recently come out, "You can be Mike, dad— here, see?"

His smile faltered at the strange, fixed expression on his dad's face as he stared at the recon vehicle lying on its side, wheels still spinning and "Bud" thrown into a deep fold of the comforter.

"Ryan..." His voice was rougher than he'd

meant and he saw his son startle. "Son," he said, as he bent down, snatching up the combat toys and tossed them into the tattered box, "I don't want you playing with these … get a book and read, like your mother's always asking you to."

Jake turned at the doorway, and paused— seeing the stricken look on his child's face.

Jake's scrubbed the back of his neck and his jaw muscle pulsed.

Christ. What am I doing to him…?

"Look, son, maybe if it's clear tonight we can get out the telescope and check on Orion. Okay?"

He left the room with the box of Army Combat Desert Action Figures tucked under his arm.

"Hey," greeted Jody as she heard Jake walk into the kitchen. She glanced up from chopping vegetables and saw Ryan's toy box under Jake's arm.

"What's up?"

"I'm just stashing these away for a while," he said, pushing the box to the back of a high cupboard. "I'll get him some new *Lego* or something to replace it."

Jody suddenly realized she was twisting the dishtowel and tossed it on the counter. "He *loves* that combat set—he played with it all the time you were gone. He'd even say that, 'as long as Buddy comes back from his battles, daddy will too.'"

"Yeah. Well, I'd just like to see him playing more with his other toys."

Jody chewed her lip, and then turned to wipe the chopping board. "Papa Joe called. They'll be here in time for dinner tomorrow."

Dad. "That's great." *'Buck-up, son—for Jody and the boy's sake...'*

"Joe fought in Vietnam, right, hon? Maybe you can talk to him, soldier to soldier," Jody's voice faltered, "about this nightmare."

Jake wandered to the fridge and stood hanging on the door as he peered in. "What's that? That looks real good..." He turned and grinned back at her.

Her heart bumped. That was the old Jake's wonderful smile—the smile she'd been missing. "It's just apple pie..." and she grinned.

"You made my favorite," Jake winked, and then turning back, he slowly closed the fridge door. He remained there a moment, bracing his arms against the door. He quietly said, "They're just dreams, Jode. They'll stop. I don't want you to worry."

***

Jody was just on the verge of sleep when Jake moaned. His body jerked in a violent spasm, and she knew he was reliving that awful event ... she rested her hand gently on his shoulder. *Dear God,* she prayed, *help him to forgive himself for having lived when the others died.*

***

The dream was different this time. It was night, not day. He was still face-down in the dirt, but there was no burning—no screaming behind him. Quiet. He rolled over onto his back with no pain. The night sky was thick with stars. One was particularly bright. *Rocket Flare?* He blinked, then squinted, trying to clear his sight. He's seen that before, back in two thousand, just before he deployed to Afghanistan. It'd been a conjunction of Venus and Jupiter, looked like the brightest star he'd ever seen. This looked just the same.

There was a small hill behind him. Maybe he could get his bearings. He did a low crawl up the hill, and nearing the top, dropped to his belly. He could hear the sounds of livestock and, faintly, human voices below. It was easy to survey—that star lit the whole area. Just a small village—much like any other. Mud buildings, no windows. The one right below him was larger than the others and had a cave dug in the limestone hill behind it. Jake observed the clay jars stacked to one side and a few sacks of grain. Obviously used as a storeroom and livestock shelter. *Huh, but the sheep are still out in the pen ... even though it's night.*

Jake checked out the town. Dead quiet. No

one around—no vehicles of any kind parked anywhere.

A donkey, browsing in the sheep pen, raised its head and brayed. It trotted to the rough fence and strained its neck toward someone emerging from the limestone cave below.

Then Jake saw a woman holding an infant. *Looks newborn.* That'd be the father waiting outside. Jake could hear their voices, though faintly. The young mother looked toward the waiting man and softly called. Jake watched the father stride eagerly forward to take and hold his new son, and felt his own throat clench as he remembered holding Ryan in his arms for the first time. The newborn was tightly wrapped in white cloth, but Jake could see the curve of the small cheek. The father kissed the child's forehead and handed him back to the woman. Another figure, a teen-age boy, approached from the shadows. Not a family member, Jake guessed, as he waited diffidently to be acknowledged by the new parents. At the father's nod, he came forward and appeared to congratulate the father. You'd think he'd never seen a baby before—the way the kid stared as the young mother tenderly laid the infant in a straw-filled trough. The kid then did a strange thing. After bending his head respectfully toward the mother and child, he lifted a ram's horn looped on a thong across his chest and blew a long, sonorous note into the night.

It was at that moment that the child's father turned his head and looked straight at where Jake lay on the hill. The man's visage was as clear to Jake as if viewed through a scope, especially the lucent brown eyes that met his with, not fear or concern, but warmth—as if he were greeting a friend. The father beckoned him, and gestured to the child in its mother's arms.

Jake's heart pounded, and he rolled on his back. *Me! I'm not worthy...what if I frighten the child...*

The eroded hills and desert expanse around him were blue-hued, bathed in an unearthly light. As the ram's horn note faded, Jake heard a strange sound, almost a hum...*like the sound the northern lights emit sometimes*, Jake thought.

The humming was getting louder—Jake felt it as a vibration coursing through him and with it a sensation of pure love. He blinked away tears as the brilliant star blurred to an all-encompassing light.

He *had* to look again.

The infant's father still patiently watched for him. He nodded, beckoned again, and then moved to stand with the mother and child.

Jake, his breath tight in his chest, rose to his feet.

***

Jake woke from the dream to find Jody leaning over him, tears filling her eyes as well.

"Jake, are you coming back to me?" She touched his face gently as she looked at him, her eyes searching and filled with wonder.

Jake clenched her to him, "Jody, it wasn't the nightmare—it was a miracle."

***

Ryan bounced on their bed, "Wake up! Wake up! It's Christmas!"

Jody and Jake disentangled, laughing.

"I'm putting the coffee on," Jody said, "that *has* to be first order of the day." She hugged Ryan, and kissed his cheek, "Merry Christmas, sweetheart! You two hang on; I've got a special breakfast pretty much ready to go. I'll call you in a couple of shakes."

Jody watched as Jake tossed Ryan in the air—it looked like a wrestling match would soon be under way. She grinned through tears at seeing Jake being playful again.

What is it Ryan called it when he squeeled with excitement—a happiness explosion? Walking down the hallway, she wrapped her arms around herself—yes, she thought, it feels just as if her happiness must explode outwards.

Their laughter followed her down the hallway.

***

When Jake scooped Ryan up and carried him to the kitchen, Jody already had coffee mugs, scrambled eggs and a plate of muffins on the kitchen counter.

Jake sniffed the air, and flashed that electric smile she so loved. "…and pumpkin muffins—mmm."

"What'd you say, little man," he looked down at Ryan, "do we execute a reconnaissance of the muffins?" Jake reached his hand toward the plate.

"Yeah! Recon!" Ryan agreed, leaning forward.

"No, you don't, you two," Jody fended off Jake's hand from hovering over the muffins. "We're eating, in the dining room, if you please." Jody took possession of the plate. Giving them an arch look, she wafted the fragrant baking under their noses, leading them into the next room.

Jake put Ryan on his feet. "Every man for himself, son," and he winked as he followed Jody to the table.

Jody halted in front of their little Nativity scene set up on the dining room buffet. "Oh—" she blinked a moment at the Nativity setting, "why, Ryan, honey, what a sweet thing to do." She touched his cheek with her fingers.

Waiting at the table, Jake pulled out her chair

with elaborate courtesy, meanwhile planting a kiss on her ear.

Jody whispered, "hon, I thought you'd put all the toy soldiers away?"

Jake raised his brows and Jody tipped her head toward Ryan and the Nativity scene.

It was Ryan's favorite task on Christmas Eve to set up the nativity. There was the small wooden stable, with Mary, Joseph and the Christ Child inside. The shepherd knelt just outside, with the three grazing lambs close by. A cow and donkey flanked the stable, resting on their ceramic grass.

Jake's brow furrowed in puzzled surprise as he continued to take in Ryan's set-up of the nativity—alongside the three Wise Men bearing the traditional gifts of gold, frankincense and myrrh—knelt Ryan's favorite toy soldier, Buddy.

Jake stared a long moment, and then dropping to his knee, pulled his son into his arms.

"Dad, you're squishing me."

"Love you, son," Jake said, his voice muffled against Ryan's shoulder.

"Love you too, dad."

Jake stood. His hand scrubbed the back of his neck as he looked again at the toy soldier.

Walking back to Jody, he wrapped his arms around her shoulders and nestled his face in the crook of her neck.

Jake smiled as he watched his parents hug, and then he too looked again at the Nativity Scene. His small brows twitched as he stared, and he sucked a small whistle through the gap where his front teeth used to be.

Finally, he whispered, "but, Buddy, *how* did you get there?"

The End

Afterword

A note from the author, Sandra Hunter

Thank you for reading our box collection – *Beneath the Mistletoe.*

And... thank you so very much for reading my short story, **Dark to Dawn.**

I hope you enjoyed reading it, as much as I enjoyed writing it.

If you liked reading this collection, please take a few minutes to leave a review. Your feedback is greatly appreciated.

Sincerely, Sandra

Memories
by Phyllis
Chubb

~*~*~

Now that I'm alone many things have changed in my life but nothing can touch my memories. Each burn as bright in my heart as when they first happened.

A short story
- Memories

Now that I'm alone many things have changed in my life, but nothing can touch my memories. Each burn as bright in my heart as when they first happened.

One event changed my life, providing me with riches beyond my wildest dreams. It started in August, thirty-two years ago, and sustains me today.

It was Friday. As my regular habit, I went to the designated place, this time an Italian restaurant in Gas Town, to meet my friends. The group of us had gone to school together. Since graduation, ten years earlier we met the last Friday of every month. This way we maintained connection and supported each other through the ups and downs of life. Everyone in the group had married and had at least one child except me. My life was the simple one. I worked and loved my work as an architect. It was my whole world.

Coming in from sunlight to the darker restaurant, it took a moment for me to see where everyone was. One member of the group noticed me and stood up so I could see where to go. Walking up to the table, I wasn't surprised to see a stranger in the midst. For some time now getting me hooked up was the main aim of the group, and this stranger might be another attempt to set me up.

As I neared the table, Evelyn stood up to greet me, and introduced Jim, who leapt to his feet as well. If I live to be a hundred, I will never forget how my heart raced as I put my hand out to this man. I couldn't remember ever feeling so clumsy, so nervous. My heart pounded hard when I shook his hand. I thought everyone heard it. I must have looked like an idiot and felt like one as I tried to balance myself by holding on to the back of a chair. Later, my friends assured me I looked the picture of composure which proves how looks can be deceiving.

I had just met the only man who touched my heart, and my befuddled brain slowed my ability to talk. According to my friends the dinner conversation went well, and I hadn't made a fool of myself. If only they knew the panic raging within me. I have no recollection of the conversation over the evening. What I do remember is how I didn't want the evening to end. I wanted Jim to stay in my world. Of course, I said nothing about how I felt. At the end of the evening, Jim and I shook hands and passed the common niceties, "Good to meet you" type of comments.

All I could remember was him saying, "We'll meet again". From my point of view, another meeting couldn't happen fast enough.

***

Six horrible days passed before a call came to my office from a Mr. MacLeod. I knew no one by that name, so answered abruptly.

"Laurie Patterson speaking, how may I help you"? The voice on the other end froze my brain as I recognized Jim's voice.

"The best thing you can do for me is to agree to go for dinner with me tomorrow night".

I wanted to yell "Yes, I've been *waiting for you to call*", but I didn't say a word. Rather, I tried to play cool, so hummed and hawed for at least three seconds before agreeing to go. I still remember how the importance my work faded after the call. The most important thing I could think of achieving was getting my hairdresser to fit me in at four pm the next day. Her schedule was always tight but she agreed. I decided I would give her a five-dollar tip! In those days five dollars was a lot of money.

Time had stood still, but as always happens, the

next day finally arrived. Lunch hour involved no food, but lots of shopping. I had to have a new outfit. Jim was to arrive at six-thirty pm and with my hair done, I arrived home with only fifteen minutes to spare. Thank God, I hadn't had time to worry about whether he would show up or not. Right on time the buzzer sounded. I still laugh when I think about how I leaped to press the open button with such force I tripped and stumbled. In my mind's eye, I could see myself lying in a lump on the floor. So much for being attractive. I was still laughing as I opened the door.

Jim was as handsome as I had remembered. It hadn't been my imagination. The evening was beautiful, but bedamned if I can remember much of our initial conversation beyond him saying he hadn't been able to get me off his mind. I found the strength to say I had the same problem.

After our dinner, we took our first of countless walks on the sea wall, and there I learned about his life and his work. His goal was to have his own construction company. Listening to him talk about his love of building, I was delighted that it fit perfectly into my dreams of designing. I know I must have shared my story too, and I still have the napkin on which we co-designed our first house in a coffee shop on Robson Street, that evening.

The first date led to more dates – all of which fed my imagination. My world and my focus changed in a dramatic way. I could see myself walking down the aisle, even though there had been no discussion pointing to such an event. I even dreamed about a honeymoon.

Christmas was coming, and I'd convinced myself there would be a ring under the tree for me. As we got closer and closer to Christmas day, Jim seemed to act strange. Two days before Christmas, he told me he had to leave. His Aunt, who lived in Edmonton, needed him. I didn't know he had an Aunt in Edmonton. He never spoke of her, but he had talked a great deal about his parents. He said he had no choice but to go, and he would try to be back by New Year's Eve. I was heart-broken, but I tried not to show him how smitten I was, or how disappointed.

Christmas day came. My heart was not into the festivities. The only bright spot I could think of would be to see my sister. She and her family arrived Christmas Eve, the first time I'd seen her in six years. Their only child, a little girl called Kara, was now five years old. I expected to enjoy her innocence over Christmas and her excitement about Santa. It had been years since a child had been present for Christmas. Mom, Dad and I all looked forward to some childish delights. We had convinced ourselves Kara's ingenuousness would put a spark into the festivities of the day. The child we got was not the child we thought we were getting.

The spark, and there was a spark, was created

by Kara's non-ending string of questions and statements. The first question she asked, shocked me.

Screwing her face up, she stared at me and asked, "Why aren't you married? My mom says you'll be an old maid."

You could have knocked me over with a feather. I swallowed hard and stared at my sister, who looked as shocked as I felt. I don't know whose eyes were open wider, mine or hers. She looked like she would say something, then slammed her mouth shut. She was aware any words she could offer would dig the hole deeper.

After taking a deep breath, I responded. "Being an old maid isn't a bad thing. Besides, I'm still young and have years ahead of me for things such as marriage".

My answer seemed to please her based on how she responded, "Me too, I don't want to marry either. It's no fun". Now it was my turn to look at my sister and frown. Was she having difficulty in her marriage? Were things not going so good for her? She had married in a rush and knew Dave only for a short time before marrying him.

Inside I affirmed to myself "*I wouldn't make such a mistake*".

The moment those words rang within me, another little voice said, "*Liar*". Yes, those words had been a lie. I had hoped Jim would at least hint at altering my status and Christmas, in my mind, was the perfect opportunity. But now he wasn't even with me. I'd tried telling myself I didn't care, but I cared, to the core of my being.

Mom noticed my usual up spirit was soggy and gave me a hug and some words of wisdom: "You never know what lays around the corner dear, have faith". My faith was thin. There hadn't even be a phone call that morning.

I told Mom about Jim the morning after our first date. I even brought him to meet my parents, and that was a first. Since then, there had been many gatherings with my parents as Dad and Jim got along like long lost buddies. Jim had even included them on our dates. Dad said he was the finest fellow he had met in a long time. The pair of them would get talking and leave Mom and I to twiddle our thumbs. After meeting Mom and Dad the first time, Jim raved about my parents. He claimed his parents would like them too. He was disenchanted about them being on the other side of the country and said it would be awhile before I got to meet them.

We'd had four months of being joined at the hip, seeing each other daily. Now he disappeared, as if he had dropped off the edge of the earth.

I spent Christmas Eve with a friend and went to my parents on Christmas day. As soon as I got there, Mom had a list of tasks she wanted me to help her with. This was unusual behavior for Mom so I asked her if she was trying to keep me busy.

"No, not really, I just need some help". Then she gave me a hug and asked me to prepare the guest room, just in case more people arrived. I agreed to help, but my heart wasn't in it.

When I asked who she was expecting, she looked at me with complete innocence, "I don't know dear, but someone might come, we never know, so best to be ready". I thought nothing of what she had said, my parents always had an open door and a busy guest room, so god only knew who would be arriving.

Dinner would not be on the table until after 4 pm, and I had done everything she asked, so I excused myself and went to my old room where I tried to sleep. I was thinking it would be better to be asleep with a broken heart then trying to tell the world everything was just fine. Sleep didn't come. What came were a multiple of replays showing the dates we'd enjoyed since meeting. Until today, Jim had always been considerate at every turn. He was a romantic clear through to his bones. He was the one to remember our anniversary of meeting. To my regret, I often forgot until he brought it up.

I heard voices, but not recognizing them I rolled over and shut my eyes again. There were always new people in the house and I would meet them when I went down to dinner. I didn't have to wait long as my sister was soon at my door.

She knocked and said, "time to come down for dinner, I suggest you come right away". She always was bossy, and I never moved fast enough to please her. After getting up I looked in the mirror. To the best of my ability I tried to paint on a happy face, but there was nothing I could do about the flat light in my eyes. Down I went to meet the new people.

As I walked into the living room Dad got up to introduce me first to Gordon and then to Sylvia. "Please welcome our new friends", he said. Nothing strange about meeting new people except it felt odd for him to ask me to welcome their friends.

No sooner I sat down then Sylvia said, "It's good to meet you, we've heard a great deal about you".

To which I replied, "our parents are biased".

Sylvia ignored my words and said, "I'm a parent and I'm biased too, so I know what it is like. When you meet my son, you'll see what I mean".

In our family, presents got opened after the dinner, but one present gets opened prior to dinner and Dad played the delivery boy every year. I could hear a fuss going on in the kitchen but paid no attention. My sister and brother-in-law were in there with Mom, so all had to be well.

As Dad was gathering up a gift for everyone, he called out to Mom, "OK guys, you better get out of here". Everyone left the kitchen and joined the rest of us. Each gift had to be opened before the next one got delivered and so we went around the room, each person opening their gift. Then something strange happened.

Dad looked confused, he reached around the parcels moving some and reading the names to whom they were for. Then he stood up and looking at me said, "the reason I can't find your gift is because I'm not the one to give it to you. Someone else will have to do that". No sooner were the words out of his mouth the kitchen door opened and Jim walked through smiling at me with a little box in his hand.

"I thought it best to ask you in front of our parents if you will be my wife"? I didn't cry that hard when I had broken my leg, as the words sunk into my thick skull.

Mom was crying and so was Sylvia as she said, "meet my son and a very Merry Christmas to you, my dear".

***

We married on February 14th. We opened our construction company in June of the same year. Two years later we had twins, Eric and Ella. Five years ago, Eric and his wonderful wife gave us our first grand-daughter who was only a month older than her cousin Dale. These were busy times. Nothing like two babies to keep life interesting.

Eric, Ella and their partners joined our business. It gave Jim and I time to travel, which we did. We lived a dream until our magical lives changed when Jim died in a car accident. Like I said before, I am alone now. The pain is excruciating, but I am not lonely. I have thirty-four years of memories, wonderful memories, to keep my heart beating, which began in full force on a Christmas Day, my favorite day of the year.

The End

Afterword

A note from the author, Phyllis Chubb

Thank you for reading our box collection – *Beneath the Mistletoe.*

And... thank you so very much for reading my short story, **Memories.**

I hope you enjoyed reading it, as much as I enjoyed writing it.

If you liked reading this collection, please take a few minutes to leave a review. Your feedback is greatly appreciated.

Sincerely, Phyllis

Please follow me on Twitter

And Facebook

Whale in the Well by Tracy L. Tinkler-Denouden

~*~*~

When Peter and David are out getting the family Christmas tree with their Dad, they learn of the whale in the well and their curiosity gets the better of them.

Dedication

I dedicate this Peter and David story to my dad,

Bruce and my son's, Bruce and Morgan

The Whale in the Well
by Tracy L. Tinkler-Denouden

"Come on boys, we need to beat the storm." John yells out to his sons. "Let's go, are you ready?"

"Dad, we need help getting our boots on." John couldn't help but chuckle when he saw his sons, struggling to reach their feet through all the layers they were wearing. This winter was proving to be a record-breaking cold one.

John and his boys kissed Peggy on the way out the door. "Bye, Mom." David says as he leaves the house, followed by his little brother Peter, "See you, Mom."

Peggy replies "I'll have popcorn balls and hot chocolate ready when you get back; I love you. Pick out a great Christmas tree."

John and his sons make their way across one of their fields to a treed area on their 350 acres. Peter, with his crooked smile and sparkling blue-green eyes, dancing up and down, "How big a tree can we get, Dad?"

David hopping from side to side, with his bright smile yells out "What about this one?"

Suddenly a loud thunderous crack rings out and can be felt rippling under foot. John has never seen either of his sons so wide eyed, as they looked at each other and then back to him. Both boys, frozen in fear, managed to get out, "What was that?"

John, without missing a beat says, "The whale in the well".

The boys in unison. "The whale in the well?"

John walks over to his sons, "See that old well house?"

Peter gives a hesitant "Yeah."

"A whale lives in there; has since I can remember. We just leave him alone. Hey, that storm is moving in, let's get us a tree."

Peter and David, while carefully keeping their eyes on the well house, carry on looking for the perfect Christmas tree.

After dinner, the family gathers in the living room. They enjoy popcorn balls, and hot chocolate while unpacking Christmas decorations. Dad strings the lights on the tree as Mom puts on her favorite Christmas music. Their dog, Reckless, joins in on all the action, dancing in between them all. Before long it was bedtime.

***

"David, David, are you awake?" whispers Peter. "No. Go to sleep." Replies David as he tosses his body over in his bed, and throws his covers over his head.

Now Peter knowing his brother is awake, was up and beside David's bed. "I heard the whale." Peter pulls back the covers and grabs David by his arm. David snaps at Peter "Let go, it's the storm, go to bed and go to sleep." as he pushes Peter away.

Peter sticks his pale, round, freckled face in to David's, "Listen, David. Shush." David sits up and stares into his brother's eyes in silence.

The sounds of a stormy night fill the room, wind whistling through the trees, tree branches banging up against buildings, and branches breaking. Then there it was, that loud cracking of ice again; it shook the ground. Peter jumps as his eyes widen, he grabs David's arm, "Did you hear that? It shook me."

David puts on a brave front, "Yeah, yeah, I heard it." Peter leans into David "I think the whale's hangry." David snickered as he brushes his fingers through his chestnut unruly hair, "Hangry, only moms get hangry."

Peter pulls again on his brother's arm, begging, "Get up, get up David, let's go feed him."

"What are we going to feed a whale in the middle of the night?"

Peter runs out of the room, and returns holding out his hand, to show his brother his feast for the whale.

"A popcorn ball? One popcorn ball, for a whale?" David jumps up and out of his bed, sending his blankets flying. Both boys race to get dressed, reminding one another to be quiet.

One behind the other they tippy-toe down the hall to the kitchen. Peter puts as many popcorn balls as he can fit into his backpack, while David gets their flashlights. They help one another get into their boots, and sneak out into the stormy darkness. David takes the backpack from his brother and flings it onto his shoulders. Leaning into the wind and snow as they make their way towards the well house.

Peggy jumps and wakes up with a jolt. "John, John." Peggy leans over John, shaking him. "Wake up, I heard the door."

"What?" John torn from sleep, is not sure of where he even is. Peggy, now out of bed, feels around for her robe at the end of the bed, and John grabs her hand.

He was now alert, "What's going on?"

"I heard the door, somethings wrong, I feel it."

John pauses and listens, "I don't hear anything,

its fine, come back to bed."

Peggy is already on her way to check on the boys. John hears the thud of Peggy falling to her knees and her cry "They're gone."

John lunges out of bed, runs in to the boy's room, and picks Peggy up off the floor.

"I'm sure I know where they are." As John and Peggy franticly put on their coats, boots, and hoods over their pj's, John tells Peggy of the story of the whale in the well. Peggy screams out, "What were you thinking? A whale, why?"

"You know Peter, afraid of nothing, into everything, his feet, I swear, as fast as his thoughts. His brother can't even keep up with him, nor can we expect him to. I had to tell him something to keep them away from the well. They are 8 and 10 now, and starting to explore more. That well is older than I am, it's a big, deep open hole in the ground full of water, fall in and you'll never get out. I've wired the door shut, but I just wanted to give them a reason to stay away from it."

Peggy looks at her husband, as though he was crazy, "Really, John, a whale?"

They didn't know they could move so fast. Once outside they call the boys names as loud as they can, but nothing could be heard in this storm, nor could much be seen, even with their flashlights. It took everything John had to keep up with his terrified wife.

Peggy could finally see the well house. The door

is no longer wired closed; it is open, blown wide open. Peggy seeing no sign of her sons, looked back at John, she cries out his name and then looked back towards the well house.

John, feeling the blood leave his face, grabs Peggy's hand and they run towards the well.

The boys unaware that their parents are near, move into the well house. David, eager to feed the whale, drops his flashlight and reaching over his shoulder for his backpack, loses his footing and falls onto the thin ice covering the open hole. Just as his fear starts to ease the ice cracks beneath him and into the freezing water he goes.

Peter screams out David's name. He is gone. Nowhere in sight. David suddenly appears once again as fast as he disappeared. Peter's eyes scan the shack for anything to help. He sees a pole of sorts hanging on the shack wall, it is covered in back soot and cobwebs. Without any thought, Peter tosses his flashlight onto the ground and grabs the pole and swings it over and down into the hole. David, looks dead, and barely moves. "Grab it. Grab the stick."

David with the last of his strength manages to lean over the pole and hang on. Peter can feel the pole slipping out of his hands, just as the pole is about to be lost, their dad flies into the shack and manages to grasp it. It takes both John and Peggy to pull David up and out of the hole. When Peter sees David can't hold on any longer he grabs the back of

David's pants and helps pull him onto the edge.

"David, David." Peter cries.

John and Peggy are quick to get David's coat off him and wrap him in their own dry coats. John picks up David in his muscular arms and holds him close as they all head for the house. No one says a word the whole way. Once they reach the house, Peggy runs for the phone and calls 911. John completely strips David and wraps him in fresh blankets. They all gather around David to warm him. David finally moves and looking up at his Dad saying, "He spit me out."

Peter bursts into tears. David looking at Peter confused, says, "What are you crying for. He was going to eat me, not you."

"I just wanted to feed him popcorn balls, not my brother."

David spends the night in the hospital, and when he comes home the next afternoon. The family all sit around the Christmas tree, after hanging their stockings above the fireplace, relaxing and very thankful they are all safe and together. All Peter can say is, "I'm glad you don't taste good, and that the whale spat you out, David. I love you more than I even knew. It's a Christmas miracle." As they all laugh, Peter couldn't resist adding, "I'm never letting him taste me."

The End

Afterword

Thank your for reading our collection – *Beneath the Mistletoe*

And... thank you for reading my story – **A Whale in the Well.** When I was a child, my Dad told my brother and I that a whale lived in our well house, in hopes of keeping us away from it and safe. We thankfully were not as curious as Peter and David. When my son's were little they would have me tell them a Peter and David story most nights before bed. I hope you enjoyed it as much as they have.

Please leave a review or contact me at ilivedit@gmail.com. I would love to hear from you.

You can also check out my blog at www.justforthehealthofitweb.wordpress.com

A word from author, Mimi Barbour

Thank you so very much for reading our first WIP group Christmas Collection – *Beneath the Mistletoe.*

WIP is a local group of authors who live on Vancouver Island in British Columbia. Many are published and work very hard to help our growing membership of mostly Indie authors learn their craft and be able to publish their own work. All of us would love to hear from you so please – if you have a minute – leave a review for this collection. Knowing you enjoyed these stories will delight every one of the authors.

Have a wonderful holiday season and a very Merry Christmas!

www.ingramcontent.com/pod-product-compliance
Lightning Source LLC
Chambersburg PA
CBHW020826030726
47496CB00001B/110